JANEWAY STUDIED THE TACTICAL DISPLAY

The Andirrim flagship and two of its fellows were still concentrating on the orbital stations, and under their onslaught four more of the dots that represented the satellites were flashing red, warning of shields stressed almost to failure. Even as she watched, another one winked out, and this time the satellites did not move to compensate. "Concentrate on the flagship," she ordered. "Treat the others as secondary targets."

Even as she spoke, the ship rocked again under Andirrim fire.

Another one of the orbital stations flashed red and vanished from the screen. The gap it left was obvious, a breach in the defense screen, and the Andirrim flagship swung toward it, maneuver engines flaring without sound. If it got inside the screen, Janeway realized, it could pick off still more stations, open a gap in the screen that the entire fleet could enter.

The Kirse, *Voyager's* friend and ally, would be destroyed. . . .

Look for STAR TREK Fiction from Pocket Books

Star Trek: The Original Series

The Ashes of Eden
Federation
Sarek
Best Destiny
Shadows on the Sun
Probe
Prime Directive
The Lost Years
Star Trek VI: The Undiscovered Country
Star Trek V: The Final Frontier
Star Trek IV: The Voyage Home
Spock's World
Enterprise
Strangers from the Sky
Final Frontier

#1 Star Trek: The Motion Picture
#2 The Entropy Effect
#3 The Klingon Gambit
#4 The Covenant of the Crown
#5 The Prometheus Design
#6 The Abode of Life
#7 Star Trek II: The Wrath of Khan
#8 Black Fire
#9 Triangle
#10 Web of the Romulans
#11 Yesterday's Son
#12 Mutiny on the Enterprise
#13 The Wounded Sky
#14 The Trellisane Confrontation
#15 Corona
#16 The Final Reflection
#17 Star Trek III: The Search for Spock
#18 My Enemy, My Ally
#19 The Tears of the Singers
#20 The Vulcan Academy Murders
#21 Uhura's Song
#22 Shadow Lord
#23 Ishmael
#24 Killing Time
#25 Dwellers in the Crucible
#26 Pawns and Symbols
#27 Mindshadow
#28 Crisis on Centaurus
#29 Dreadnought!
#30 Demons
#31 Battlestations!
#32 Chain of Attack
#33 Deep Domain

#34 Dreams of the Raven
#35 The Romulan Way
#36 How Much for Just the Planet?
#37 Bloodthirst
#38 The IDIC Epidemic
#39 Time for Yesterday
#40 Timetrap
#41 The Three-Minute Universe
#42 Memory Prime
#43 The Final Nexus
#44 Vulcan's Glory
#45 Double, Double
#46 The Cry of the Onlies
#47 The Kobayashi Maru
#48 Rules of Engagement
#49 The Pandora Principle
#50 Doctor's Orders
#51 Enemy Unseen
#52 Home Is the Hunter
#53 Ghost Walker
#54 A Flag Full of Stars
#55 Renegade
#56 Legacy
#57 The Rift
#58 Face of Fire
#59 The Disinherited
#60 Ice Trap
#61 Sanctuary
#62 Death Count
#63 Shell Game
#64 The Starship Trap
#65 Windows on a Lost World
#66 From the Depths
#67 The Great Starship Race
#68 Firestorm
#69 The Patrian Transgression
#70 Traitor Winds
#71 Crossroad
#72 The Better Man
#73 Recovery
#74 The Fearful Summons
#75 First Frontier
#76 The Captain's Daughter
#77 Twilight's End
#78 The Rings of Tautee
#79 Invasion 1: First Strike
#80 The Joy Machine
#81 Mudd in Your Eye

Star Trek: The Next Generation

Kahless
Star Trek Generations
All Good Things
Q-Squared
Dark Mirror
Descent
The Devil's Heart
Imzadi
Relics
Reunion
Unification
Metamorphosis
Vendetta
Encounter at Farpoint

#1 Ghost Ship
#2 The Peacekeepers
#3 The Children of Hamlin
#4 Survivors
#5 Strike Zone
#6 Power Hungry
#7 Masks
#8 The Captains' Honor
#9 A Call to Darkness
#10 A Rock and a Hard Place
#11 Gulliver's Fugitives
#12 Doomsday World
#13 The Eyes of the Beholders
#14 Exiles

#15 Fortune's Light
#16 Contamination
#17 Boogeymen
#18 Q-in-Law
#19 Perchance to Dream
#20 Spartacus
#21 Chains of Command
#22 Imbalance
#23 War Drums
#24 Nightshade
#25 Grounded
#26 The Romulan Prize
#27 Guises of the Mind
#28 Here There Be Dragons
#29 Sins of Commission
#30 Debtors' Planet
#31 Foreign Foes
#32 Requiem
#33 Balance of Power
#34 Blaze of Glory
#35 Romulan Stratagem
#36 Into the Nebula
#37 The Last Stand
#38 Dragon's Honor
#39 Rogue Saucer
#40 Possession
#41 Invasion 2: The Soldiers of Fear
#42 Infiltrator
#43 A Fury Scorned

Star Trek: Deep Space Nine

Warped
The Search
#1 Emissary
#2 The Siege
#3 Bloodletter
#4 The Big Game
#5 Fallen Heroes
#6 Betrayal
#7 Warchild
#8 Antimatter
#9 Proud Helios

#10 Valhalla
#11 Devil in the Sky
#12 The Laertian Gamble
#13 Station Rage
#14 The Long Night
#15 Objective Bajor
#16 Invasion 3: Time's Enemy
#17 The Heart of the Warrior
#18 Saratoga
#19 The Tempest

Star Trek: Voyager

Flashback
#1 Caretaker
#2 The Escape
#3 Ragnarok
#4 Violations
#5 Incident at Arbuk

#6 The Murdered Sun
#7 Ghost of a Chance
#8 Cybersong
#9 Invasion 4: The Final Fury
#10 Bless the Beasts
#11 The Garden

STAR TREK®
VOYAGER™

THE GARDEN

Melissa Scott

POCKET BOOKS
New York   London   Toronto   Sydney   Tokyo   Singapore

An *Original* Publication of POCKET BOOKS

POCKET BOOKS, a division of Simon & Schuster Inc.
1230 Avenue of the Americas, New York, NY 10020

A VIACOM COMPANY

STAR TREK is a Registered Trademark of
Paramount Pictures.

This book is published by Pocket Books, a division of
Simon & Schuster Inc., under exclusive license from
Paramount Pictures.

ISBN: 0-671-56799-3

First Pocket Books printing February 1997

10 9 8 7 6 5 4 3 2 1

POCKET and colophon are registered trademarks of
Simon & Schuster Inc.

Printed in the U.S.A.

THE GARDEN

CHAPTER
1

CAPTAIN KATHRYN JANEWAY STARED AT THE IMAGE IN her viewscreen, and the holographic doctor stared back at her with an expression that she could only call dyspeptic. Not that he wouldn't be the first to correct her misuse of a medical term, she added silently, but he still lacked a certain level of self-awareness in his interactions with other people. But then, he hadn't been designed for full-time, nonemergency function; if one took that into consideration, she thought, he was doing better than she would have expected. In the screen, the hologram shifted impatiently, and she brought her attention back to him.

"Well, Doctor?"

The doctor looked at her, his mouth compressed into a thin line. "I have to report two cases of scorbutus—ascorbic acid deficiency."

"Scorbutus," Janeway repeated. The word was

vaguely familiar; ascorbic acid deficiency was more so, and she frowned. "Isn't that—"

The doctor nodded once, jerkily. "Scurvy. That's the common name, anyway."

Janeway's eyebrows rose at that, and she reached for her datapadd, calling up the file that gave the supply situation. *Voyager's* food stocks were spelled out in intricate detail, each item cross-referenced for its nutritional values as well as caloric content and availability. "According to my files, Doctor, there's no shortage of vitamin C in the stores we have on board. Are you sure these crew members are eating a balanced diet?"

"I've questioned both Ensign Renehan and Lieutenant Imbro about their eating habits over the past month, and both claim to have been following Starfleet nutritional protocols," the doctor answered. "Indeed, by his account, Lieutenant Imbro should have exceeded the requirement for ascorbic acid to a significant degree. Nonetheless, both are suffering from scurvy. I've put them on supplemental dosages of ascorbic acid, which should correct their condition, but I cannot satisfactorily account for it."

Janeway took a deep breath, let it out slowly, keeping her face without expression. Nutritional deficiencies had been something to worry about from the moment the Caretaker had brought them into the Delta Quadrant: *Voyager's* crew, human and nonhuman alike, had evolved in a very different part of the galaxy; there had always been a chance that the planets of the Delta Quadrant would not provide the various necessary minerals and trace elements in the quantities *Voyager's* crew required. Still, ascorbic acid was one of the basics, one of the things that the away teams scanned for automatically, and as automatically rejected flora that did not provide it. "All right, Doctor," she said aloud, "keep me informed of Lieutenant Imbro's and Ensign Renehan's conditions—"

"Excuse me, Captain." The hologram's gaze was focused suddenly on her wrist, where the sleeve of her uniform was pushed up against the edge of the datapadd. Janeway followed his look, and realized that he was staring at the bruise just above the bones of her wrist.

"It's nothing, Doctor."

"It looks painful," the hologram answered. "Would you mind telling me how you did it?"

Janeway frowned. "Now that you mention it, I'm not entirely sure. I must have hit it against something. . . . " Her voice trailed off as she realized what she was saying, and the doctor nodded briskly.

"I would appreciate it if you would come down to sickbay for an examination. Bruising can be an early symptom—particularly if you don't remember injuring yourself. How are your teeth and gums feeling?"

"They're fine." Janeway's frown deepened. She rarely spent much time worrying about her body; she did what was necessary to keep herself fit, but otherwise tended to ignore her physical self until illness demanded her attention. And so far, at least, she felt well enough, had observed no unsettling symptoms. . . . She looked at the bruise again, ugly beneath her skin, and nodded to the doctor. "All right, Doctor, I'm at your disposal."

"Sooner would be better," the hologram said, and Janeway allowed herself a smile.

"I'll be there in an hour. Compile a report for me on the other cases, and anything else you think is relevant, and have it ready for me. Janeway out." She closed the viewscreen and stared for a moment at the Starfleet logo that had replaced the image. When she had taken command of her first ship, that symbol had been a reassurance, a reminder that she was not alone, was part of an entity greater than herself. Here and now, it served more to remind her of just how far she—all of them—were from home. Not for the first time, she wondered if she should remove it from the standard screen, and once again rejected the idea. It was better for everyone, even the ex-Maquis, to keep to the familiar as much as possible. She shook the thought away, impatient with her own sense of loss, and reached for her datapadd. "Computer," she said aloud. "Give me everything you have on ascorbic acid deficiency. Scurvy."

There was a surprising amount of information in the computer's memory banks, considering that the disease hadn't been a problem in Federation space for generations, but none of it explained why people would become ill when there was plenty of vitamin C available. Unless, she thought, the affected crew members hadn't been following the nutritional protocols. She steepled her hands on the desktop, wincing at the sight of the bruise on her own wrist. On the other hand, if she herself were somehow affected, when she knew she had been careful to follow the recommended diet, then they, *Voyager,* could be in serious trouble. It was probably nothing, she told herself, just a few careless crew members—and it was easy to get careless without the replicators to provide the full range of needed vitamins and minerals—and her own clumsiness that added up to an unnecessary worry. She couldn't convince herself, and shook her head slowly, dismissing the files that filled her work screen. She would know soon enough; until that time, there was no point in letting herself worry.

The doctor was already present in sickbay when she arrived, and she wondered briefly who had forgotten to turn him off this time. His expression when he turned to face her was less irritable then usual, however, and she guessed he'd asked to be left on-line.

"I have your report ready, Captain," he said, "but I'd prefer to begin with your examination."

Janeway frowned, more reflex than anything, but then allowed herself an inward shrug. "Very well. But I can assure you I'm feeling perfectly well—"

She broke off as the doctor aimed a medical tricorder in her direction, and waited while the diagnostic cycled. The doctor grunted at the information on his screen, and then gestured to the nearest table. "If you'd have a seat, Captain. And please roll up your sleeve."

Janeway complied, with a lift of the eyebrow that would have warned most of her crew that her patience was reaching its end. The doctor ignored it, and her, focusing his considerable attention on the tiny cylindrical scanner. He frowned at the reading it produced, touched a button, and applied it again to the skin of Janeway's forearm. After a moment, it beeped discreetly, and the doctor removed it, his frown deepening.

"Well?" Janeway asked, after a long moment.

"I wish I could say it was good news," the doctor said, his attention already diverted to another console, and Janeway slid off the table, smoothing her sleeve back into place.

"I would appreciate a full explanation, Doctor. Now."

"I don't have a full explanation," the doctor began, and then stopped, as abruptly as he'd begun. "Oh. You mean of the diagnosis. Well. There's no surprise there, I'm afraid. You're showing the same deficiency as Imbro and Renehan, only not as advanced."

"My teeth feel fine," Janeway said, and was obscurely glad that she'd decided to search the ship's memory on the topic. "And I haven't noticed bleeding from my gums or any of the other symptoms that I understand are characteristic of the problem."

The doctor nodded, his attention once again on the screen in front of him. "Oh, your condition is much less advanced than theirs. I suspect your own guess about the origin of this bruise is at least partially correct. I think you probably did strike your hand against something, not so hard that you would notice, in the ordinary course of events, but hard enough that, coupled with the weakening of the blood vessels created by the deficiency, a substantial hematoma formed."

Janeway glanced at her wrist again, her annoyance fading as the implications of the doctor's words began to sink in. "And yet, Doctor, I know I have been following the recommended diet. I shouldn't be getting scurvy."

"I agree." The doctor looked up from his screen at last. "And the same thing seems to be true of Imbro and Renehan. All three of you are getting plenty of ascorbic acid, but nonetheless you show signs of deficiency."

"What's your explanation?"

"At the moment, I have none." The doctor's lips were compressed into a tight line, his eyebrows raised to crumple the skin of his forehead. "I'm in the process of creating a test protocol, which, with your permission, I'd like to implement for the entire crew. Once I've determined whether or not this is an isolated problem, I'll have an easier time finding the cause. In the meantime, Captain, I would like to begin by giving you supplemental vitamin C—a fairly high dose, I think we're better off treating this aggressively—and ask you to return for further tests in, say, three days' time."

"All right," Janeway said. "Go ahead with the test protocol, and keep me informed of your results. And let me know if there are any new cases."

"Of course." The doctor walked to a storage shelf, studied the containers for a moment, and then selected a flat box from among them. "Take two of these tablets twice a day, preferably with a meal."

Janeway nodded. "How are your supplies?"

"We can synthesize more in the replicators, or conceivably extract it from some of the foodstuffs we have on board," the doctor answered. "Though of course the latter would eventually affect our overall supply levels."

"Right," Janeway said. Neither option was particularly appealing—one consumed power, the other the food supplies, both of which were limited—but as short-term solutions, both would work. In the long term— She cut off that thought. The only acceptable long-term solution was to find the cause of the deficiency. "Keep me informed," she said briskly, and left the sickbay.

Ensign Harry Kim considered the plate in front of him, and the bland round grains that substituted for rice, and was glad he'd accepted an extra spoonful of Neelix's vegetable curry. It was bright green, almost the color of a cheap, sour-lime flavored candy he'd been fond of as a boy, but at least it tasted of turmeric and ginger. Those flavors came naturally from the bright-yellow fruit they'd gathered on the unnamed, uninhabited planet where they'd last stopped for supplies, and for a moment he could almost feel the touch of the cool breeze that had swept across the grassy plain. It had been a beautiful world, rich in vegetation, and almost completely lacking in animal life: as Janeway had said, a perfect place to restock

their larder without having to worry about upsetting
the natives, especially once they'd run the tests and
discovered that the fruits and grains not only met
their nutritional needs but almost certainly tasted
good as well. Kim closed his eyes, conjuring up the
headland where his landing party had done their
survey. The air had smelled of the sea's alien salt; the
plain had swept down from the headland until it met
a low line of trees laden with the yellow fruits. A
perfect place, he thought, except for the silences. It
had been odd to be so close to the sound of surf, and
not hear seabirds. Their noise had always been part of
the family's seaside holidays.

"Not up for the curry tonight, huh?" a familiar
voice said, and Kim opened his eyes as *Voyager*'s
helmsman dropped into the seat opposite him. "Can't
say I blame you, I'm getting a little tired of these
gingered tomatoes myself."

"That must be why you took such a small helping,"
Kim said, dryly, looking at the other's overflowing
plate, and Lieutenant Tom Paris grinned back at him,
not the least discomfited.

"Oh, got to be sure I'm getting all my vitamins,
Harry. Haven't you heard?"

"Heard what?" Kim said, suspiciously, and grimaced as Paris's grin widened. He ought to know by
now not to take everything the helmsman said at face
value, and yet somehow he always asked. . . .

"We've got a little problem," Paris said, cheerfully,
and shoveled in a mouthful of the curry. His eyes
widened, and he reached hastily for the nearest glass
of water.

Kim allowed himself a smile. "Neelix has been
experimenting with the spices again."

"You might've warned me. My god, where did he

get goat peppers in the Delta Quadrant?" Paris took a deep breath, and another cautious taste of the curry.

"Who knows?" Kim leaned forward, planting both elbows on the table. "What little problem, Tom?"

Paris smiled again, his taste buds apparently already adjusting to the curry. "You'll never guess, so I'll just tell you. Some of the crew have come down with scurvy."

"Scurvy?" Kim shook his head, and reached for his fork again. "No way, Tom, I won't bite this time."

"It's true," Paris protested. "I heard it from Ensign Renehan—she's one of the ones who has it."

"Maybe she just said it so you wouldn't ask her for another date," Kim said, and smiled as Paris made a face at him. "Seriously, Tom, it's just not possible. I mean, scurvy's preventable—completely preventable. And I worked on the team that checked the last load of food we brought on board, so I know the analysis was good."

"Maybe you screwed up," Paris said, "or somebody missed something, because Rennie says she knows eight other people who're having problems." He smiled again, this time with cheerful malice. "How are your teeth feeling, Harry?"

"Fine." Kim frowned, Paris's friendly barbs fading as he tried to remember the details of the analysis. Everything had been well within normal limits; nothing had stood out, and nothing stayed in his memory. He shook his head again. "Damn it, Tom, people can't have scurvy."

"A demonstrably untrue statement," a cool voice said from behind Kim, and in the same moment he saw Paris smooth his expression into something more decorous. "Though based on logical assumptions."

Kim stood quickly. Lieutenant Tuvok was one of the few people on board who could still make him feel as though he were at the Academy, and he still couldn't imagine how the Vulcan had functioned as part of Chakotay's Maquis crew. He heard the chair scrape as Paris copied him, less automatically, and Tuvok acknowledged the courtesy with the flicker of an eyelid.

"The captain would like to see you both in the ready room," the Vulcan continued.

"Now?" Paris asked. Kim glanced back, and saw him looking with regret at his unemptied plate.

"Now," Tuvok agreed. He added, "The matter is urgent."

"Or at least sensitive," Paris said, "since we're not using communicators."

"Just so," Tuvok said, apparently without irony.

Kim reached for his plate and utensils, bundled them into the nearest cleaning slot, and stepped out of the way to let Paris do the same. Tuvok waited, not hurrying them, and Kim decided he could risk the question.

"So there is scurvy on board, sir?"

"Several crew members are suffering from an ascorbic acid deficiency," Tuvok said. "The captain will explain the situation in more detail." He turned without waiting for an answer and strode toward the nearest turbolift. Kim followed, Paris at his heels, and heard the man murmur something under his breath. He couldn't quite make out the words, but Tuvok answered without turning, "No doubt it will, Mr. Paris."

"Crushed again," Paris said, and took his place in the turbolift.

Serves you right, Kim thought, but under Tuvok's curious and uncomprehending stare decided to keep silent.

The others were already present in the ready room

by the time they arrived. The captain acknowledged their arrival with a curt nod and, mercifully, no further comment, and Kim slipped hastily into his seat next to the chief engineer. Lieutenant B'Elanna Torres gave him a look—no smile, but no overt hostility—and returned her attention to the datapadd in front of her. Kim slanted a glance at it, but couldn't make out the lines of text and didn't dare look too closely. He looked around the room instead. Everyone was there whom he'd expected to see: Tuvok and Paris, of course; the first officer Commander Chakotay; Torres; the alien Neelix, perched between discomfort and eagerness on the very edge of his chair—everyone, Kim realized abruptly, except the holographic doctor. Even as he thought it, however, a wallscreen lit, and the doctor's image peered out of it. Seeing him, Janeway nodded and leaned forward, drawing everyone's attention with the simple movement.

"I'm sure the news of our present crisis has spread throughout the ship by now," she said, "but, to summarize, to date over thirty crew members are suffering from some form of ascorbic acid deficiency—scurvy to those of you with a historical bent—while analysis of our stores shows that there is an ample supply of vitamin C in the food we have on board. Naturally—" She gave a small, austere smile. "Naturally, I'm concerned. Doctor, let's begin with your conclusions."

"Certainly."

Kim shifted in his chair to face the hologram, uncomfortably aware that he had left a message from the doctor unread and unanswered in his personal files. At the time, he'd thought it had to do with his annual physical—the ship's computer was still keeping its records up to date despite their unscheduled trip to the Delta Quadrant—but now he wondered if it had had to do with the discovery of scurvy on board.

"So far," the doctor went on, "I have examined a little more than ninety percent of the crew, and have made firm appointments with most of the remainder. As the captain said, I have found thirty cases of actual clinical deficiency, and another forty-two crew members show signs that they are not getting enough vitamin C. I have been treating the deficiency cases with supplemental doses, but so far only Lieutenant Imbro has responded positively to the treatment, and I had to give him dosages that bordered on toxicity before he responded. In other words, Captain, I think we've got a problem."

"Not responding—?" Chakotay began, and broke off abruptly, glancing at Janeway.

The captain nodded. "Could you be more specific, Doctor?"

"I'm not sure how," the hologram answered. "I have given each of the affected crew members enough vitamin C to reverse the condition, but it hasn't worked. I'm running tests now, but right now my best guess—and it is only a guess—is that something is impeding the absorption of the ascorbic acid."

"It's not my fault," Neelix said hastily. "I've followed your protocols, I've done everything exactly the way you told me to—"

"I'm sure, Mr. Neelix," Janeway said firmly. "We'll get to you in a moment."

Neelix started to protest further, met her steely look, and shut his mouth again without making a sound.

"I take it you don't have any idea what's causing the problem?" Chakotay asked, after a moment, and the hologram shook his head.

"Not yet. I'm investigating, of course, but I haven't found anything untoward in the affected crew members' systems. This suggests that, if a contaminant is impeding absorption, it, too, is broken down fairly rapidly by the body." The doctor paused, seeming to consider something only he could see. "It may or may not be significant that only human crew members have been affected so far."

"Unsurprising," Tuvok said. "Not all species make use of ascorbic acid. Vulcans, for example, do not metabolize it at all."

How very helpful, Kim thought, and heard a soft noise from Paris. Janeway glanced in his direction, but apparently decided to ignore him.

"Very well, Doctor, continue with your tests, and let me know as soon as you find anything."

"Of course."

Janeway nodded again, still with that slight smile. "In the meantime, gentlemen, I'm open to further suggestions."

There was a little silence, and then Torres tossed aside her stylus. "Don't look at me, I'm an engineer. I don't know a thing about biological systems."

"I've been following the protocols," Neelix said again. "I swear, I've done everything just the way you told me—"

"I don't doubt that Mr. Neelix is entirely correct," Tuvok said. "Nonetheless, the food supply is, logically, the place to begin this investigation."

"I agree," Chakotay said. "And we did take on a lot of food in one place this last time. Not that we had a choice, given how rare M-class planets have been lately, but reliance on a single source is never good."

Janeway nodded. "With hindsight, I'm beginning to wonder if we should have been concerned about the absence of animal life."

Kim made a face, thinking about that lovely, empty planet. Rich it had been, but perhaps not as perfect as it had seemed. He thought he could guess what was coming next, and was not surprised when Janeway turned her gaze on him.

"Mr. Kim. You ran the analysis of the first samples we collected, is that right?"

"Yes, Captain." Even though he knew there was no need to defend himself, he found himself rushing on. "There was nothing anomalous in our findings, though."

"Except that we didn't know what we were looking for," Chakotay said.

"A number of things can interfere with vitamin C absorption," the doctor said impatiently.

"But I assume you've already tested for the most obvious ones," Janeway said.

Kim looked away from the wallscreen, trying to collect his own thoughts. The analysis had been done quickly—it had had to be done quickly, they had had to come into the fringes of Kazon-Ogla space to find any class-M planets at all, and they had had to reject two others before they had found this one. And it had been a good thing they'd been able to hurry it along: the sensors had detected Kazon-Ogla activity nearby almost before they had finished the harvest. But as a result, they had looked only for positive dangers in the food, and known negatives like shortages of the crucial trace minerals. "Captain," he said aloud, "could something else be, well, masquerading as vitamin C?"

Janeway looked at the hologram, who shrugged. "That would be one possible explanation. Something that the human body perceives as vitamin C, and is therefore picked up preferentially over vitamin C— yes, that could happen."

"And if it looked enough like vitamin C, chemically speaking, to fool our bodies," Kim went on, "could it have fooled the computers as well?"

There was a little silence after he'd finished speaking, and then Chakotay said, "That's a frightening thought, Mr. Kim. And frighteningly plausible." He looked at Janeway. "That could explain it. If there's some difference at the submolecular level?"

"Like the left-handed amino acids," Kim said, dredging his memory for details of an already-forgotten Academy course in nutrition and diet.

"Look into it, Mr. Kim," Janeway said, and, too late, he remembered something else he had learned at the Academy. *Never even look like you might volunteer,* the senior cadets had said, and, all too often, they'd been right.

"Yes, Captain," he said, and managed to keep the resignation from his voice.

"Commander Chakotay, Lieutenant Tuvok," Janeway went on, "I want you to review the records of the worst-affected crew members, see if there's any common factor among them besides being human. Lieutenant Torres, run a study of the minimum crew required to keep *Voyager* operational. I want answers—" She glanced again at her datapadd. "—in forty-eight hours."

There was an awkward murmur of acknowledgment, almost drowned in the shuffling of chairs, and Kim followed Torres and Paris from the ready room. The engineer was shaking her head, already deep in the parameters of her problem, but she looked up as Chakotay came abreast of them.

"I'll run the study, but I already know we need at least seventy-five people—seventy-five healthy people—to run the ship."

"Do what you can to bring it down, B'Elanna," Chakotay said.

"There isn't anything," Torres answered, but sounded oddly satisfied as she turned away.

Kim turned to the turbolift, and was not surprised when both Neelix and Paris crowded in with him. "Shuttlebay," he said, to the computer, and looked pointedly at the others.

"Shuttlebay," Paris said, cheerfully. "I thought I might be able to give you some help."

"Thanks," Kim said, surprised but pleased, and Neelix cleared his throat.

"Galley," he said, to the computer. "I mean, deck three. Officers' lounge. You know, gentlemen, I simply don't understand how this could have happened. I steered you to a perfect planet, one that met all the captain's criteria—no indigenous population, she said, and outside the Kazon-Ogla sphere, or almost, and it had to be rich in edible plant life. Not exactly easy to find, especially not in this quadrant, but I did exactly what was required."

"I'm sure it wasn't your fault," Kim said. Out of the corner of his eye, he saw Paris grin, and fixed the other man with a disapproving stare. If Paris started one of his practical jokes now . . . At that moment, the turbolift slowed, and he gave a sigh of relief as the door opened.

"I've done my best," Neelix said, and stepped out into the corridor. The turbolift doors closed again, and Paris snorted.

"Why is it that his best never quite works out the way we expected it to?"

"Or that he did," Kim answered, and then shook his head. "You're not being fair, Tom."

"I suppose not," Paris said, reluctantly abandoning his joke. "So, what do we do now?"

"I wish I knew."

The turbolift slid to a stop again, and the doors opened onto the dimly lit lower corridor that gave access to the shuttlebays. Power had been rerouted from the corridor lighting to the hydroponics trays and the special lights that helped to feed the plants, and to the preservation fields that kept the provisions stored in the second, smaller shuttlebay, and the corridor was not only dim, but oddly chilly. It was probably purely psychological, Kim knew, or at best the contrast with the warmer air of the hydroponics room, but he always found himself shivering when he came down to the converted shuttlebays.

"All right," said Paris, "then where do we start?"

Kim touched the wall controls, disengaging the locks on the storage room door, and then reached for his tricorder. "I guess with whatever Neelix has been using most of—the tomato-things, maybe."

Paris reached for his own tricorder, and Kim heard soft machine beeps as the other man consulted his data. "I just got the computer to check the menus for the last six weeks, since we took this stuff on board. You're right, the tomato-things have showed up in nearly every meal since then, and then he's used a lot of the sour-cane—"

"Sour-cane?"

"The stringy stuff that tastes like onions and lemons. And there's a big bean that comes in third."

"Those are all things that we were afraid would spoil." The soft, female voice came from the doorway of the hydroponics room. "Hello, Harry. Is something wrong?"

Kim turned to face the Ocampa woman, his lips curving into an automatic smile. "Hello, Kes."

"What, no hello for me?" Paris asked, grinning, and Kes smiled at him politely.

"Hello, Tom. Is something wrong?"

"Hasn't the doctor told you?" Kim asked. Kes had been studying with the holographic doctor almost since she came on board.

Kes shook her head, frowning now. "He's been very busy lately, and so have I, trying to get the new seedlings established. I haven't spoken with him in days."

"A lot of the crew are suffering from a vitamin deficiency," Kim said. "Even though there should be enough of the vitamin in the food we're eating. We're trying to find out why."

"Is it serious?" Kes asked.

"It could be fatal," Paris answered.

"Can I help?" Kes looked at Kim, who nodded.

"Another pair of hands can only speed things up."

"Let me get my tricorder," Kes said, and disappeared back into the hydroponics room.

Kim looked at his tricorder again, checking the menu of preprogrammed tests. He had run the more common ones when they brought the food on board; that left the less common ones, and then the specific examination of the ascorbic acid in the food. Kes emerged from the other shuttlebay, holding up her tricorder, and Kim nodded. "All right," he said aloud. "Tom, you'll run the first five tests on this list, and, Kes, you'll take the rest of them. I'll set up the tests for ascorbic acid. We'll start with the foods Neelix has made most use of, and then work our way down the list."

"Shall we synthesize the results as we go along?" Kes asked.

Kim nodded. "But don't bother reporting anything until you find an anomaly." He looked from her to Paris. "Everything clear?"

"Reasonably," Paris said, and Kes merely nodded.

"Then let's get on with it," Kim said, and opened the door to the storage room. For an instant, it was lit only by the pale blue glow of the stasis fields, and then the overhead lights came on as well, fading the fields to near-invisibility. Kim could feel them, though, a chill presence that raised the hairs on his bare skin as he moved into the room. This had been a repair bay; it was smaller than the shuttlebays to either side, but the shelves of food—some wrapped in clingfilm, some boxed, some preserved in containers—rose to nearly three times his height.

"I'll take the left aisle to start," Paris said. "Harry, you want the middle?"

"I doubt it makes much difference," Kim said, but nodded. "Kes, that leaves you the right."

"All right." The Ocampa disappeared down the side aisle.

Kim took a deep breath, and started down his corridor. The presence of the stasis fields was much stronger here, enough to raise goose bumps on his arms even through the uniform. He suppressed a shiver as he consulted the tricorder's plan for the area. He would begin with the tomato-things, he decided—at least three tons of them were stored in this aisle, and he had a feeling that they were somehow involved—and then sample the beans and the sourcane, and move on to the other food as necessary.

The tomato-like fruits were stored in gas-filled cylinders at the middle of the aisle. Kim found the nearest control box and adjusted it until he had a window in the field through which he could drag one of the cylinders. Even with antigrav assistance, it was heavy, and he was sweating by the time he had it sitting in the middle of the aisle. He resealed the stasis field behind him, and turned his attention to the cylinder. The bright green fruit—somehow less virulent than he remembered from the curry—bobbed gently in the preserving gas, clearly visible through the transparent walls. They certainly looked all right, he thought, and worked the controls to retrieve one fruit. The selector mechanism whined softly, numbers flickering across the checkplate, and a small lockplate slid back at the top of the cylinder. A single fruit sat in the opening, wisps of gas curling away from its bright rind. Kim took it, cautiously, wondering if something that small, that innocuous-looking—*that tasty,* he admitted silently—could really be the cause of their problems, and set it carefully on top of the cylinder. The access lock closed again with a soft hiss, and Kim reached for his tricorder.

He had run the standard tests before, but he cycled quickly through them again, just in case something on the planet, some peculiarity of the local condition, had interfered with their survey. As he'd expected, however, the results were the same as they had been before: the fruit was perfectly edible, and even actively healthy for humans. The band that sampled ascorbic acid glowed bright green, at the upper end of the desired range. Kim made a face at that, and adjusted the controls, defining a new test. It, too, came back green, showing normal molecular structure. He ran two more tests, each one designed to target structural oddities that might not appear on the first test, but they, too, came back green. *So it's not the ascorbic acid that's the problem,* Kim thought, *but something that's blocking its uptake—assuming, of course, that these fruits are actually the source of the trouble.*

He adjusted the tricorder controls, calling up the next battery of tests, and waited while the machine cycled though them. This time, the telltales showed bright red all across the board: there was nothing in the fruit's makeup that should interfere with absorption of vitamin C. *And since something very obviously is interfering,* Kim thought, hearing Tuvok's voice in his mind, *then one must assume that these fruits are not the culprit.* He reopened the gap in the field, wrestled the cylinder back into place, and turned his attention to the next item on the list. The beans, massive, mottled spheres a little larger than his fist, were stored in open boxes, protected by their hard rinds, but they, too, showed both an abundance of ascorbic acid and a complete absence of anything that might block its uptake. He got the same results from the sour-cane, and stood for a moment, staring at the tricorder's screen. He had been sure it would be one of those three foods—they were the ones that Neelix used most, the ones that nearly everyone agreed tasted good, the ones that had become the staples of nearly everyone's diet—but then shook his disappointment away. The tricorders didn't make mistakes; if they said there was enough ascorbic acid in these foods, then there had to be some other factor involved. *Maybe,* he thought, *one of the other foods interacts with these, which might explain why some people are more affected than others.* The idea cheered him slightly, and he lifted the package of sour-cane back to its shelf. He would begin at the nearer end of the aisle, and test everything.

It took him almost five hours to test everything else in the aisle, but at the end of it he still hadn't found a likely cause for the deficiency. He stood at the end of the aisle for a long moment, sharply aware of his own hunger and fatigue, then made himself turn back toward the door, touching his communicator as he went. "Kim to Paris."

"Paris here."

It was only a minor consolation, Kim thought, that

Paris sounded as tired as he did. "I'm done with my aisle. How are you doing?"

"I've just finished," Paris answered. "I haven't found anything, Harry."

Kim swallowed hard, telling himself that the sudden emptiness in his gut was just hunger. "Neither have I. Maybe Kes—?"

"Kes here," the Ocampa said. "I'm sorry, Harry, all my tests haven't turned up anything either."

"Damn." Kim bit off the rest of what he wanted to say. *That can't be right, we've made some mistake, we should do the tests again—* There was no point in that, and he straightened his shoulders, trying to think what he—what a Starfleet officer—should do next. "All right," he said, "meet me back by the door, and let's compare notes. Maybe something will show up in the test protocols."

"I sure hope so," Paris answered. "I like my teeth where they are, thank you."

Kim grimaced, annoyed at the other man's flippancy, and as he reached the door was meanly pleased to see that Paris was no longer smiling. "So," he said, "let's link tricorders and see what we can come up with."

Paris offered his tricorder, and Kes copied him, but she was frowning slightly. "Something's just occurred to me, Harry," she said, and Kim looked up from trying to mate the three machines.

"Oh?"

"Yes. We're not testing the right things. I mean, these—" Kes gestured to the shelves behind them. "This isn't what we eat, not in this form. What we eat is cooked. Could that make a difference?"

Kim stared at her for a moment, the tricorders forgotten in his hands. "It could," he said. "My God, it really could."

Paris gave a little yip of impatience. "Then what are we waiting for? Let's check out the galley."

Kes nodded, but her mobile face was sad. Kim hesitated. "Is anything wrong?"

Kes shook her head, forced a rather wan smile. "No, not exactly. It's just—if it is the cooking, Neelix will feel terrible."

"Better to find out what's wrong," Paris said, brutally cheerful, but Kim touched the Ocampa lightly on the shoulder.

"It isn't Neelix's fault, Kes, and no one will blame him. If anybody's to blame, it's us—the away team, I mean. We should have tested for that."

"Oh, don't you start," Paris said, and touched controls to summon the turbolift. "First, you couldn't've known either, and second, we don't even know if that's the problem yet."

Neelix's makeshift kitchen was actually a surprisingly efficient and pleasant space, despite the constant fuss and bustle from Neelix himself. The second dinner shift had just ended, and Neelix was watching jealously as a trio of human crew members fitted the first of the cooking pots into the cleaning belt. A second team was busy setting out the trays of cold food that would be available for anyone whose duties had kept them from eating during a regular serving period, and, seeing that, Kim heard his stomach growl.

"Dammit," Paris said, "he's put everything away."

"Just in cold storage," Kes answered. "Don't worry, Tom."

Neelix turned sharply at the sound of her voice, and came toward them, smiling, his eyes darting from Kes to Paris and then back again. "I was looking for you, Kes. I could have used your help with dinner—it would have been very helpful, in fact."

"I'm sorry." Kes didn't sound particularly repentant. "I was helping Harry in stores."

Neelix turned a suspicious glare on Kim, who said hastily, "We've spent most of the day testing the food supplies. We think that the ascorbic acid in the food from that last planet may be affected by the cooking process, so we need to test the food you served tonight."

"Well, there's not much left," Neelix answered. "The curry was very popular tonight—it was the green leeabi nuts in the piquant yduvari salsa, very tasty, if I do say so myself—and I don't know if there's enough—"

"Even something left on a plate would do," Kim said, breaking firmly through the chatter, and Neelix gave him a look of horror.

"Oh, no, I can do better than that. This way, please."

Kim followed him behind the improvised serving station, and Paris and Kes leaned on the nearest counter, peering past the trays. Neelix ignored them all, rummaging in a stasis box until he finally produced a covered container. He held it out to Kim with a flourish. "I made this specially for the captain. I know she liked the leeabi nuts when I made them this way the last time, so I thought—"

Kim nodded, letting the wave of talk roll over him, and pried off the tight-fitting lid. Inside the dish was a darker green version of the curry he had had at lunch, tastefully cupped inside a thick dark-red leaf.

"—so if there's anything wrong with it, anything at all," Neelix went on, "I want to know about it. I want you to test it—in fact, I insist you test this. Nothing but wholesome food goes to the captain from my kitchen, nothing else."

"Right," Kim said, and aimed the tricorder at the curry. He held his breath and pressed the button that would initiate the test. For a long moment, nothing happened, and then the bar light appeared. It glowed pale red, and beneath it letters and numbers spelled out the details that confirmed its news: there was little or no ascorbic acid in the curry. Kim gave a whoop of joy, and then sobered as abruptly. They might have found the cause of the deficiency, but they were no closer to its solution.

"Good news?" Paris asked, and Kim gave him a wry smile.

"Depends on your definition of good. It looks like you were right, Kes, the cooking process does somehow destroy the vitamin C."

"What?" Neelix shook his head, nearly sending his tall hat flying. "Gentlemen, I assure you, everything is properly cooked here—"

"It's not your cooking," Kim said, and turned his tricorder on another dish. "It's something about the food itself that's the problem."

"But—" Neelix broke off as Kim touched his communicator.

"Kim to bridge."

"Chakotay here. Go ahead, Mr. Kim."

"I have a preliminary report for the captain," Kim said. "I'll be entering more detailed information into the computer, but I think she should hear this now."

"I'm here, Mr. Kim." Janeway's tart voice was perversely reassuring. "What have you found?"

"It looks like the problem isn't precisely in the food," Kim said, "but with the cooking. Somehow, cooking seems to destroy some of the nutrients we need."

"I see." There was a little silence, and then Janeway's voice came briskly. "Very well. File your report as soon as possible. I'll have the doctor and Mr. Neelix investigate our options. Janeway out."

"Well," Paris said.

"But what am I going to do?" Neelix demanded. "I've worked like a slave to come up with these recipes, recipes that have pleased even the most finicky of the crew, and now I'm supposed to, what, do it all over again?"

"I'm sure you'll come up with something," Kim said.

Neelix ignored him. "I've done everything in my power to make this work. I've experimented with taste and texture, using myself for a guinea pig when no others were available, and now you tell me all this is for nothing?"

"Think of it this way, Neelix," Paris said. "Now you can really prove what a great cook you are."

The ready room was unusually quiet, each of the officers bent over a datapadd, no one willing to meet the others' eyes. Even Kes was quiet, her pretty face for once unsmiling. Janeway looked around the room, and felt her lips tighten at the sight. Things were bad, certainly, but they had been worse; she would not tolerate this level of pessimism even in the privacy of the senior officers' gathering. "Well, gentlemen," she said, and was pleased by the sudden shift in alertness as all eyes turned to her. "I gather the news is not promising. Mr. Kim, will you begin?"

"Yes, Captain." The young man looked nervously down at his datapadd, and Janeway gave him an encouraging smile.

"I don't have a whole lot to add to my preliminary report," Kim went on. "To summarize, all of the food that we took on board at the last stop seems to be affected by, well, I guess you'd have to call it weak molecular bonding. We're still not fully sure how it works, or what causes it, but the results are pretty clear. The ascorbic acid in the food breaks down into unusable compounds once it's heated—in fact, the doctor says those compounds actively block the uptake of real vitamin C. Some other important nutrients seem to have the same problem. So my conclusion is, unless we can eat this food without cooking it, we have a real problem."

Janeway nodded. She had already read Kim's detailed report, had expected and received no surprises there. In the screen, she could see the holographic doctor shifting, preparing to speak, but at the same moment Neelix leaned forward, his stubby fingers knotting nervously. Better to get him out of the way first, she thought. "Mr. Neelix?"

"Captain, I've tried to find ways of making these foods palatable without cooking, but it's just not working—"

"More to the point," the doctor said, "they're not digestible. I've run experiments, including live trials on volunteers, and the result has been consistent. Unless the food is cooked, the subjects suffered stomach cramps, bloating, and frequent and debilitating diarrhea. I cannot recommend such a course of action."

"Live trials?" Janeway said, in spite of herself, and Paris shifted in his chair.

"Um, I was one of the volunteers, Captain. I'd say the doctor was understating the case."

Janeway eyed him thoughtfully. He was looking paler than usual, and there were dark circles under his eyes. "So what are our options, Doctor?"

"Limited." In the screen, the hologram gave a thin smile. "In fact, practically speaking, I can see only one: find a new food source."

"That's not all that easy," Chakotay said. "Captain, we've already established that this is an unusually barren sector, and we don't know how much further this extends. We haven't spotted an M-class planet in weeks—not since we took on food this last time, in fact—and we've been looking."

"Yes, I know," Janeway said. She looked down at her own notes, mentally crossing off the first two possibilities as no longer viable. "What about the new long-range scans?"

"So far, nothing," Chakotay answered. "I've asked Torres to try to boost the gain on at least the forward sensors, but it doesn't seem to have done much good."

"I've achieved a seven-point-eight-percent increase so far," Torres said, "and I'm trying for eight."

"Unfortunately," Chakotay said, "all we're seeing is still just empty space. A few uninhabitable rock-balls and the occasional gas giant. Nothing else. I can't even predict which direction would be more likely to support M-class worlds, though I'm working on that now."

"All right," Janeway said, and matched the doctor's smile. "Assuming that it's likely to take us some time to find food again, Doctor, what can you do to keep the crew healthy and functioning?"

"That is where we run into some further problems," the hologram answered. "You'll remember that I told you before that Lieutenant Imbro's condition responded only to near-toxic doses of ascorbic acid? That's proved to be a common factor in all the cases I've detected so far. Not only does this weakly bound molecule refuse to act like vitamin C, it inhibits the body from absorbing the proper chemicals. I do not yet know if it's a permanent effect, but as a result, I need to give ascorbic acid in massive doses before it has any effect on the subjects—patients, I should say. At the current rate of use, I will run out of ascorbic acid in ten days."

"Run out?" Paris echoed.

Janeway lifted an eyebrow at him. "Can you make more?"

"Only through the replicators," the doctor answered.

"What will that do to power consumption, Mr. Torres?" Janeway asked, and was pleased to see the engineer already busy with her datapadd.

"Well, we can do it," Torres answered, after a moment, "but it's going to bring down our overall output by almost four percent. And if we have to make really large quantities. . . ."

Her voice trailed off, and the doctor said, "Which we will, almost certainly."

"Four percent's not so bad," Neelix said, and Torres fixed him with a long stare.

"We don't have four percent to spare, unless you want to find us a new fuel source as well."

"Sorry, I'm sure," Neelix said hurriedly, and Torres looked back at her padd.

"I also ran the figures for going completely to the replicators for our food supply. If we strictly rationed consumption—and I mean at or below the minimums necessary to function—we could feed the entire ship for three weeks before we begin to touch the fuel supplies. That's not counting the cost of replicating vitamin C tablets, too."

"May I see your figures?" the doctor asked, and Torres nodded. She touched her padd to feed the files to his terminal, and the hologram cocked his head to one side. "Captain, use of these numbers would certainly lead to serious illness among the crew."

"If we ate any better—" Torres broke off, getting herself under control with an effort. "Unless we go to this level, and, yes, I know it's well below the recommended minimum, the sacrifice won't do us any good."

"Any other alternatives?" Janeway asked.

Torres paused. "I've also worked out a power conservation schedule that spreads the power-down periods around the ship. We can save some power that way, but it won't make enough difference in the long run—it just postpones the inevitable for a little."

"Then let's postpone it," Janeway said. "Keep rationing as a last resort, and go to the power-down schedule. Chakotay, about the long-range scan—"

"I'll keep working on it," the first officer answered. "But right now, Captain, space looks pretty much the same in all directions."

"I would also add that, according to Mr. Neelix, most of the habitable planets in this sector are claimed by either the Kazon-Ogla or their allies," Tuvok said. "If we go looking for food in those areas, we risk having to fight for it."

It was not an encouraging statement, and it produced a moment of profound silence. Then Kes cleared her throat. "Excuse me," she said, her small clear voice seemingly very loud in the quiet, "but has Neelix already mentioned the Kirse?"

Janeway blinked. "No, he hasn't."

"I was going to," Neelix began, with a defensive glance at Kes, "but I really can't recommend it as a course of action. They're not the sort of people I like to deal with, and I can't imagine that the captain would want to meet them, either—"

Janeway leaned back in her chair, steepling her fingers. "Mr. Neelix. Tell us about the Kirse."

Neelix sighed. "I really don't know that much about them, Captain. The information I have is, well, thirdhand at best."

"That's quite all right," Janeway said, and kept her patience with an effort. "Please go on."

Neelix swallowed hard, responding more to her tone than her words. "The Kirse, as I understand it, are both the trading partners and the sworn enemy of the Andirrim—they're a Kazon-Ogla client race, I mentioned them to Mr. Tuvok."

"Warlike, semifeudal, and xenophobic," Tuvok said. "Quite similar to the Kazon-Ogla, in fact."

"Only not as good at it," Neelix said. "The local Kazon-Ogla leaders aren't exactly the most ferocious in the galaxy, but they were able to deal with the Andirrim pretty handily—"

"Mr. Neelix," Janeway said. "What about the Kirse?"

"But I'm trying to tell you about them," Neelix said. "I only know about the Kirse because of the Andirrim. The Andirrim say that the Kirse planet is an incredible place, a paradise, even, with everything anyone could desire available just for the asking. The entire world is a garden, lush and fertile, and the Kirse live without work—or so the Andirrim say, anyway. They also said that the planet is ringed by an almost-impenetrable defense system, and breaking through it to conduct raids is their adulthood test."

"I thought you said they traded with the Kirse," Chakotay said.

"They do that, too," Neelix answered. "Just not to prove they're adults."

"The Kirse are still willing to trade with them, in spite of the raiding?" Janeway asked.

Neelix nodded. "The Kirse enjoy driving a hard bargain, or so the Andirrim I talked to said. Very sly people, the Kirse—they always keep the letter of their word, so you have to be very, very careful what you agree to."

"If the Kirse world is such a paradise," Chakotay said, slowly, "what exactly do they want from the Andirrim?"

"Ah, that's the interesting part," Neelix said. "And this I do know for certain, because the Andirrim were buying their trade goods from me, to resell to the Kirse. The Kirse buy metals. Apparently—or at least according to the Andirrim captain I talked to—the Kirse built their gardens after they built their technology, and the gardens have spread and pretty much taken over the planet. The Kirse don't like to disturb them if they can help it, so they trade for some of their metals rather than tear up the planet's surface. Or maybe there isn't any left. The captain wasn't very clear on the subject."

"So they're high-tech, too?" Paris said. "They sound too good to be true."

"They do maintain the defense system," Neelix said. "That's a definite fact. And they buy metals."

"They could be a people in decline from a technological high point," Tuvok said. He was frowning slightly, considering the evidence, a familiar expression that made Janeway once again glad to have him on board.

Chakotay shook his head. "Not if they're still holding off the Andirrim's raids. Besides, respect for their land—their planet—isn't evidence of decadence."

"It is if it's at the expense of their own safety," Torres muttered.

Janeway leaned back in her chair again, putting the

voices out of her mind. The Kirse world sounded rich beyond anything she had hoped—rich enough to meet the needs of the ship, great as those were; even if the Andirrim had exaggerated, and Neelix then exaggerated on top of that, in his desire to fit in with the crew, it should be possible to trade for food that would at least keep them all healthy until *Voyager* could find a further source of supply. And if the Kirse had a technological base that let them create a nearly impenetrable defense system for the planet . . . She hesitated for a moment, weighing what she'd seen of Kazon-Ogla technology. Its uses might be crude, and it might not match the Federation's, but it was effective. If the Kirse could hold off the Andirrim, then they would almost certainly be advanced enough to synthesize the vitamin C the ship needed. *Of course,* she added, with a wry and inward smile, *the fact that I don't see any other alternatives does make the decision easier.*

She cleared her throat, and all eyes turned to her, Paris pausing in midsentence, a slightly guilty look on his face. She decided to ignore it, and said, "As far as I can see, gentlemen, the Kirse planet seems to be our best option. Unless someone has a compelling argument against it—" She paused, but no one answered. "Very well. Mr. Paris, get the information from Mr. Neelix, and set a course for the Kirse planet. Mr. Tuvok, Mr. Chakotay, Mr. Kim—and you too, Mr. Neelix, when you're finished with Mr. Paris—we need to discuss what we can offer the Kirse in exchange for these supplies."

CHAPTER
2

EVEN AT WARP SEVEN, A FULL WARP FACTOR FASTER THAN their standard cruising speed, it took almost ten days to find the Kirse planet. Tom Paris, who had extrapolated the course from Neelix's charts and memory, found himself glued to the sensors, unable to stop himself jumping every time the long-range scanners spotted a new star system. None of them were the Kirse world, of course—they were too far out, wouldn't come into range for some hours yet even at the most generous predictions—but even so he found himself extending his time on the bridge until the captain banished him, pointing out that his watch had ended almost an hour before. There was no arguing with that, but at the same time, he was too keyed up to return to his stateroom, especially alone. That left the officers' lounge, and he ordered the turbolift to take him there, hoping he would find some company there.

Since the discovery of the shortages, the mess hall

had been less busy than usual. It was depressing, most people found, to sit at tables where they ate only the necessary minimum while Neelix's cooking tables were piled high with useless food, and it had suddenly ceased to be the center of everyone's social life. Paris hesitated in the doorway, seeing the rows of empty tables, but then, just as he was about to turn away, he saw a familiar pair of square gold shoulders sitting at a corner table. The woman opposite Kim lifted her head and smiled, beckoning him over. Paris gave a sigh of relief that he didn't let himself feel, and moved to join them.

"How's it going?" the woman asked. She was tall, good-looking in a full-bodied, fair-skinned way, and even though she'd turned him down more than once, Paris felt a twinge of jealousy as he seated himself next to Kim.

"About the same. Still no sign of the Kirse planet, but if our projections are right, we should be seeing the first signs of it in about four hours."

"Not bad," Kim said, and reached across to pour himself another cup of tea. He winced as the movement caught his sore elbow or wrist, and Paris looked away, not knowing what to do. There was nothing he could do, of course—they were all showing signs of scurvy now, the sore joints, the bruising; he himself had spat blood for almost fifteen minutes that very morning, just from cleaning his teeth—and even sympathy had become more annoying than useful. The signs weren't really bad enough to keep them from doing their jobs, but they were an alarming taste of things to come—unless they found the Kirse planet.

"Do you want a cup, Tom?" Kim went on, and Paris shook his head.

"Not at the moment, thanks. I'm supposed to be off-duty, and I should get some sleep sometime."

"That doesn't sound like you," the woman said, and gave a sly smile. "Are you feeling all right?"

"Very funny, Renehan," Paris said, and her smile widened slightly.

Kim said, "I wonder what the captain will do if the defenses are as good as Neelix says?"

Paris shrugged. "Presumably we can talk the Kirse into letting us through."

Renehan nodded. "I think we can count on the old 'The enemy of my enemy is my friend' to get us at least a hearing."

"And we do have trade goods," Kim said. "More than I thought we would."

"Oh?" Paris asked. "I didn't know you were part of that team."

Kim nodded. "It turns out there's a decent amount of scrap metal on board. I guess it was intended for engineering repairs, or at least that's how the computer has it filed in the manifest."

Renehan chortled. "I bet Torres was happy to give you her spare parts."

Kim grinned in answer. "She wasn't best pleased, no. But she finally agreed that she could spare some of the tonnage."

Paris smiled, too, but wondered what would happen if there wasn't enough metal, or if it turned out not to be what the Kirse wanted. *Voyager* needed the supplies badly already; if the Kirse refused them, if they had to find another source of food—most of the human crew were already feeling the effects of the deficiency, and there weren't enough nonhumans on board to run the ship. The obvious possibility loomed large in his mind: *Voyager* was one of the most powerful ships they had seen in the Delta Quadrant, its technology superior to anything the Kazon-Ogla possessed. If it came to it, they could probably take what they needed— He shook his head, rejecting the thought. He couldn't imagine Janeway, or even Chakotay, Maquis and renegade though he was, giving that order. *Would I?* he wondered. *Could I? Oh, yeah, I'm a real hard man, done my time and everything, but this, pure piracy . . . even in the best of causes, I'm not sure I could. The risks are too great.* It was an odd discovery, almost disconcerting— Starfleet training lasting longer than he'd ever thought possible, he told himself—and he shook the idea away. Besides, the other point of Starfleet training was to avoid getting into impasses in the first place, and Janeway had obviously learned her lessons well. It shouldn't come to that. "So how's Neelix handling it?" he asked, almost at random, and earned an odd look from Renehan.

"What are you talking about, Tom?"

"I know he was upset about the cooking situation," Paris answered. "I wondered if he'd calmed down."

"He seems to have," Kim answered, and whatever else he would have said was cut off by the beep of their communicators.

"Mr. Kim, Mr. Paris, report to the bridge." Chakotay's voice was controlled, but Paris thought he could hear an edge of excitement in it. "We've found the Kirse planet."

"On my way," Paris answered automatically, and the ship's computer spoke over him.

"All off-duty personnel, report to your stations. All off-duty personnel, report to your stations."

"That's me, then," Renehan said. "Let's hope we find something."

"We'd better," Kim said, and looked embarrassed by his own fervor.

Renehan's blue-team station was on the lower decks, near the engine room. Paris and Kim took a turbolift, reaching the bridge as the computer announced, "All crew members in position." Paris settled into position behind the helm as the thin-faced ensign who had had the conn slid aside, and called up a quick review of the ship's status. Everything seemed normal, all systems at maximum efficiency, and he switched to a sensor feed. The unenhanced view seemed unimpressive, a tiny disk barely larger than the nail of his little finger, too small as yet to show the clouds and colors of an inhabited world, but he heard Kim whistle softly to himself as he examined the sensor readouts.

The captain obviously heard it, too, though Paris didn't dare look back to check her expression. "Report, Mr. Kim."

"Still scanning, Captain," Kim answered. He was learning, Paris thought. Not long ago, he would have apologized, or rushed to finish, but he'd learned to take his time. "Sensors confirm this is a class-M planet. The atmosphere is almost identical to Earth's, down to trace gases, and the oceans are also remarkably Earth-like, including mineral content."

"Vegetation?" Janeway asked.

"Still scanning," Kim answered. "There's a lot of it, Captain, and all complex. It looks like Neelix didn't exaggerate at all."

"Take us in closer, Mr. Paris," Janeway said. "Impulse speed. Mr. Tuvok, any sign of this defense system Neelix mentioned?"

"Not yet, Captain," the Vulcan answered. "All security scanners are at maximum."

"Maintain that," Janeway said. "Proceed when ready, Mr. Paris."

Paris touched his controls, setting up an easy course

into the Kirse system. The planet lay between them and the diamond-bright pinpoint of the sun; as he fed the numbers into the computer, the image on the screen shifted, the disk of the planet slowly eclipsing the distant star. "Course locked in," he announced. "Engaged."

For long minutes, nothing happened. In the main screen, the disk swelled fractionally, revealed a hint of blues and pale grays that Paris guessed would resolve into the familiar streaks and whorls of a class-M planet's cloudy atmosphere. At his own station, the course numbers clicked past, registering otherwise all-but-invisible progress, and the screens that relayed vital sensor indications stayed monotonously empty.

"I'm picking up metal in orbit," Kim began, and Tuvok cut him off.

"Captain, there are defense stations in orbit around the Kirse planet."

"All stop," Janeway said instantly, and Paris was quick to obey. "All right, put it on the main screen, Mr. Tuvok."

"Yes, Captain." The Vulcan manipulated his controls, and the planet vanished, to be replaced by a highly colored version of the same image. Flecks of brighter light appeared as well, most clustered around the planet's equator, but some in what seemed to be circumpolar orbits. There were dozens of them, Paris realized, and at the same time realized that they were seeing only a part of the system. There would have to be as many similar stations on the far side of the planet to provide the coverage the Kirse seemed to want.

"Each of those dots represents an orbiting phaser platform," Tuvok said. "They are positioned so as to create overlapping firezones that cover all approaches to the planet. It seems that Mr. Neelix was correct in reporting an all but impenetrable shield around the planet."

Janeway didn't answer for a moment, and Paris glanced over his shoulder, to see her staring thoughtfully at the screen. "What's the range on those things?"

"Uncertain." Tuvok's hands were busy on his console as he spoke. "The power apparently available would indicate that the phasers are capable of reaching some distance, particularly if they were linked in series. However, the configuration of the firing points suggests that the stations are designed primarily for short-range use, and not for linked fire. If that is the case, then the range is actually quite limited, less than half the planetary radius, but the actual phaser fire would be correspondingly strong."

"Captain," Kim said. "I've isolated the command frequency for the platforms. It seems to be mostly machine language, platform-to-platform communication."

"I can confirm that, Captain," Tuvok said. "The computer indicates that these are a constant test pattern."

"Test pattern?" Paris asked, in spite of himself, and looked away in embarrassment as the Vulcan looked at him.

"The defense zone seems to be intended to be largely self-maintaining. The communications we are receiving are simply each platform confirming its own status and inquiring the status of the next platform in the series. The pattern also indicates the presence of smaller components which I cannot identify at this distance."

"I wonder what happens when they get a negative answer," Chakotay said.

"I don't think we'd like to be there to find out,"

Janeway answered. "Mr. Kim, can you pick out a communications channel? Not for the machines, I mean."

Kim shook his head. "I've been trying, Captain. I'm not getting communications from any higher life-forms. In fact, I haven't been able to pick up any life-forms at all on the planet."

"None?" Chakotay said, sharply.

Janeway frowned. "Sensor error?"

"I don't know," Kim said, "but I don't think so." His hands moved over his console again, confirming his previous readings. "We could simply be out of range—we are close to our limits—but usually we can pick up gross life signs from a planetary population at this point."

"Interesting," Chakotay said, and Paris rolled his eyes. The first officer had, it seemed, a gift for understatement.

Janeway acknowledged the comment with a nod. She stared at the screen for a moment longer, her hands on her hips, then turned back to her chair. "Well, there's no point in hovering out here wondering. Mr. Tuvok, find the likely range of those platforms."

Tuvok touched controls, and the planet in the screen was suddenly surrounded by a red haze. "This represents the zone of greatest danger from the platform-mounted phasers. As long as we stay outside of that, our shields should be able to handle an attack, and our far greater mobility will move us quickly out of danger."

"Very well," Janeway said. "Take us on in, Mr. Paris, just to the edge of the red zone—and be ready to raise the shields at the first sign of an attack."

"Aye, Captain," Paris answered, and touched his controls to adjust the course. "Going in."

Voyager eased forward, sliding easily along an invisible line in space. Paris watched the image swell in the viewscreen—a lovely planet, more green than blue, streaked with clouds that obscured the surface from their visual scans—and wondered just what was hiding under those pretty clouds. Already, the first of the platforms was just visible, a boxy, odd-angled shape studded with antennae and a single shallow dish that had to be the phaser mount. It looked like an old-style ship's phaser, the kind that Starfleet had declared obsolete a hundred years ago, but Paris wasn't sure if he found that reassuring. Those phasers had worked well enough, after all, and there were a lot more of them on the orbiting stations than there were phasers on *Voyager*.

A buzzer sounded softly, warning him that they were approaching the end of the preprogrammed course, and he took a deep breath, switching from autopilot to manual controls. "We're coming up on the defense zone's boundary now, Captain."

"Any response from the platforms?" Janeway asked, and Paris found himself tensed for the answer.

"Nothing, Captain," Tuvok said.

"You don't suppose they haven't seen us?" Paris said, and heard Chakotay laugh softly.

"I hope not. I wouldn't want to surprise them."

"I have no information on that," Tuvok answered. "We have not been scanned on any frequency that we normally monitor."

"I've finished our preliminary scan," Kim said, "and I'm getting very odd readings, Captain."

"Such as?"

"I'm still not getting clear life signs," Kim said, "but I have found definite signs of habitation."

"Put it on the main screen," Janeway said.

Paris caught his breath as the planet's disk vanished

from the screen, to be replaced by a series of towers that rose from an elliptical complex of shorter buildings. Their surfaces gleamed, as though they were washed with rain, but the sky shone clear and blue behind them. "What the hell are they made of?"

"I can't tell," Kim answered. "It could be either metal or stone or something in-between that the computer can't recognize."

"Well, it took an advanced civilization to build it, whatever it's made of," Janeway said. "What about life signs, Mr. Kim?"

"Still inconclusive, but—"

Whatever Kim would have said next was drowned in the sudden flat crack, more light than sound, that filled the screen. Paris flinched away, keeping his hands on his controls with an effort, but the white brilliance seemed to pass over and through him, blinding him completely. He bit back a cry, of fear or warning, he wasn't sure which, and groped for the controls again, finding them by touch alone.

"What the devil was that?" Janeway demanded, and to Paris's amazement she sounded more annoyed than anything. He blinked, tears filling his eyes, and the haze faded from white to green, began to clear a little. "All stations, report!"

"All systems normal," Paris said.

"Same here, Captain," Kim answered.

"Hull integrity and environmental systems are unaffected," Tuvok said.

"Everything's all right in engineering," Torres's voice said, from the intercom, "but that was a hell of a shock. What happened?"

"That's not yet clear, Lieutenant Torres," Janeway answered. "We'll keep you informed." She lifted her finger from the intercom button, and looked at Chakotay. "Any guesses?"

"A scan of some kind," the first officer answered.

"I can confirm that, Captain," Tuvok said. "We seem to have experienced a full-spectrum scan from the planet."

"Its source?" Janeway demanded.

"I cannot be certain," Tuvok said, "but all indications are that it came from the structure presently on the screen."

Well, that was no surprise, Paris thought, still rubbing his eyes. Where else would it come from? A dozen other alternatives instantly presented themselves—underground installations, the platforms, almost anything—and he was glad he hadn't spoken.

"And I'm still not reading life signs," Kim said. "Or a power base sufficient to have sent that pulse."

"Can you trace a communications spectrum?" Janeway asked.

Kim shook his head. "Everything reads dead now, Captain. There was just that pulse and then—nothing."

"Open hailing frequencies," Janeway said. "Our own standard set, plus anything we've seen used in this quadrant."

"Including Kazon-Ogla frequencies?" Kim asked.

"A good question," Janeway said, and Paris glanced over his shoulder to find her smiling slightly. "Yes, use them. That's one set the Kirse will be sure to monitor."

Kim nodded, hands busy on his controls, and Paris swung back to his own station. "Hailing frequencies open, Captain."

"This is Captain Kathryn Janeway of the Federation starship *Voyager*," Janeway said, pitching her voice to carry to the communications relays. "We come in peace, and would like to establish trade relations with the inhabitants of this planet. Please respond."

Paris fixed his eyes on the main screen, waiting for it to dissolve into the familiar larger-than-life figures of full communications. Instead, the complex of buildings remained on the screen, empty of life and movement. Their surfaces shone in the local sun's pale light, an odd, oily brilliance that was like nothing he'd ever seen before. Stone or metal, the shapes were graceful, weirdly beautiful—they looked, he thought, like the city sculptures he'd seen once on Delphis IV, celebrations of the Delphians' crowded, transurban world.

After a moment, Kim said, almost apologetically, "There's no response, Captain."

"Keep trying." Janeway pushed herself out of her chair, stood hands on hips, staring at the screen with narrowed eyes. "And carry on with the science scans."

"Yes, Captain."

"Check for any sign of recent fighting, too," Chakotay said, and came to stand beside Janeway.

She lifted an eyebrow at him. "Surely if the Andirrim had done enough damage to prevent the Kirse responding to our hail, we'd be able to see signs of it from space."

Chakotay shrugged. "We don't know how large a population the Kirse actually have. One good reason for spending resources on an automated defense system as elaborate as this one could be a small or a declining population."

"It's possible," Janeway said, but shook her head. "And right now, Mr. Chakotay, we've got too many possibilities to be useful."

She sounded almost Vulcan as she said that, and Paris hid a grin, imagining Tuvok's startled approval.

He realized that Chakotay was looking at him then, and hastily fixed his attention on his own controls, running an unnecessary diagnostic just to have something to do. The navigation sensors were as empty as the rest of the sensor screens, only the phaser platforms moving in their careful orbits, chattering to themselves, apparently oblivious of the ship hanging just outside their range. *Or I hope we're outside their range,* Paris amended. *At least they don't seem all that interested.*

"I'm not picking up any tracks of recent phaser fire," Kim said. "Or anything else that could mean a recent attack."

"The defense platforms do not seem to have fired recently, either," Tuvok said. "Their current configuration suggests that they have been on standby for some time."

"The preliminary science scan shows that nearly ninety percent of the land in the temperate zones is under cultivation," Kim said, "and we haven't even begun to classify everything. It looks as though there are plenty of plants carrying hexuronic acid, though, so we ought to be able to get everything we need. I am picking up what might be lower life-forms, but my readings are inconclusive. It could be sophisticated organic-based machinery."

"What about the citadel?" Janeway asked.

Paris could almost hear the shrug in Kim's voice. "I'm not picking up anything there, Captain. There is power in some kind of storage cell, but it's very low level. No life-forms at all."

"Captain, the pattern of power use suggests that the building may be on standby," Tuvok said. "Its condition is similar to that of the platforms."

Janeway was silent for a long moment, so long that Paris ventured another glance over his shoulder, to see her staring at the screen, a faint, thoughtful frown on her face. "Very well," she said at last. "We'll give the Kirse another chance to show themselves. Mr. Paris, put us into orbit outside the optimum range of those platforms, and, Mr. Kim, set up an automatic contact transmission. We'll give them twelve hours to respond, and then we'll see. In the meantime, keep scanning. Let's get as complete a picture as possible of this planet."

"Aye, aye, Captain." Kim's response was still Academy-perfect, and Paris knew his own acknowledgment sounded even sloppier by comparison. He felt his cheeks burning, and turned his attention to his console, fingers moving easily over the complex controls, setting up the optimum orbit. *At least I know how to do this,* he thought, *and there's not an Academy graduate who can match me.* The bravado rang a little hollow even in his own mind; he made a face, and touched the controls again.

"Moving into orbit now, Captain."

"Excellent, Mr. Paris," Janeway said. "Twelve hours, gentlemen. Let's see if we can find the Kirse."

Not entirely to Janeway's surprise, the twelve hours passed without any further sign of life from the surface. In part, she thought, it was a good thing—she had been able to get a full eight hours' sleep for once—but all things considered, it would have been simpler if they had made some sort of contact. She pushed Neelix's latest effort at breakfast aside and concentrated on her datapadd. The reports flashed past as she scanned through them, all monotonously the same, except for the doctor's. More than half the human crew were seriously affected by the deficiencies, and the level of supplemental dosage needed to stave off problems for the rest of the crew was approaching toxicity—and even that would be impossible to sustain without using the replicators. At least the news from the science scan was good. The Kirse world was lovely, filled with vegetation that would almost certainly supply their every need, but there was no sign of the inhabitants, no sign of the sophisticated culture that had built the citadel. She touched controls on the datapadd to recall the report that covered the massive structure, and the image filled the little screen. Towers rose from a central hexagon, each one different from the rest—one topped with thin structures like old-fashioned radio antennae, another glittering as though sheathed in ice or glass, still another sporting a bulbous, gold-washed shape that looked vaguely familiar, if only from holograms—and dozens of outbuildings spread from that center, creating a pattern like a slanted spider's web or early frost on a windowpane. It was strikingly beautiful, an artificial structure as lush as the flourishing plant life, and obviously the work of skilled engineers, the same skilled engineers who had created the network of defense platforms—who were nowhere to be found.

She shook her head, leaving the image on the screen, and addressed herself to the plate in front of her. Neelix had done his best to create something both palatable and nutritious that didn't use too much of the defective foodstock, but his best efforts still left much to be desired, and she regarded the grainy mess—roughly based, she suspected, on Tom Paris's unenthusiastic description of oatmeal—without pleasure. Still, it was carbohydrates, and she took a careful bite. It was less sweet than she had expected, and bland to the tongue; she swallowed hard, almost wishing for some of Neelix's more dramatic spices, and reached for the vitamin supplement the doctor had provided from his dwindling supplies. It was orange, a failed attempt to mimic a natural juice, and she drank it as quickly as she could, putting aside the glass with a grimace of distaste. Here in the privacy of her quarters, she could at least indulge her own dislike without worrying that she was setting a bad example, and she tossed the glass into the collection bin with more force that was strictly necessary. Even taking into account the fact that the doctor was a hologram, without taste buds and not yet used to full-time interaction with human beings, it simply tasted bad. She drew a glass of water to wash away the bitterness, and turned back to her desk.

"Computer, contact the duty officers, and tell them I want them in the ready room in—" She glanced at the nearest chronometer. "—fifteen minutes."

"Confirmed," the computer answered, and Janeway reached for her datapadd. She glanced at her image in the mirror beside her cabin door, making sure that she looked as collected—as unaffected by mere human frailties—as a Starfleet captain should be. Especially now, it was a necessary illusion.

She was the first one in the ready room, as she had intended, but almost as soon she had seated herself at the head of the table the door opened and Chakotay appeared. She nodded a greeting, and he gave her one of his rueful smiles.

"Nothing new so far," he said. "Either no one's home, or they're hiding from us. Kim hasn't been able to raise anyone on the planet, except the machines, and they don't want to talk to us either."

"So what do you think?" Janeway asked.

The first officer shrugged, and took his place at the table, adjusting his datapadd as he did so. "As I said before, it could be that the Kirse have been eliminated—I don't know why else they wouldn't respond at all to our presence. If they think we're hostile, well, they've got that defense system just waiting for us, and if they think we're friendly, there's no reason not to respond to our overtures." He spread his hands. "Except, of course, that there's no sign of damage to the citadel or to anything on the planet."

"I suppose something else could account for the disappearance," Janeway said, halfheartedly. "Disease, natural waning of the population—for all we know, they could have emigrated en masse, we'd never know the difference." She touched her controls, projecting the image of the Kirse world onto the larger of the viewscreens. The blue-green disk, cloud-streaked, seemed an almost mocking presence behind the cage of its defense network. "One thing I am sure of, though, Chakotay. We're going to have to get supplies here."

"I agree." Chakotay nodded, his tattooed face somber. "I've been over the latest figures with the doctor twice already. We don't have a choice anymore."

"No." Janeway broke off as the ready-room door opened again, admitting the rest of the junior officers in a cluster. An instant later, a second viewscreen lit, and the doctor looked out at her, Kes just visible over his shoulder. Janeway squared her shoulders and folded her hands on the table. "Gentlemen," she said. "Let's have your reports. We'll start with yours, Mr. Kim."

The young ensign glanced quickly at his datapadd, then back again. He looked exhausted, Janeway thought, and he moved with a care that suggested that his joints ached. "I can go into details, Captain, but it's pretty much what we saw in the first scan. There's plenty of food down there, food that we can eat which also contains hexuronic acid—that's the precursor to vitamin C—and most of the other elements we need.

Most of it seems to have been cultivated, at least originally. The whole planetary land mass, except for the area around the citadel, is like one big garden, or at least a series of linked gardens. It looks almost as though the continents have been modified to provide specific habitats and microclimates to grow the various plants. I think I've picked up traces of irrigation systems and artificially created land forms—mostly barrier hills and things like that, but some of the lakes look artificial, too." He touched his datapadd and a holographic globe appeared to float above the tabletop. "Of course, the area right around the citadel—" As he spoke, colors brightened on the image. "—there, for about a hundred kilometers all around, is heavily cultivated, and there are definite irrigation channels just under the surface. Some kind of sophisticated drip system, I think."

"But no sign of the builders," Janeway said.

Kim shook his head. "None, Captain."

Janeway studied the image, trying to imagine what could make a people abandon a world like this. "What about life-forms? Any more detail?"

To her surprise, it was Chakotay who answered. "Nothing conclusive. Mr. Kim and I have been over the readings a couple of times, and Lieutenant Torres rerouted systems power to try to improve the resolution, but we're still pretty much where we started. There are things that might be animals down there, but they could be complicated machines."

"Organic based machines," Torres corrected. She looked at Janeway. "I think Neelix was probably right about the Kirse needing to trade for metals. There doesn't seem to be a whole lot on the planet."

"But no intelligent life?" Janeway asked.

Kim shook his head. "Not that we can find."

"You're sure these are animals?" Paris asked. "I

mean, if you can't tell for sure what they're made of, how can you tell if they're smart?"

"They're engaged in what look like highly repetitive, probably food-gathering activities pretty much all the time," Kim answered.

Paris gave a fleeting grin. "So if they are intelligent, they're probably bored?"

Kim smothered a smile of his own. "Probably."

Janeway allowed herself a smile as well—after all, if they could still make jokes, however bad, they had to be doing better than she'd thought—and looked at Tuvok. "Have you been able to find out anything more about the defense platforms, Mr. Tuvok?"

"I've run a complete analysis," the security officer answered, "and I've been able to make a partial assessment of their capabilities. Our present orbit is just outside their optimum focus, which means that, should the Kirse or their machines decide that we are a threat, our shields would be able to withstand their strongest attack for the time needed to take us out of orbit."

Paris cleared his throat, the smile vanishing from his face. "Mr. Tuvok and I have programmed an escape pattern into the navigational computers. If we're fired on, that'll take us out of range by the quickest route."

"Excellent," Janeway said, and meant it.

"Also," Tuvok went on, "the spacing of the orbits and the weaponry aboard the platforms suggests that they are designed to intercept an attacking force by phaser fire only. In other words, they have no shields."

"How do they defend the platforms themselves, then?" Chakotay asked.

"Each platform is heavily armored," Tuvok answered. "It appears to be a collapsed metal sheathing.

Also, there are molecular differences among the various pieces of armor that suggest they were installed at different times."

"So what you're saying," Janeway said, "is that they don't have the transporter, either."

Tuvok nodded. "That is correct, Captain. Neither the defense platforms nor what I assume to be the citadel's defense mechanisms are configured to block a transporter beam."

That was good news, and Janeway leaned back in her chair. An away team on the Kirse planet would have the margin of safety that the transporter had been invented to provide. For an instant, she felt as though she were caught in a timeslip—her crew suffering from scurvy, the transporter a significant advantage, the Federation out of range even of subspace radio—and then put the feeling firmly aside. The transporter was an advantage only as long as they were able to lower their own screens to receive the crew, but there should be enough of a communications lag between the planet and the defense systems to allow *Voyager* to retrieve the away team before it came under attack.

"Very well," she said aloud. "I assume you've all seen the doctor's report?" There were murmurs of agreement around the table, and she went on, "The gist of it is that we have to replenish at least some of our supplies here—we have no choice in the matter."

"Based on the estimates Lieutenant Torres gave me," the hologram said, "and the observed frequency of M-class planets in this sector, there will not be enough healthy crew members left to collect the food once we find a suitable planet if we don't resupply here."

"Exactly." Janeway gave a rueful smile. "So I intend to take an away team down to the planet—to the citadel, for a start—and see if we can find the Kirse. Mr. Paris, Mr. Kim, Lieutenant Torres, you'll accompany me."

"Captain," Tuvok said. "May I suggest that I be part of the team as well?"

Janeway shook her head. "I want you on the ship, Tuvok, where you can keep an eye on the defense platforms."

The Vulcan nodded, his face as impassive as ever, but Janeway thought she caught a hint of disapproval in his eyes. "Then may I suggest you take a larger security contingent?"

"I will take two more people," Janeway said. "But I don't want to suggest that our presence is hostile." She looked around the table. "Any further comments? Then let's go find what's happened to the Kirse."

CHAPTER
3

THE GROUP THAT GATHERED IN THE TRANSPORTER ROOM was quiet. Even Paris seemed subdued, and that, Kim thought, was hard to imagine until you saw it. He shrugged his shoulders, hoping to ease the aching joints, and grimaced as the pain redoubled. Across the compartment, Renehan did the same thing, and managed a rueful smile when she saw him watching.

"Lovely day for a landing party, don't you think?" Her voice was far more cheerful than her pale face.

"Lovely," he echoed, and Paris tapped him lightly on the shoulder.

"Oh, come on, Harry, what more could you ask for? An alien planet, a mysterious invisible race, the ship in desperate need—isn't that what you joined Starfleet for?"

"No." Kim smiled in spite of himself, and Renehan laughed aloud, drawing a curious look from the other security man.

"Well, I did join to see the galaxy, but I have to say this is more than I bargained for."

"Where's your sense of adventure?" Paris began, and broke off as the door slid back, revealing the captain and Chakotay. Kim looked hastily at his tricorder, triggering a final calibration run, but he could still feel the captain's sharp stare as she looked around the compartment.

Chakotay took his position behind the transporter technician, glancing over the woman's shoulder at the settings displayed on her board. "All ready here, Captain."

"And here," Janeway answered. "You have the conn, Mr. Chakotay. We'll check in every thirty minutes. If we miss a check, beam us up."

"Absolutely, Captain," Chakotay answered.

Janeway nodded, and stepped up onto the transporter platform. Kim took his place with the others, bracing himself for transport. It wasn't that the process was unpleasant, precisely, or even frightening, but more that the instant drop from one place to another could be disorienting—

"Energize," Janeway said, and the transporter room disappeared.

Kim blinked hard, and opened his eyes to brilliant sunlight and the deep green of a perfectly manicured lawn. In the distance, perhaps ten meters away, a row of trees no taller than his shoulder hung heavy with pale yellow fruit; he looked down, and stepped carefully away from a stand of saucerlike flowers streaked with red and yellow. A breeze touched his face, soft with sunlight and the faint sweet smells of the trees, and in the distance he heard a faint, strangely musical clicking, like the ghost of birdsong.

"Report," Janeway said, and Kim shook himself, brought up his tricorder.

He touched the control pad to run a standard scan, and watched the checklights flick from the orange of standby to the green of positive readings. At the same time, the first analysis scrolled past in the tricorder's tiny screen: no sign of poisons, no signs of harmful insects or animals, just the rich, unfamiliar plant life stretching for kilometers on every side. He looked up again, unable to suppress his pleasure in the sheer physical beauty of the planet, and said, "Nothing unexpected here, Captain. Just plants, nothing more."

"The same here," Renehan said, and the other security man echoed her.

Torres didn't answer, and Kim glanced curiously in her direction. The engineer was pacing slowly toward the line of trees, her brow even more furrowed as she frowned at the readings in her tricorder's screen.

"Lieutenant Torres?" Janeway said, and Torres swung back toward them.

"Sorry, Captain. I set my tricorder to scan specifically for signs of construction, and I found what seems to be a pipeline, directly underfoot. It could be an irrigation pipe, but it's pretty big for that."

Kim adjusted his own tricorder to match her scan, then touched controls to correlate those readings with the maps he had made from orbit. "It runs directly toward the citadel, Captain."

"Interesting." Janeway set her hands on her hips and turned slowly, surveying the parklands. "Still no life-forms?"

"Not on my scan," Renehan answered, and Kim swung his own tricorder in a full circle, confirming her results.

"I'm picking up something," Torres said, her frown deepening. "Toward the citadel. It could be those machines the scanners picked up back on *Voyager*."

Janeway nodded. "Well, there's no point in staying

here." She touched her communicator. *"Voyager,* this is Janeway."

Chakotay's response was reassuringly prompt. "Chakotay here, Captain."

"We're starting for the citadel," Janeway said. "Janeway out." She glanced at her team. "Mr. Kim, keep scanning anything that looks like a food crop. We might as well make sure we can eat what we trade for."

"If there's anybody to trade with," Paris murmured.

Janeway lifted an eyebrow. "We'll cross that bridge when we come to it, Mr. Paris. For now, this is an inhabited planet, and we are as yet uninvited guests."

"Sorry, Captain." Paris didn't sound particularly regretful, but Janeway seemed to take his words at face value.

"Right. Lieutenant Torres, does this—pipeline— go all the way to the citadel?"

"As far as I can tell, it does," Torres answered.

"Then we'll follow it, at least until we find a road." Janeway started along the line the engineer had indicated, but paused to glance back over her shoulder. "And, for those of you who are not from agricultural worlds, be careful of the growing crops. Don't walk on or among them if you can help it."

There was a ragged chorus of acknowledgment, and Kim stepped cautiously away from the saucer-shaped flowers. They were certainly lovely, but not, he thought, terribly practical. Then, reconsidering— how could he make that assumption on form alone?—he turned his tricorder on the nearest cluster. To his surprise, the tricorder registered a large, bulbous root system, and suggested further that it was edible by humans. He touched another set of keys, refining the analysis as far as he could without taking samples, and produced a profile that looked very like a terrestrial potato. He blinked in surprise, and touched the controls to run the test again.

"Hey, Harry! You coming?"

Kim looked up, still amazed by the results, and saw Paris beckoning from the far side of the lawn. "Sorry," he called back, and hurried to catch up. To his embarrassment, the captain looked over her shoulder at his approach.

"Something interesting, Mr. Kim?"

"Maybe, Captain," he answered, and suspected he was blushing. "One of the flower types back there, the ones that look like saucers, they have an edible root."

"Good," Janeway answered. "Keep scanning."

Kim murmured an answer, looking ahead toward the line of trees. Torres had almost reached them, her head down over her tricorder, following the trace of the pipeline beneath the surface of the lawn, and he lengthened his stride to catch up. As he got closer to the trees, he could smell the rich fragrance that rose from their leaves—very faintly like roses, he thought, and a little bit like lemons or pears. The pale yellow fruit, nestled among the thickly curling leaves, seemed by contrast to have no scent at all. He swung the tricorder at one anyway, and was not surprised to see that it was edible as well.

"Two out of two," Paris said, looking over his shoulder, and Kim suppressed a start.

"So far," he answered, and looked at the trees again. They stood in neat parallel rows, no one tree taller than his shoulder, and he stooped to examine the ground under them. It was as tidily empty as the lawn, and he hurried after Janeway. "Captain, about the trees . . ." Janeway paused, a look of inquiry on her face, and Kim hurried on. "Captain, I noticed that there aren't any drops under the trees—there doesn't even seem to be any blemished fruit on the branches."

Janeway looked at him. "I think we knew that these weren't wild plants, Mr. Kim."

"That's not my point." For an instant, Kim couldn't believe he'd said that, but Janeway nodded, and he went on, "It's not just that they're cultivated, but they've been tended recently. These fruits are really ripe, but there aren't any on the ground—and I do find insects in the branches, so there should be some. Unless something's cleaning them up."

Even as he spoke, a thumb-sized creature launched itself from the curled edge of a leaf with a loud clacking sound. Kim ducked in spite of himself, and the thing bumbled past, to settle on a higher branch. The green of its carapace blended with the leaf, so that it was all but invisible. Only the way the leaf sagged under its weight betrayed its presence.

"So I see," Janeway said, with a slight smile. She sobered quickly. "And you're right, Mr. Kim, that's a good point. So wherever the Kirse are now, they were here recently enough that the trees are still tended."

Kim nodded, and in the same instant, Torres called from beyond the row.

"Captain, I think I've found a road to the citadel."

Kim turned, and saw the engineer waving from a band of stone set into the perfectly manicured grasses. The ground sloped gently away behind her, the grass hidden by what he would have thought were low-growing weeds except for the way they met the grass in a perfect, tidy edge. It looked almost as though there were more fruits tucked under the heart-shaped leaves, and he ducked through the last row of trees to join Torres. Janeway followed more slowly, and Torres looked down at her tricorder.

"As best I can tell, this road goes to the citadel by the most direct route. At least I guess it's a road."

Kim scuffed his boot against the pale gold surface. From a distance, it had looked almost like an igneous inclusion in a bed of sedimentary rock, but up close, the edges looked too neat for it to be anything except an artifact. But if it was, he thought, how had it been laid? It looked like natural stone, like granite or flecked tergonite, but he couldn't see any seams where blocks could have been butted together to create the almost polished surface. "It looks like a road," he said aloud, and knew he sounded far less certain than his words.

"It certainly does," Janeway agreed. "And you say it runs to the citadel?"

Torres nodded. "The pipeline I mentioned, it runs under it, a little more than half a meter down."

"Well," Janeway said, and smiled. "We might as well follow it." She glanced at her own tricorder. "And we'd better get a move on. We're still almost three kilometers from the nearest building."

She started off without waiting for an answer. The others followed, but Kim paused to point his tricorder at the low-growing foliage beside the path. The spots of red that he'd though were fruit seemed to be tiny, spherical flowers, but the thick, almost-black leaves were rich in calcium, and seemed otherwise edible. He shook his head, amazed again at the fertility of the land, and Paris passed him, whistling a seven-note phrase.

"Come on, Harry," he called, over his shoulder, and Kim filed the tricorder reading for later study. Paris's whistling floated back to him, teasingly familiar, and he frowned, trying to remember the words that went with the tune. A children's film, he thought, and a very old one, but he couldn't remember any more. He shook the memory away, and lengthened his stride to catch up.

The stone road ran under an arch that seemed to grow from a pair of living trees, and then curved gently down a slope covered with more of the dark-green leaves. At the bottom of the slope, the ground was divided by low-growing hedges, none of them taller than Kim's knee, into a complicated pattern that seemed to be based on hexagons. Each of the sections was filled with a different plant, and in the center of the pattern a tree rose from a carpet of vivid blue flowers and spread into an almost flat canopy of bright yellow leaves. Or were they flowers? Kim wondered, and then caught his breath as something moved at the base of the tree. He trained his tricorder on it instinctively, and saw a phaser appear in Renehan's hand as if by magic.

"What is it?" Paris said, and Kim shook his head, watching the readings shift and change on the tricorder screen.

"I can't tell—"

Even as he spoke, the figure straightened to its two hind legs, reaching up to paw at the golden canopy overhead. It looked more humanoid in that position, definitely bipedal, despite the bowed legs and awkward, almost anthropoid stand. From this distance, it was hard to see if the dull gray was skin or scales or even short fur, though the color seemed to darken on the limbs, deepening almost to black in the clumsy, two-fingered hands. Kim glanced at his tricorder again, unable to make the readings match what he thought he was seeing. The tricorder called it a machine, or at least claimed there were machine parts in it, but at the same time, the system gave a weak life-form reading. The creature shook the tree, hard, and sent a shower of gold over itself. Something larger fell with the leaves, and the creature squatted to retrieve it, glancing over its shoulder as it did so. It saw the *Voyager* party, and started to its feet, dropping the fruit it had gathered half-eaten.

"Damn," Janeway said under her breath, and the creature leaped gracelessly over the nearest of the little hedges and bolted for the shelter of a distant stand of trees.

Torres shook her head in frustration. "The readings are still inconclusive, Captain. But it didn't look like a machine."

"I got the same results," Kim said. "A weak life-form reading, but also machine parts."

Janeway shook her head, staring at the trees where the creature had vanished. "Well, let's at least take a look at what it was eating—if it was eating."

Luckily, the road brought them to within two fields of the tree. Even at that distance, Kim could smell the odor that spilled from the tree. It was sweet but not sickly, a delicate perfume that promised the taste of nectar and made his stomach growl in response. He stepped carefully through the fields, and ducked under the low-growing canopy. The smell was even stronger there, and it was all he could do not to pull a fruit from the tree and taste it then and there. He pointed his tricorder at it instead, and was not surprised to find that it was well within the required parameters. A breeze stirred his hair, bathing him in a sudden gust of scent—like peaches and pears, he thought, or honeysuckles—and he swallowed hard as his mouth filled with saliva.

"They've got to be edible, with a scent like that," Renehan said, and Kim glanced again at the tricorder screen.

"Oh, yes, they're edible." He stooped to pick up the

dropped piece, and turned it curiously. Where the creature had bitten into it, the pale ivory flesh was already darkening, and a glint of dark red showed at the core. A seed, he guessed, and touched the tricorder's sampling wand to the exposed fruit. The results flashed back almost instantly: high in ascorbic acid and in several B-complex vitamins, as well as containing several highly rated flavor esters. "Not only that, it should taste good."

"Did you try it?" Paris asked.

Kim shook his head. "That's according to the tricorder."

"That's hardly conclusive," Paris said. "I propose we test one of them now. And I'll make the ultimate sacrifice and go first." He reached up, searching for fruit among the golden leaves.

"Hold it," Janeway said.

Paris froze. "Why not, Captain? Harry says they're edible."

"They may be," Janeway answered, "but they're also growing in somebody's garden. We're not touching anything until we've either gotten the Kirse's permission, or found out what's happened to them."

Paris withdrew his hand as though he'd been stung. Out of the corner of his eye, Kim saw Torres nodding thoughtfully, and set the half-eaten fruit carefully on the ground. It was already several shades darker than it had been, and growing less appetizing with every second.

Janeway allowed herself a rather wry smile. "And since I'm sensible of the appeal, let's get a move on. I'd like to find the Kirse myself."

Kim waded carefully through the smaller garden plots, but as he reached the road, he glanced back wistfully at the tree. The golden leaves were stirring, though he couldn't feel a breeze, and an instant later there was a flash of green light and a thin curl of smoke rose from the ground where he had left the fruit. "Captain!"

Janeway swung around, her eyebrows rising as she saw the smoke. "And I wonder what caused that, Mr. Kim?"

Kim was already examining his tricorder. "No information, Captain. When I examined the fruit, it registered traces of phosphorus, but they were literally traces. Not nearly enough to do something like that."

Janeway nodded. "So there's some other mechanism at work here."

"A cleaning system, maybe?" Torres asked. "To get rid of trash?"

"It seems something of a drastic remedy," Janeway said, "but I can't think of a better answer. I think we should stay away from the food plants from now on—stay on the road. We don't want to run into the equivalent of, say, a deer fence."

"What's a deer?" Renehan murmured. She had been talking to Paris, but Janeway heard.

"A large herbivore, noted for raiding gardens back on the part of Earth I come from. My point is, Ensign, we don't know what plants the Kirse particularly want to protect."

"Yes, Captain," Renehan said, and Kim could see color rising under her clear skin.

"So we stick to the road," Janeway went on. "Mr. Kim, you can scan from here."

"Yes, Captain." Kim adjusted his tricorder for a long-range scan, and started toward the citadel again.

The seamless stone ribbon led through another stand of trees—these taller, the smallest rising nearly ten meters from the ground, with silver-gray trunks and tiny, tri-lobed leaves that clung close to the stubby branches—and then into a field of waving grasses that rose to shoulder height on either side. The slim stalks were topped with bright pink plumes that tossed with the slightest breeze, and Torres smiled.

"They look like circus flags, from when I was young —or cotton candy."

Kim aimed his tricorder at them, and was almost relieved when the readout appeared. "Not these. There's sugar in them, but not a kind we can eat."

"What about the vine?" Janeway asked.

Kim looked down, startled. The ground between the edge of the road and the first stands of grass was covered with a low-growing, dove-gray vine, interspersed with narrow, trumpet-shaped flowers so dark that it was hard to tell if they were purple or blue. Tucked beneath one of the leaves, he thought he could see a smooth, egg-shaped pod, and he trained the tricorder sensors on it. "It might be good cooked, there's a lot of carbohydrates in it, but we'd have to do a certain amount of processing to get at them."

Janeway nodded, her attention already elsewhere, and Kim returned his tricorder to his belt. The breeze he had felt before was picking up again, ruffling his hair, and he could see faint puffs of pale yellow dust rising from the plumes as the wind took them. Pollen, he guessed, and was not surprised when Paris sneezed. The breeze strengthened further, bending the grasses into graceful arcs, the plumes nearly touching the ground. The sudden gusts sent a drift of pollen across the road's polished surface at his feet, and Kim held his breath as he stepped through it. Even so, he caught a whiff of a harsh, pungent odor— skunk and asafetida—and grimaced.

"Lovely stuff," Paris said, and Kim glanced back just in time to see the taller man stagger and sink to one knee.

"Captain!" Kim hooked his tricorder back on his belt and ran to help. Paris shook his head, hard, and Kim caught him by the shoulders, pulling him upright. "What happened, Tom?"

"Are you all right, Mr. Paris?" Janeway called. She was keeping her distance, Kim thought, and very properly, too. The last thing they needed was for the captain to be affected by whatever it was that had hit Paris.

Paris shook his head again, but took a step without falling. "Damned if I know. I smelled that stuff, the dust, and then, wham, I went down."

Kim shifted his grip on Paris's shoulders, freeing one hand to work his tricorder. "Nothing—no, wait. Hold your breath, Tom." He closed his own eyes for good measure as a spray of pollen washed past them, opened them again only as the breeze faded from his face. The readings glowed red in the tricorder's screen. "It's the pollen," he called. "It's not really harmful unless you breathe a whole lot of it, but it'll make you dizzy for a minute or two if you get a direct hit of it."

"Lovely stuff," Paris said again, and freed himself from Kim's grip. "I felt like I'd been drinking with Klingons."

"Are you all right now?" Kim asked, and touched keys to switch the tricorder to medical mode.

Paris nodded. "Yeah, I'm fine."

"Report, Mr. Kim," Janeway called, and Kim looked quickly over his shoulder.

"He's fine now. The pollen seems to be very quick-acting—quick to wear off, too."

"Will filter masks block it?"

Kim glanced again at the tricorder. "Yes, Captain. It's a pretty big grain."

"Good." Janeway touched her communicator. "Janeway to *Voyager.*"

"Chakotay here, Captain." The first officer's voice sounded tense, and Kim saw the captain's expression change.

"Is everything all right, Mr. Chakotay?"

"Everything's fine here, Captain. Are you all right? We've been picking up faint power fluctuations in your area, but we can't pinpoint the source."

"No real problems," Janeway answered, "just a plant with some—interesting—pollen. Beam down a set of standard filter masks, one for each of us. Get your fix from our communicators, we may be moving on."

"Aye, Captain," Chakotay said.

"Thank you, Chakotay. Janeway out." She looked at her team. "Come on, gentlemen, there's no point in standing here."

Maybe not, Kim thought, *but I'll be glad to get those filters.* He covered his nose and mouth with his hand as the wind shook another drift of the pale dust across the road, and heard Renehan cough and stumble. He turned back to help, but the other security man had already caught her by the elbow and was urging her along. Then the air shimmered, and a white-wrapped package appeared on the road surface perhaps a meter ahead. Torres—she seemed least affected by the pollen, Kim thought, maybe because of her Klingon blood—made a little noise of satisfaction and sprinted to retrieve it. The others hurried to join her, and Torres handed out the masks, folding the white wrapping into a neat packet that she tucked into her belt pack. Kim took his gratefully, fitting the cool plastic over his nose and mouth, and took a cautious breath. It was mostly imagination, he knew, but he felt more levelheaded already.

"Captain," Torres said, her clear voice only slightly muffled by the mask. "Do you suppose this is deliberate action?"

"A defense mechanism of some kind?" Janeway asked. Kim stiffened at the thought. It would make sense, explaining the increased power use Chakotay had registered from orbit, and why a plant would possess a soporific pollen— He stopped then, shook his head, annoyed at his own assumptions. The pollen hadn't necessarily evolved to be soporific; it was probably a side effect of something else, an unpredictable interaction with human metabolism. Besides, it would be all but impossible to control the release of the pollen, and equally easy to defeat. The captain shook her head then, echoing his thoughts. "It's possible, B'Elanna, but it seems, well, rather—subtle—for a defensive tactic. What good is a defense that you can circumvent with something as simple as these masks?"

"It still seems like a coincidence," Torres muttered, and shook her head. "But at least the masks work."

The wind died down even before they reached the end of the grass field, and the last sprinkles of pollen drifted slowly across the road, slick as powder underfoot. Another line of trees marked the end of the field, their dark gray trunks, each easily as thick as Kim's upper arm, winding around each other like vines to form a solid barrier. Only the road was clear, the vine-trees lifting into a delicate arch above the stone ribbon. Beyond it, the ground dropped suddenly away into a wide, steep-sided ravine, and Kim could hear water running somewhere nearby. Steps led down to the road's continuation, a wider path with a water-filled channel carving running along its center. It ran straight across the ravine, supported presumably on invisible pylons, and Kim, squinting, thought he could just make out a second set of steps leading up to another vine arch on the far side.

Torres pointed her tricorder at the bridge, and Renehan copied her, her own free hand never far from her tricorder. "The structure seems sturdy enough," Renehan said, after a moment, and Torres nodded.

"It's like a classic aqueduct. It'll hold double its own weight, easily." She frowned at her readings again. "That channel is the continuation of the pipeline we've been following."

"Any sign of booby traps?" Janeway asked. "Or any security devices?"

"Nothing," Torres answered. "And I'm not getting any of the power readings Chakotay mentioned."

"Right." Janeway glanced at the knotted vines to either side of the road. "Well, we don't seem to have much choice, in any case. Let's go."

The sound of water grew louder as they came down the stairs and onto the bridge, louder than seemed reasonable from the channel alone. Kim moved cautiously toward the edge of the road—there were no railings, just a low stone lip—and peered over, to see a river a dozen meters below at the bottom of the ravine. The water frothed white in patches, boiling over rocks, and spray rose from a short waterfall just above the bridge. It was a beautiful sight, strangely Earthlike, and Kim was suddenly overcome by the realization of just how far they were from home. Seventy-five years of travel, most of a human being's lifetime, and even then they would barely be in range of home. . . . He shook himself, hard, forced away the memories, and followed the others along the bridge.

"It's interesting," Torres said, abruptly, her tricorder pointing at the river. "This seems to be the first really natural feature we've seen, but there still aren't any native life-forms in it. At least there's nothing that the tricorder recognizes as unambiguously organic."

"Is there something ambiguously organic?" Paris asked, and Torres shook her head.

"Not even that."

Janeway paused, and Kim heard her sigh. "I am very much looking forward to meeting the Kirse," she said, to no one in particular, and moved on toward the far shore.

The tree-vines that formed the barrier on the far side were paler, and bore clusters of bright red flowers. No, not flowers, Kim amended, training his tricorder on the nearest cluster, but leaves that mimicked flowers. Then he looked up, and all thoughts of Kirse plant life vanished from his mind. The field ahead stretched unbroken to the horizon, and the towers of the citadel were clearly visible, eight, a dozen primary towers soaring in a group above the jagged lower roofline. The sun glinted off them as though they were made of metal, drowning all guess at their color. Kim looked away again, dazzled, and heard Paris swear under his breath. Something was moving among the low-growing trees—more than one something. Several creatures like the one they had seen foraging beneath the golden-leafed tree were rooting beneath a thickly berried bush, one squatting on its haunches, industriously scratching at the dirt, the others searching through the leaves. Even as Kim watched, one reached up and shook the branches vigorously, sending a spray of bright green berries over the others. The squatting creature squealed and covered its head, while the other bounced excitedly up and down for a moment before it stooped to the fallen berries.

"I'm reading at least twenty more of them," Torres said.

"Phasers, Captain?" Renehan asked, and Janeway shook her head.

"Not yet, Ensign. But be ready. All of you, keep close together." She touched her communicator. "Janeway to *Voyager.*"

"Chakotay here."

"We've stumbled across a group of the creatures," Janeway said. "Stand by to beam us up if there's trouble."

"We're standing by, Captain," Chakotay answered.

"Janeway out." The captain tipped her head to one side, considering. "Keep an eye out, everyone. Though I must say they don't seem hostile."

"Yet," Paris muttered, and Kim jumped at the voice in his ear. "Sorry, Harry."

"Don't mention it." Kim felt for his phaser, making sure it was loose on its holder, ready for use.

The creatures didn't seem to notice their presence—or rather, Kim thought, watching one lift its head, turning great yellow eyes to follow them, they didn't seem bothered by the Starfleet presence. Experimentally, he turned his tricorder on it, and saw it hunch its shoulders as though it expected a blow.

"Look at that," he said aloud, and Janeway turned to face him.

"What is it, Harry?"

"The—creature." Kim pointed, careful not to use his tricorder this time. "When I turned my tricorder on it, it flinched. See?" He lifted the tricorder again, and the creature ducked away. At the same time, the other two turned to face him, crouching a little, too, as they saw the leveled tricorder.

"All right, that's enough," Janeway said, sharply, and Kim lowered his tricorder. "It was a good guess, Lieutenant Kim, but once you saw the reaction, you shouldn't have repeated it. Suppose you'd angered them, or frightened them enough so that they attacked? We can't risk hostilities, not until we've found the Kirse."

The captain was right, and Kim felt himself blushing. "Sorry, Captain. It won't happen again."

Janeway nodded. "But you are right, it is an interesting reaction."

"So they've seen people more or less like us before," Paris said, thoughtfully, "and they don't like tricorders."

"Which they associate with something unpleasant," Janeway said. "But they aren't necessarily afraid of us, just the tricorders."

"Captain," Kim said. Beside the bush, one of the creatures had straightened to its hind legs, revealing its midsection. It was heavily furred, unlike the first creature, but the fur was missing across its abdomen, replaced by a plate of dark brown metal. Even at this distance, Kim could see what looked like rivets, and the tips of its fingers seemed sheathed in the same material.

"A cyborg?" Paris said, and a second creature rose to its feet. It was less furry than the other, and one of its arms seemed to be partially replaced by a brighter, golden metal.

"I can't tell," Torres said. She was shielding her tricorder as best she could, but the creature saw it, and bolted away, leaving their berries scattered across the ground. "They're not really cyborgs, at least not by our definition—in fact, I don't think they're really animals at all."

"What do you mean?" Janeway asked.

"Well, every one of them that we've seen has been doing something that could be construed as taking care of the crops," Torres said. "I think they're—well, for lack of a better word, a kind of organic machine, designed to tend these fields."

"They could also have been gathering food," Kim protested. "That's more what it looked like to me."

"The two can overlap," Janeway said. "It's an interesting idea, B'Elanna. Let's see if we can prove it one way or the other. Keep scanning, as discreetly as you can, and pay particular attention to their behavior, but stay on the road." She glanced at the sky. "I'd like to reach the citadel well before local nightfall."

Kim glanced up as well, into a sky bluer than his homeworld's, streaked with thin trails of cloud. The sun, a hot white disk, seemed to be near the zenith, but whether it was rising or setting was unclear. *Still,* he thought, *it shouldn't take us too long to get to the Kirse city—even as careful as we've been, we're nearly halfway there already.* He adjusted his tricorder, letting it hang at his waist, the autorecord function fully engaged, and started after the others. The creatures seemed to be keeping their distance now, slipping away from the roadside fields before the *Voyager* team could get too close to them; they caught glimpses of various creatures in the distance—more of the anthropoid creatures, but also some that looked taller and thinner, without the heavy fur, once something that might be a quadruped—but no one was able to get a decent fix on any individual. The readings remained frustratingly consistent, not organic, not mechanical, and Kim shook his head, shading his eyes to get a better glimpse of one of the tall, smooth-skinned creatures busy in the distance. It seemed to be pulling something—fruit? leaves or flowers? It was hard to tell without the tricorder's help—from the lower branches of a small tree, but even as he watched, it dropped to all fours and began scrabbling in the dirt beside the trunk. When it straightened again, its clumsy paws seemed to be empty.

"Maybe you're right, B'Elanna," he said, "that looks more like caretaking than looking for food."

The engineer looked over her shoulder at him, her serious face curving into a reluctant smile. "I was thinking exactly the opposite myself. You can't plant in the shade of the parent."

"But I wouldn't want to bury a food cache there, either," Paris said. "I mean, why bother? The tree's there, ripe for the picking."

"Storing it for another season, maybe?" Torres answered. She shook her head. "I wish I knew."

Kim opened his mouth to continue the discussion, but the fickle breeze strengthened then, bringing with it the sound of running water. "Listen," he said instead, and saw the others pause as they heard the same sound.

"Another river?" Paris said, and Torres reached for her tricorder.

"Probably. This reading's a little unclear, though. It could a lake of some kind. But it's beyond those—trees."

She pointed to the line of thickly interlaced plants that formed a natural fence at the edge of the cultivated area. Kim eyed them uncertainly, not liking the way the gnarled limbs twined around each other, springing from trunks that were twisted into a thick spiral, or the way that the limbs grew together to form a canopy above the road. He couldn't make out the shapes of any leaves, or indeed if there were any, just the heavy, thick-scaled bark and the twisting limbs. Then something moved in the sky above the treeline, a scattering of white, bright in the sunlight, and gone as quickly as it had appeared.

"Look!" He pointed, but the light, whatever it had been, was already gone.

"What it is?" Janeway demanded, and Kim shook his head.

"I'm not sure, Captain. It— I saw something beyond the trees, rising above them, but I couldn't tell what it was." He shook his head again. "It looked almost like, well, fog, but I couldn't be sure."

"I don't see anything," Paris said.

"It's gone," Kim answered, and Janeway looked around.

"Anything on sensors, anyone?" There was no answer, and she sighed. "Keep an eye out, all of you. Let's move on."

The trees looked no better as they got closer. They weren't completely leafless, as they'd first appeared, but the leaves, tiny dark-green lobes the size of Kim's fingernail, clung so close to the limbs that they looked almost like a coat of coarse fur. There were fruits as well, dark red, cupped in hemispherical caps at the end of the most twisted branches, and Kim trained his tricorder on them uncertainly. They weren't edible, he saw to his relief—in fact, they weren't really fruits at all, but thick-skinned, hollow blossoms. Hollow, he amended, watching the numbers change on the tricorder's screen, but not empty. There seemed to be a fine particulate suspended in the shells, pollen, perhaps, or very fine seed. He frowned at the reading, trying to determine what it might mean, and there was a tremendous ratcheting sound from the trees ahead of him. He looked up just in time to see one of the twisted limbs whip forward, unwinding so fast that it was little more than a gray blur. The dark red flower-sphere snapped out of the cup and shattered on the roadway a few meters ahead of Renehan, releasing a pale cloud. Renehan leaped backward, covering her mouth and nose, and Kim trained his tricorder on the rapidly fading cloud.

"Another soporific," he said. "Similar to the grass pollen, but probably longer-lasting."

"Masks," Janeway ordered, and the *Voyager* team reached hastily for the protective gear. "What the hell set it off?"

There was a little silence, and then Paris, his voice only slightly muffled by the mask, said, "Um, I think it was me."

Janeway turned to face him, both eyebrows rising in mute but pointed question, and Paris made a face. "In the grass there, beside the road. You see those things that look like roots? I was trying to get a better look at the flower on it, and I think I touched it. Then the tree—went off."

Kim moved closer, peering past the taller man's shoulder at the gray-brown spike that protruded from the rich dirt. It looked like a miniature version of the trees, the same warty, crinkled bark, but there was no flower, nothing at all, in fact, to set it off from the ground around it. "I don't see any flower."

"There was one." Paris's voice trailed off, and he swung from side to side, scanning the ground beside the road. "There, like that one."

He pointed to a bright blue flower, long and narrow, with a deep gold throat, and Kim crouched to examine it more closely, careful to keep well away from its surface. It grew from a root-spike like the one Paris had indicated before, but it seemed oddly fuzzy, as though it was more furred than a flower should be. Kim frowned, and leveled the tricorder at it, already suspecting what he would find. Sure enough, at high magnification, the fuzziness resolved itself into a cloud of fine hairs extending almost seven centimeters from the surface of the plant. "Captain! I think Tom's right, these—things—are the trigger mechanism."

Janeway took the tricorder he held out to her, and scanned the readings herself. "So if you touch those hairs at all, the tree flings one of those pods at you."

"That's what it looks like," Kim answered, and Janeway nodded, handing him back the tricorder.

"And there seem to be quite a lot of those flowers around here."

Kim straightened, still careful to keep his distance from the plant, and realized that there were indeed dozens, maybe hundreds, of the bright blue flowers in the grass around them. "Should we test it?" he asked, and Janeway nodded.

"Move back, everyone. Give us at least a ten-meter clearance."

Kim blinked at that—he hadn't expected Janeway to do it herself—and Paris frowned.

"Captain—?"

"That's an order, Mr. Paris," Janeway said, briskly, and the pilot backed away with the rest. The captain looked down at Kim. "All right, Mr. Kim, let's see what happens if you touch one of them."

"Yes, Captain." Kim fumbled in his tool kit and finally found a thin extension rod. He tugged it out to its full two-meter length, and glanced back at the captain.

"Mask in place?" Janeway asked, and adjusted her own. Kim tightened his, and nodded. "Lieutenant Torres, you're recording all this?"

"Aye, Captain."

"Then let's go, Mr. Kim."

Kim took a deep breath, and reached out cautiously

with the rod, aiming at a large bloom nearly two meters from the roadway. He extended the tip toward the flower, stopped when he thought he must be in contact with the very tips of the invisible hairs. Nothing happened, and he eased the rod forward. There was another snapping sound, a heavy noise like gears suddenly releasing, and he saw two more branches snap forward, slamming their fruits against the stone of the road. The pollen or seeds rose like smoke, and Kim held his breath until the plumes faded, teased to nothing by the wind.

"This is not a natural phenomenon," Torres said.

"I'm inclined to agree with you," Paris said.

Janeway nodded thoughtfully. "The first branch is starting to rewind."

Kim could hear a faint creaking as she spoke, and looked to see one of the longer branches slowly twisting back toward its original position. The scaly bark seemed to contract along one side—the sunlit side, he clarified, so maybe the sun provided the necessary energy, or at least the stimulus—pulling the branch back into its taut spiral. The cup at the end of the branch was empty, and he wondered how long it would take to grow another gas-filled flower.

"Hey," Paris said, coming up beside him, "that flower's gone, too."

He was right, Kim saw; the blue flower he had touched had vanished, leaving only the gray-brown stump that blended perfectly with the dirt around it.

"I've traced the root system," Torres said. "It doesn't seem to run under the roadway."

"So if we stay on the road itself, we should be safe?" Renehan asked.

"Unless they have something else waiting for us," Torres answered.

Janeway folded her arms, and considered the arch

of the branches. "Not a natural phenomenon," she said, so softly that Kim barely heard the words. "No, I would say not, B'Elanna." She looked back over her shoulder. "Any sign of nonorganic components, Lieutenant Torres?"

"Not in this area," the engineer answered. "Or at least not as part of this tree. The only things I'm picking up are the same pipeline we've been following and the road itself."

"Right." Janeway turned back to the trees. "There seems to be a clear message involved here. Stay on the road, and you won't get hurt."

"Not very friendly," Paris said, almost in spite of himself, and Janeway fixed him with a quick stare.

"But not precisely hostile, either, Mr. Paris. We press on."

CHAPTER
4

THE REMAINING CREATURES KEPT THEIR DISTANCE AS THE away team crossed the last kilometer to the citadel. Kim could see them hovering watchfully among the heavily fruited bushes, or peering from the stands of tall grain, but they kept away from the road itself, and any attempt to lure one closer sent them scurrying deeper into the protection of the fields. Ahead, the citadel seemed larger than ever, its dull, waxy walls barely reflecting the sunlight. And the sun was setting, Kim realized, declining from the near-zenith where he had last noticed its position. The citadel cast a lengthening shadow now, reaching out to engulf them—already, the shadow of the tallest tower lay along the road less than five meters ahead of him. Kim hesitated, suddenly unwilling to step into that shade, and then shook himself, angry that he'd indulged such an unscientific thought. There was nothing menacing about the shadow; it was a natural phenomenon, perfectly benign. If he should be worrying about anything, it should be the citadel itself.

"Pretty intimidating place," Paris said, at his shoulder, and Kim frowned, worried that his own fears had been obvious. He looked back, but Paris's eyes were fixed on the linked buildings, brows drawn down in a frown of his own. "And, you know, I think it's meant to be."

"What do you mean?"

"The proportions—at least I think that's what it is. The way it's put together, I think it's deliberately trying to look intimidating, at least from this angle."

Kim squinted up at the citadel, its towers very dark now against the bright afternoon sky. The buildings did have an oddly organic look, each structure budding from the others like the lobed melons his family had grown in the recreational gardens. The towers clustered around the central spire with its glassy disk, looking a bit like pistils around a stamen, their spiked tips tilted outward defensively. The whole construction did look like a single, hostile entity, a monstrous hybrid of plant and animal crouching across their path. He shook his head then, trying to put the image out of his mind. "It doesn't have to be," he said. "The builders are aliens, who knows what their ideas of architecture are like?"

Paris jerked his head toward the fields. "Those things are mostly humanoid. I think the builders know exactly what they're doing."

"I hope you're wrong, Mr. Paris," Janeway said. "Otherwise we may find it a little difficult to trade with them. Now, if you could put your architectural studies on hold for a moment, we'd like to continue."

"Sorry, Captain." Paris sounded only mildly abashed, and Kim shot him a look of envy, knowing his own cheeks were red.

"He's got a point, though," Torres said. "This does look, well, unfriendly."

"From what Neelix said, the Kirse have been suffering raids from the Andirrim for quite some time," Janeway answered, and shook her head. "But if this is a fortress, where are the gates?"

It was a good question. Kim scanned the dark-green walls, but could seen no sign of barriers, nothing but a single arched opening at the base of a mushroom-topped tower. He leveled his tricorder at it, scanning for forcefields, for any hidden defense or weapon, but found nothing. In the same instant, Renehan said, "All clear. I'm reading very low-level power use inside, but not enough even to power a phaser."

"The light's on, though," Paris said.

It was true, Kim saw. The arch wasn't dark at all. Instead, the opening was exactly as bright as the shadowed ground at the base of the walls, as though the local sun's light somehow seeped through the waxy stone.

"How does that light compare with the power reading?" Janeway asked.

It was Torres who answered, frowning over her tricorder. "A little more than it should take to create that light, but not much more. And for what it's worth, the power source is a long way in."

Janeway nodded, contemplating the opening, and touched her communicator. "*Voyager,* this is Janeway. We're entering the citadel."

"We have you on our sensors," Chakotay answered promptly.

"Keep us there. Janeway out." The captain smiled back at the away team. "Let's consider it an invitation." She started for the door.

Kim touched his phaser again—making sure it was loose and ready, he told himself, though he suspected it was more for reassurance. He saw Paris take a deep breath, and Renehan's hand was very close to her own phaser. Torres was looking more Klingon than usual, her lips curled back in the first stages of a snarl. Even as he thought that, the engineer seemed to realize what she was doing, and smoothed her expression.

The arched door was less a door than a tunnel through the thickness of the outer wall. Kim swung his tricorder at it, curious, and saw Torres doing the same thing. "I make it nine-point-seven meters," he said, and Torres nodded.

"The same on this side. And it's solid to the sensors. If there is conduit or anything like that in it, I can't read them."

Nine, almost ten meters of solid—what? Kim thought. The tricorder was inconclusive, didn't recognize and couldn't categorize the molecular structure. From the look of the surface, the walls could be made of anything from polished stone to heavy plastic, and he reached out to trail his fingers over the surface. It wasn't as smooth as it looked, had instead an almost metallic texture, but weathered metal, metal that had been out in the elements for some time. Kim frowned at that, wondering if it could be made of metal, but rejected the thought almost at once. Neelix had said that the Kirse were metal-poor, that they had to trade for most of what they needed—and was this why they were metal-poor? he wondered suddenly. If the citadel was made of metal, some light, alien alloy that the tricorders couldn't analyze, it would have taken an enormous amount of it to create a structure this size, maybe even all the planet's accessible resources.

The tunnel opened into a rectangular hall, where the ceiling soared nine meters to a barrel-vault. The same apparent sunlight filtered down from an invisible source, and the walls and ceiling and the ribs of the vault glowed in its diffuse light. They were all obviously metal, but the range of color was astonishing, from the green-brown of bronze to the rose-tinged gold of the vault's ribbing to blued steel. In contrast, the floor was almost black, and dull-surfaced. Kim crouched, curious, and felt the same pitted texture he had found in the tunnel walls.

"It's all metal," Torres reported. "Still a lot of strange alloys, though. I can pick out some of the components, but not many."

"It's—pretty," Renehan said, and sounded almost surprised.

"Can you get a fix on the power source, Lieutenant Torres?" Janeway asked, and the engineer shook her head.

"Not a good one. It's ahead of us, maybe a hundred meters, but the reading is very diffuse. This—metal—seems to interrupt the signal."

"Ahead of us," Janeway repeated. "This way?"

"Yes, Captain."

There was another doorway in that direction, still without a door to block it, and Kim looked closely at the frame as he passed through its arch. There were no visible openings, no slots or guides where a barrier could be inserted, and he shook his head. "You'd think there'd be doors or something, after what Neelix said."

"You mean because of the Andirrim?" Janeway asked.

He hadn't meant to speak that loudly, but nodded. "I would expect more security."

"I agree," Paris said.

Torres tapped her tricorder lightly, the gesture holding a controlled violence that made Kim flinch. "For all the data I'm getting from this, there could well be security hidden in these walls—there could be a whole fleet of war machines, and I wouldn't be able to tell them from the wall."

"We'll go carefully," Janeway said. She touched her communicator again. "Janeway to *Voyager*. We're getting some interference with our tricorders, Chakotay. Are you still able to maintain your fix on us?"

There was a moment's silence before the ship answered, and when at last he spoke, Chakotay's voice was thin and faintly glazed with static. *"Voyager* here. Your signal is weakening, Captain, but we still have you. Indications are that the interference will increase as you go farther in, so I suggest you check in more frequently. We'll alert you if the passive signal drops too close to the edge."

"Do that," Janeway said. "Janeway out."

In the sudden silence, Kim caught a distant rushing sound—like water, he thought, or blowing air, but too steady for either. He tipped his head to the side, frowning, and Paris said, "I think I hear something."

Torres waved him to silence, adjusting her tricorder. "Captain, I'm showing an increase in power use, through that doorway."

"Let's go." Janeway turned to the open door.

Kim followed with the rest of the away team, trying to divide his attention between his tricorder and the rushing noise. It still didn't seem right that there should be so many open doors, without any sign of any barriers against the Andirrim. But then, maybe Neelix had gotten it wrong, he thought. Neelix had been wrong before, and this was at best a secondhand story. He glanced at his tricorder in the vague hope of seeing something that would confirm that idea. There was nothing, just the same monotonous not-found, not-recognized messages that he'd been seeing since they beamed down to the planet, though the bars that tracked power output were longer than they had been.

He caught his breath as he came into the next room, heard Paris swear admiringly under his breath. The room was long and narrow, more like a very wide hallway, and the walls were banded with more strips of metal that alternated with sculptures of strange machinery in bas relief. Then one of the ruddy gold flywheels spun, giving off a hissing whir, and he heard Paris swear again. Kim leveled his tricorder at the nearest sculpted strip, and saw a set of pistons shift, rising and falling in an unfamiliar rhythm before they froze again. They were so well lubricated that they made almost no noise, barely adding to the soft rushing sound he had heard before. The sound was more or less constant, coming from everywhere and nowhere. All the sculptures were movable, he realized, were moving in odd rhythms, first the pieces of one band and then another—they weren't sculptures at all, despite their gleaming beauty, but parts of some much larger machine. A series of antique gears swung into motion, the smallest, about the size of his hand, spinning frantically, teeth blurring, just to move the largest, easily more than a meter in diameter, a few clicks farther on around its circle. All the gears were made of some blue-toned metal, bluer than steel, not as bright as treated titanium, and Kim stared for a moment in fascination before he remembered to check his tricorder. The readings were still inconclusive, power expended to no discernible end, and he shook his head in frustration.

"I wonder what it does."

"If it does anything," Paris said. "That big gear doesn't seem to connect to anything."

"It could be a regulator," Torres began, and then shook her own head. "No, there's no use speculating." From her scowl, Kim thought, she was as annoyed by her own guess as she was by the missing information.

"Is this the power source you've been reading?" Janeway asked. She had been staring curiously at the bands of machinery, but now she turned back to face the engineer.

"No, Captain." Torres shook her head for emphasis. "The source—or at least the highest level of use— is at least another fifty meters west of here."

Kim glanced down the length of the hall, gauging distances. "That's not much beyond the end of this room."

Even as he spoke, a section of the new-copper pink wall faded, and then disappeared, leaving another of the perfect arched doorways. Kim looked automatically at his tricorder, and saw the red spike of a power surge frozen in the time-elapsed display. He touched controls to analyze it, and to his surprise the machine flashed back a recognizable pattern. The energy spike was similar to a transporter beam, though far more primitive. "Captain," he began, and was cut off by a signal from the communicators.

"Chakotay to away team."

Janeway held up her hand to Kim, and touched her communicator. "Janeway here."

"Captain, we just picked up the largest power reading we've received from the surface so far, located less than fifty meters from your position."

"Yes, Chakotay, we know." Improbably, Janeway was smiling, but she sobered quickly. "Someone's just opened another door for us."

"Captain," Kim said again. He could feel the old dread rushing in as he spoke, the fear that he was going too far, interrupting with something that would turn out to be trivial, but stuffed it down again. "The energy we saw is related to our transporter beam."

Janeway looked sharply at him, and he braced

himself for a reprimand. Instead, she touched her communicator again. "Did you hear that, Chakotay?"

"I did, and we can confirm that," Chakotay answered. "Tuvok has just finished the analysis."

"Let me see that," Torres said, at Kim's elbow, and Kim handed her his tricorder. She mated it briefly to her own machine, transferring data, and then handed it back without a word, her attention already concentrated on the readings in her own screen.

"No one else we've encountered has had anything close to our technology," Paris said. "Particularly the transporter."

"And yet there's an open door waiting for us," Janeway said. "Keep a fix on us, Chakotay. We're going on."

Kim took a careful breath. One of the few things *Voyager* had had going for it in the Delta Quadrant was its technological superiority; if the Kirse had a transporter, even a more primitive version, that would make them the most advanced civilization the ship had yet encountered. And that, he added silently, made them also the most potentially dangerous species as well.

"Do you smell something?" Renehan said, abruptly, and out of the corner of his eye Kim saw Paris nod.

"Yeah. Bread—fresh-baked bread."

Even as he spoke, Kim caught the same aroma, and beneath it the scent of garlic and onions, strengthening even as he identified them. He swallowed hard, tasting hunger, saw even Janeway quicken her step as they approached the door. He was suddenly, irrationally certain that food, human food or something that smelled very like it, waited in that room, and had to make an effort to keep from breaking into a trot.

They crowded through the doorway, into warm gold light and the complex scents of cooking, and this time it was Paris who swore out loud. A table stood in the center of the room, directly under a multi-armed chandelier like an antique candelabrum that gleamed in shades of silver. The tabletop was covered with platters, deep and shallow dishes that stood on footed holders over disks that glowed red-orange, even an enormous steaming tureen, and the uncovered plates were clearly piled high with food. Kim swallowed again, hard, almost sickened by the sheer quantity, the incredible opulence after the weeks of close rationing, and heard Renehan murmur something, either curse or prayer. He recognized some of the food as plants he had scanned on the way through the gardens—the peach-pear fruit, for one, a good dozen of the pale globes piled into a pyramid that was topped with a vivid red bell-shape that was probably a flower—but the rest smelled too appetizing not to be edible. And that, he told himself, trying to get a grip on his emotions, was a dangerous fallacy, but the temptation to reach out, take something, anything, from the groaning board was almost overwhelming. He reached for his tricorder instead, and trained it on the table. The results flashed back instantly: everything on the table was indeed edible.

"Captain," he began, and to his horror heard his voice crack. In the same instant, Torres cleared her throat.

"What—are those hands?"

Kim looked quickly at her, and saw that she was staring at the table.

"There," she said, impatiently. "On the—big bowl—and on the rest."

Kim looked more closely. What he had taken for an elaborate filigree stand holding the tureen wasn't a stand at all, but a pair of delicate, three-fingered shapes very like robotic hands. They clung to the sides of the tureen, two fingers curved beneath the base, the third steadying the rim, balancing it above a glowing disk that seemed to be a heating element. Another hand-shape, this one with spidery, multi-jointed fingers, held eight round shapes that looked like the sweet-bean cakes of his childhood between its thin fingers. Even as Kim watched, the "hand" swiveled on its wrist, rotating a different cake over a smaller glowing disk. Another hand, this one smaller, golden rather than the functional pewter-gray of the rest, uncoiled itself from the edge of a plate and took the cake, setting it delicately onto the empty plate.

"My god," Paris said, and sounded almost faint. "Harry, is all that edible?"

Kim nodded, made himself answer. "All of it," he said, and was remotely grateful that his voice didn't fail him.

"Then let's go," Paris said. "Captain, this is just sitting here waiting for us. Let's eat."

Kim nodded again, in spite of himself, in spite of the strangeness of the banquet. It was too much to withstand, too much to expect them to wait, after they'd come so close not merely to hunger but to slow death, the slow poison of the scurvy. He saw Renehan nodding with him, and Torres's brow was drawn into a tremendous scowl of concentration.

"Hold it, Mr. Paris," Janeway said, and her voice was like the crack of a whip, breaking the spell of the food. Kim blinked, shook his head, the suffocating hunger easing. They wouldn't die if they didn't eat this second, no matter how good it smelled or how much he wanted food that didn't taste of Neelix's spices or the not-quite-perfect products of the replicator. Even the scurvy could wait, could and would be cured later, after they'd figured out why this banquet had been laid out like this.

"We don't know if this is for us," Janeway went on, "or even if it is, it could be a trap."

"But, Captain, it's just sitting there." Paris waved a hand, the sweeping gesture taking in the table and all its piled contents. "Who else could it be for? God, we may never get another chance like this."

"Chance for what?" Janeway retorted. "To gorge yourself on alien food? That's likely to happen more than once in your lifetime, Mr. Paris, and I'd like to see you survive the experience. Have you forgotten the trees in the gardens?" She shook her head. "We've not been invited to this dinner, Mr. Paris. No one is to touch any of it until we know what's going on here. That's a direct order."

Paris took a breath, as though he would have protested further, and Kim laid a hand on his arm. "The captain's right," he said, and laid delicate stress on the title. Paris subsided, though Kim could feel the muscles still taut under his hand.

"Very good, Captain." His tone still sounded faintly grudging, but Janeway ignored it.

"Right—"

"Captain!" Torres called, looking up from her tricorder. "I'm picking up a power surge, located just below this room—"

Even as she spoke, there was a sound, deeper and harsher than the familiar treble whine of the transporter, and the floor beyond the table vanished in a haze of dark blue light. A round hole maybe six meters across appeared, and through it rose a group of shapes. For an instant, a blinding light from below obscured the details, so that Kim could see only a cluster of tall bipeds, and curving shapes that might be wings. Then the light winked out, cut off by the rising platform, and he could see clearly. There were two slim, gray-skinned humanoids, one with wings folded close to its sides, the lower edges curving forward around its thighs, the other wingless, any external indicators of gender concealed by a longer, bright-red tunic, reaching almost to its ankles, that glittered with metal bands like embroidery. At its side stood a human male.

Kim caught his breath, unable for an instant to believe what he was seeing—another human, caught in the Delta Quadrant, a human whose way in might become *Voyager*'s way out—and the man took a step forward, his thin face curving into a grin.

"Congratulations," he said. "You passed the test."

The taller, wingless alien tipped its head to one side, an oddly indulgent expression flickering across its face. It was very human in its features, Kim thought, striving for perspective, but an idealized, genderless humanity, variations smoothed into the gentle planes of the puppet-heroes he had enjoyed as a child. "On behalf of the Kirse," it said, "I welcome you to this planet."

The voice was more male than female, Kim decided, though he knew better than to act on his guess until he knew more about the Kirse.

"You've passed the test," the Kirse speaker went on, "and are clearly worthy of being called people. Once again, I bid you welcome."

"Thank you." Janeway drew herself up to rigid courtesy, not even a glance straying to the man at the speaker's side. "I'm Captain Kathryn Janeway of the Federation starship *Voyager*. We're delighted to meet the inhabitants of this planet."

"As am I to meet space travelers who can be called something more than animal," the speaker answered. He waved his hand, and the table shifted slightly, began to walk away, its eight legs giving it a strange, rolling gait. Kim tried not to watch it go, not wanting to seem as desperate as he felt, but he could feel the human watching him, and met his gaze to see the man smiling very slightly, as though he could read Kim's emotions. The heavy wail of the Kirse transporter sounded again, and the table stepped through the opening that had appeared in the far wall. The door closed again behind it, and Kim suppressed a sigh. None of the food had fallen, or even shifted on its plates.

"What brings you to this planet, Captain Janeway?" the Kirse speaker continued.

"We've come here to trade," Janeway answered, after a barely perceptible pause. "We're particularly interested in foodstuffs."

The speaker inclined his head gravely. "I am always interested in trade, particularly with people who have come such a distance. But I would prefer not to discuss such things until we've become better acquainted, person to person. May I suggest, Captain, that you and I—"

"And her officers," the human said.

The speaker gave him a quick glance, then inclined his own head gravely. "That you and your officers and I eat together first, to put things on a proper basis, before we move on to the details of negotiation."

"We would be delighted," Janeway said.

The speaker nodded again. "In the meantime, as an earnest of my intent, let me offer you something less—extravagant—than what was laid out for you before."

The winged Kirse lifted a hand, wings stirring to counterbalance the movement, and another door opened, this time in the opposite wall. Another walking table, smaller than the first, but as heavily laden, waddled into the room, and the door beamed closed behind it. The winged Kirse gestured again, and the table settled into place, hands and less-human appendages deftly arranging the dishes across its surface.

"Thank you," Janeway said, and the human spoke before she could finish.

"They'll be offended if you refuse, Captain."

Janeway looked at him, not quite masking her curiosity. "No offense, but just who are you?"

The human gave her an easy smile. He was handsome in a bony sort of way, Kim decided, a tall, pale man with dark brown hair pulled back into a loose tail. There was a streak of silver at one temple, but otherwise it was hard to guess his age.

"My name's Thilo Revek. I crashed here a while ago, and the Kirse took me in. Adamant there asked me to help greet you."

"Adamant," Janeway repeated, with a quick glance at the Kirse speaker.

The speaker bent his head—not a native Kirse gesture, Kim guessed, but one learned from Revek— still with that oddly indulgent expression on his face. "He calls me Adamant. You are welcome to do the same."

"Thank you," Janeway said.

"And he calls me Night-Whispers," the winged Kirse said. His voice was lighter, though still not quite feminine, and there was a note in it that might have been a whistle of laughter. "Will you eat with us, Captain?"

"We would be honored," Janeway said, without hesitation, this time. "But if you don't mind, I'd like to ask Mr. Revek a few questions first."

"Of course," Adamant answered. "You will have much to share. And we can't have much to say to each other yet, I know, until we have become better acquainted. I trust Thilo will facilitate the process."

There was an almost admonishing note to the Kirse's voice. Kim glanced at Revek, curious, and saw the man's smile turn wry. "Don't worry, Adamant, you know how I feel about this place."

"Indeed. Then I trust you will make your cohorts feel at home." Adamant turned away, moving toward the new table. "Please, Voyagers, help yourselves."

Kim looked at Janeway again, uncertain, and the captain nodded to him. "Go ahead, Mr. Kim—all of you. I'll join you in a minute, once I've spoken to Mr. Revek."

There was a note in her voice that did not bode entirely well for the stranger. Kim hesitated for a moment longer, wondering if one of them should hold back to give her support, but Paris clapped him on the shoulder.

"Come on, Harry, we're not going to get a better offer any time soon. Just smell that stew!"

Kim took a deep breath, inhaling odors he hadn't smelled since he came on board *Voyager*, and his resolve vanished. The Kirse certainly weren't hostile, whatever Revek's origins might be. The captain could deal with it; he would eat.

Janeway glanced warily at the man in front of her. Behind her, she could hear voices and the chime of metal on metal as the rest of the away team helped themselves to the food spread out on the newly arrived table. They sounded subdued, and she hoped they were being cautious. No matter how friendly the Kirse seemed, there was still a great deal that was unexplained about them. Not least of which, she added silently, was this Thilo Revek.

"Mr. Revek," she said. "How precisely did you end

up here?" It was the voice she used at admirals' receptions, polite, cool, and completely noncommital, and she allowed herself an inward smile at the recognition.

Revek's mouth twitched upward, and she wondered for an instant if he recognized the social voice. "Do you mean here in the Delta Quadrant, or here on the planet?"

"Both." Janeway moderated her words with a faint smile. "But let's start with the Delta Quadrant." The winged Kirse—Night-Whispers, Revek had called it—was standing just within earshot, its wings just slightly raised, dividing its attention between her and the rest of the away team at the table. It—he?—seemed friendly enough, but she was very aware of his listening presence.

Revek ignored it, however, gave her a shrug and another easy grin. He had odd eyes, Janeway saw, a color between gray and hazel that looked almost yellow in the golden light. They didn't quite match, either, the left drifting slightly, not quite aligned with the right. That was the sort of thing that Federation medics usually corrected in childhood, and she filed the observation for later.

"I'm a native of the sector the Federation ceded to the Cardassians, had a good business there and no particular desire to pull up stakes or go to work for the local Gul, so I ended up working for the Maquis."

"And what is it that you do, Mr. Revek?" Another echo of party chat, Janeway thought, and felt suddenly light-headed. She could smell the food more strongly than ever, a butter-and-onions smell warring with the sweeter scents of fruit, reminding her how little she'd been eating, and it was suddenly all she could do not to excuse herself and attack the table.

"Computers, mostly," Revek answered, and she

dragged her attention back to him. "Shipboard systems, specializing lately in autopilots—anything that would help the Maquis pare down the number of people they needed on any one ship. I was testing one of the program/hardware matrices when I was hit by a coherent tetrion beam. When I got free of it, I was looking at this alien lighthouse that also didn't much like me, or at best couldn't be bothered with me. And the people on the planet weren't exactly friendly, either. So I started putting the ship back together— luckily I'd done a good job with the autosystem, it stayed reparable—and then I headed back home."

Janeway swallowed a stifling sense of disappointment. Until that minute, she hadn't realized how much she had been hoping that Revek had reached the Delta Quadrant by some other means, something that *Voyager* could use to get home again. Now, hearing the Caretaker's Array described, however crudely, she felt that hope die. Revek had come in by the same door they'd used, the same door that had closed forever at the destruction of the Array. "This hardly looks like home," she said, and heard her voice sharper than she'd meant. Night-Whisper's wings lifted slightly, a soft rustle of leathery skin, but Revek laughed.

"No, not a lot like. I came here because some people several systems back said it was a dead world, full of self-perpetuating tech, and I thought I could make something from it, maybe even figure out a way to boost my speed enough to make a difference getting home. My sense of timing being what it is, I arrived in the middle of an Andirrim raid, and while I was yelling 'Don't shoot, I'm a neutral' I got shot down on the far side of the planet. By the time the Kirse sent Night-Whispers—no, I'm wrong, it was Treekeeper, wasn't it?"

Night-Whispers moved closer, gave the stiff-necked Kirse nod. "It was."

Revek nodded. "By the time the Kirse sent Tree-keeper to see what kind of a mess I'd made of their *irri'a'a* orchard—"

Night-Whispers made a soft whistling noise, and Janeway glanced at him, startled. Revek grimaced. "Night-Whispers hates my accent."

"I think it's funny," Night-Whispers corrected, and Janeway realized that the sound she heard had been laughter.

"Anyway!" Revek shook his head, but the gesture hid laughter of his own. "I wasn't in great shape after the crash—the automed did its best, but it had been damaged, too. Still, that kept me from foraging, which intrigued Treekeeper enough to bring me back here to see if I was person or animal. To make a long story short, I've been here ever since."

He was making a long story very short, Janeway thought, and leaving out most of the interesting bits. It would be nice to know just how long it had taken him to figure out Kirse society, and how he had gotten to be on such good terms with them. "How long have you been here?"

Revek shrugged again. "Let's see, fourteen seasons, that's a little under four local years—three standard Earth years, give or take a few thousand hours."

Janeway nodded, hiding the suspicion that flared at his words. A human being, a member of the Maquis, out of touch with the rest of his species, with a cause that he'd been willing to die for—surely, she thought, surely he should have asked about the war before this. Her eyes strayed to Night-Whispers, still listening, though at least part of his attention seemed to have been diverted by the group around the table. Or maybe he didn't want to ask with one of the Kirse listening? It was hard to tell, harder still to know what could be safely asked.

"Captain?"

That was Kim's voice, and Janeway turned to find the young ensign at her elbow. He held out a small plate—gold in color, Janeway thought, and very possibly gold in substance—that he had loaded with both sliced fruit and some kind of pastry. "I thought you might like something while you were talking."

"Thank you, Mr. Kim." Janeway accepted the plate, guiltily glad of the gift. She took a cautious bite of the pastry, and her mouth filled with flaky crust and the warm, garlic-tinged filling.

"Believe it or not," Revek said, "that cheese comes from a tree—I don't know if you would have seen it, it's a tall evergreen, with red-tipped fronds. The sap gets rendered down into a curd."

"It's very good," Janeway said, her wariness momentarily banished by the taste of the food. She finished the pastry in two more bites, and looked up, mildly embarrassed by her sudden hunger, to see both Night-Whispers and Adamant regarding her with distinct approval.

"Eating is one of the Kirse's major forms of communication," Revek said. "You might even think of it as a kind of communion. It's the high point of the whole act of hospitality, and that's the central point of the culture."

Adamant, who had wandered over with Kim, nodded in thoughtful agreement. Janeway picked up a piece of the fruit, took a careful bite, hoping to buy time. The explosion of flavor—melon, honey, perhaps a touch of mint—almost drove that intent out of her mind, but she forced aside the pleasure. Revek was plausible enough, but she couldn't help wondering why he was telling her so much, and how much of it was provided by the Kirse themselves—and indeed what Revek's relationship was to the aliens around them.

"You're wondering why I'm telling you this," Revek said.

Janeway nodded.

Revek nodded toward Adamant, who was looking away again, his attention visibly elsewhere. "Frankly, they asked me to. They're interested in trading, and it's not often they have a native translator to help them out." A shadow seemed to pass across his face then. "Assuming I've got it right, of course. But they've been both open and consistent in their dealing with me."

Janeway nodded again, less warily this time. So far, everything Revek had said fit the stories Neelix had heard and repeated, allowing for the inevitable distortions that occurred with each retelling. "Tell me about—I'm assuming it was a test? The first banquet that was waiting for us."

"You're exactly right," Revek answered. "Like I said, hospitality is very important to the Kirse—think of any human culture that ever valued the concept, and then triple that concern—and I think as a result there are a lot of complex rules surrounding giving and withholding anything, but especially around food. People don't touch that which doesn't belong to them without explicit invitation, and that goes double for food. If you had helped yourself to that food—if you'd picked anything in the gardens, for that matter—the Kirse would have decided you were animals and you would have been attacked and probably killed." He grinned suddenly, glancing again at Adamant. "I'm personally glad you didn't. Not only is human company a refreshing change, but I've won a bet with Night-Whispers on the subject."

Adamant made the whistling noise that was Kirse laughter, and moved away.

"So how did *Voyager* end up here, anyway?" Revek went on.

"One of my crew heard some stories about the Kirse," Janeway answered. She knew better than to hesitate, even as she tried to choose her words carefully, to give away as little as possible. "But we'd also heard that they were under attack from a people called the Andirrim, and one rumor said that they'd been destroyed."

Revek laughed. "Hardly. The Andirrim are the best of the raiders, that's true, but they're not nearly good enough to beat the Kirse. Though of course that colors the question of trade."

"Which we can discuss at a more—" Adamant hesitated, a slight frown creasing his forehead. "—friendly? when-we-have-become-better-acquainted? —time."

Revek shrugged. "Suit yourself."

"Do you have many raiders, Adamant?" Janeway asked. She knew she risked offending him by being so direct, but this was important, particularly with *Voyager* in orbit. Certainly the elaborate network of orbiting platforms suggested a recurring danger.

"This is a rich world," Adamant answered. "It is— attractive to animals, I suppose. But only the Andirrim pose a consistent problem. And they are a nuisance, but not a threat."

"I see." Janeway tried to match his words to the orbiting platforms, the heavy weaponry Tuvok had deduced from the power signatures, and failed.

"But all of this can be discussed once we have eaten together," Adamant said. "It would make a better beginning that way."

Janeway took a deep breath. Clearly, they wouldn't get anywhere with the Kirse until they had shared a meal—*and the way we're all feeling,* she added silently, *that's hardly a hardship.* "Very well," she said. "We'd be—honored—to eat with you." For a moment, she thought she might have overdone it, but then she saw Revek's smile, at once wry and admiring, and guessed that had been the right note to strike.

"Tonight?" Adamant asked, and Janeway blinked.

"Surely you would want more time for preparation—?" she began, and cut herself off in the next breath, annoyed at her own assumption. Adamant tipped his head to the side, visibly perplexed.

"Adamant's helpers are very quick," Revek said. "And efficient."

They would have to be, Janeway thought, and fought back her instinctive distrust of the situation, born more of a hundred admirals' dinners than any rational response to Adamant's invitation. "Tonight would be good, then. But we have no desire to inconvenience you."

Adamant's expression cleared. "Ah. There will be no inconvenience."

"I'd suggest you bring your senior officers," Revek said, with a quick glance at Adamant, who blinked again.

"Indeed. Thank you, Thilo. You are indeed welcome to bring your compatriots-of-appropriate-status."

He slurred the words together, and Janeway was sure it was a literal translation of some Kirse term. Revek had said senior officers, which was logical and appropriate if they wanted to establish decent relations with the Kirse, but potentially dangerous if the Kirse turned out to be hostile. She would bring the minimum number, she decided; herself, Tuvok, maybe Torres or either Paris or Kim, and Chakotay only if she had to. "Thank you," she said, and thought she had spoken quickly enough to allay any suspicion. "I'll be bringing three others."

Adamant bowed then, spreading narrow, four-fingered hands in a graceful gesture. By the table, Night-Whispers copied the movement. "You will be most welcome, Voyagers. We will expect you an hour after sundown."

"That would be about eighteen-hundred hours by your reckoning," Revek said. His tone was almost demure, but there was a glint of mischief lurking in his eyes.

"Thank you, Mr. Revek," Janeway answered, with deliberate austerity, and looked over her shoulder to find the rest of the away team waiting by the table. They had emptied a number of the plates, and her own stomach growled jealously. "Gentlemen." She touched her communicator. "Janeway to *Voyager*. Beam us up, Chakotay."

"—and as a result of this discussion, I, Lieutenant Tuvok, Lieutenant Paris, and Ensign Kim will be beaming down to the citadel to dine with the Kirse at eighteen hundred hours." Janeway touched the key that ended the log entry, and looked up to see Chakotay frowning slightly across the ready-room table. He smoothed his expression, but not quickly enough, and Janeway sighed.

"You disagree, Mr. Chakotay."

Within Starfleet tradition, the words were permission, but not an invitation. She saw Chakotay hesitate, weighing the importance of his protest—as she'd expected, as she'd intended—but then he nodded. "I do, Captain."

He said no more, and Janeway rested her elbows on the table. "All right, Chakotay, let's hear it."

Chakotay gave her a wry, fleeting smile, momentarily shifting the tattoo that marked his face. "To get to the point, I think I should be part of the group." Janeway lifted an eyebrow, and the first officer went on, ticking the points off on his fingers. "First, it's a matter of protocol. Both the captain and the first officer are expected to attend local functions, as a matter of courtesy to the indigenous people, and I don't think we should change that when there's a human being down there who can tell the Kirse whether or not we're following standard procedure. Second, you haven't picked any ex-Maquis to go with you, and that's likely to start up the conflicts you and I have been at such pains to smother."

"I am, of course, leaving an ex-Maquis in command of my ship," Janeway murmured.

Chakotay nodded. "Agreed. But the people who are still looking for trouble aren't going to see it that way. But it's also worth remembering that Revek is ex-Maquis, too. One of us might be able to get something out of him that you can't. Finally, I think it's important that both of us get a look at these Kirse." He fixed her with a sudden serious stare. "There's something about them that doesn't feel right, Captain. I don't know what it is, where this comes from, but I want to see them face-to-face. I need to see them."

Janeway considered his words, her fingers still steepled on the tabletop. His points were good, she admitted—much as she hated having to consider the former Maquis separately, not to do so would undo everything they'd done to meld the two crews into a single entity, and he was right about Starfleet protocol, too, not to mention the healthy respect she'd developed for Chakotay's hunches. *I'll think about it,* she started to say, and bit back the words. He had played by the rules, Starfleet rules; she owed him as direct an answer.

"Very well, Mr. Chakotay," she said aloud. "You'll replace Mr. Paris in the away team."

"Thank you, Captain." Chakotay did not smile, but she could read the relaxation in his rigid shoulders, knew he was genuinely relieved. *And that,* she thought, *should probably worry me.*

"Have we established subspace contact with the Kirse yet?" she asked, and Chakotay nodded.

"Yes. They're answering our hails now, and they've given us coordinates for tonight—not the same place we were picked up."

Janeway raised an eyebrow.

"Tuvok says they're having us beam down to a courtyard, near the center of the citadel. It means we don't have to go through their walls."

"All right." She put that question aside, and said, "The other issue is this primitive transporter the Kirse seem to have. Has Torres finished her analysis?"

"Not yet," Chakotay answered. "Tuvok has been running that data as well, checking the security angles. It's interesting that this is the one planetary culture that has anything like a transporter, and it's the one where we find another human here ahead of us. And a Federation technician, at that."

"That had occurred to me," Janeway answered. "I've asked Torres to see if she can tell whether or not this system has been influenced by Federation technology, but she wasn't sanguine about the chances." She paused. "Revek is ex-Maquis, at least by his own account. Do you know anything about him?"

Chakotay made a face. "I'd heard of him, anyone who commanded anything bigger than an orbital shuttle had heard of him. But I never worked with him."

"Would there be any mention of him in the files we transferred from your ship?"

"Possibly," Chakotay answered. "We didn't keep too much on record, for fear of the information falling into Cardassian hands."

Janeway nodded. "I'll see what there is later, then. But let's start with what you know."

Chakotay leaned back in his chair, made a sound that was not quite a whistle. "Do you want what I knew officially, or off the record?"

"What do you mean by off the record?" Janeway tempered the question with a smile, received an equally knowing smile in answer.

"Gossip, mostly, crew members' scuttlebutt. But relevant, I think."

Janeway nodded. "Then let's hear it all."

"Thilo Revek comes from one of the really marginal settlements—the ones I suspect the Federation was glad to cede to the Cardassians. That's about all I ever heard about his background; when I first heard of him, he was running a repair lab on the NSTN-2 station."

"The Maquis base," Janeway said.

"One of them," Chakotay corrected. "As I said, I never had any work done there—the Cardassians found it first—but the people who did use it said he was an absolute genius with computer systems. Not as good with the hardware, maybe, but he had a technician who handled that. He was particularly good with automatic systems, figuring out ways to let the computer handle routine work without compromising crew control, or interfering with emergency procedures. And we needed that, there were never enough trained crew to handle our ships—" He broke off, shaking his head, went on in a tightly controlled voice. "The only thing anyone ever complained about officially was that he had a real bias toward computer-controlled systems, and not every captain liked giving the computers that much power."

"And unofficially?" Janeway asked. "I haven't heard anything that could be called gossip so far, Chakotay."

The first officer smiled, the expression wry. "Unofficially . . . he wasn't well liked, and I'm not completely sure why. As far as I know, he didn't have a wife or partner, or any family that he acknowledged, and I never met anyone who mentioned even a close friend. There was a general feeling that he liked his machines, the raw programs, mind you, not holodeck simulations, a good deal better than most of the people he met. Some people didn't take this well."

"I can imagine," Janeway said. She had met technicians like that before herself, could remember the disconcerting sense that the woman had been looking through her, all her interest focused not on the captain but on the ship she represented.

"The other thing I heard," Chakotay said, "may or may not be relevant, but it certainly interested me at the time. A couple of my colleagues claimed that he wasn't exactly committed to the Maquis, that he was more interested in testing his programs than helping us, and that he was on our side just because we were a bigger challenge."

Janeway lifted her eyebrows. That was a serious complaint, even a possible sign of psychosis—if it was true, of course. "And what did you think?"

"I told you, I never met him." Chakotay shrugged. "At the time, I don't know. I suppose I thought Ger— the captains involved—were overreacting. This was right after NSTN-2 fell, and they'd lost good people in the fighting, friends as well as crew. Nobody ever went so far as to say that he betrayed us, that he was a Cardassian agent, or even just against us. I know the leadership employed him afterward, on various of the smaller planets, so they trusted him, anyway."

"I see." Janeway frowned, trying to match Chakotay's description to the man she had met. Revek had seemed comfortable enough with her, with the rest of the away team, even amusingly irreverent at times; *still,* she thought, *if this is his record, he'll bear watching.* "If you get the chance," she said slowly, "see if you can draw him out about his background. I'm interested in how he got here, of course—anything new he can tell us about the Caretaker or the Array—but I'd also like to get an idea of how trustworthy he is."

"Whose side he's on?" Chakotay asked.

"Exactly." Janeway sighed. "You know, Chakotay, I think the thing that I find strangest about him is the one thing he didn't ask." Chakotay frowned, and Janeway pushed herself to her feet. "He didn't ask to come with us. Oh, maybe it was early for that, maybe he's been happy with the Kirse, but still—it strikes me as odd."

Chakotay nodded.

"But we can deal with that once we've opened negotiations for the food," Janeway went on, forcing a briskness she didn't entirely feel. "I'll meet you and rest of the away team in the transporter room at seventeen-fifty. Until then, I'll be in my cabin."

"Aye, Captain," Chakotay answered, and Janeway swept past him into the corridor.

The cabin seemed less welcoming than usual when Janeway stepped through the open door, and she frowned at the environmental panel on the bulkhead beside the door. "Computer, return the lights to my previous setting."

"Your cabin is part of the power-down cycle, a command override is necessary to return to your preferred levels."

The computer's voice sounded almost smug in its refusal, but Janeway shoved that thought aside, recognizing it as born of her own fatigue and the lack of decent food. "Cancel that. Find everything in our databanks, both of Federation origin and those files taken from the Maquis ship, that relates to Thilo Revek—" She spelled the name. "—and patch it to my desktop viewer."

"Confirmed. Searching."

There was a pause, and Janeway moved to her desk, debating her next move. She desperately wanted a cup of coffee, something normal to balance her worries about the planet and the ship, but wondered if she should—could—spend her limited rations on something so self-indulgent. On the one hand, she did have to think about setting a good example for the rest of the crew; on the other, to see that the captain was relaxed enough to spend a replicator ration on coffee was bound to have a positive effect on morale. She smiled then. *And if I'm thinking like that, I think I really need the coffee.*

"Coffee," she said, turning to the alcove that housed the replicator unit. "A small black coffee."

There was a pause, longer than had been usual before they'd ended up in the Delta Quadrant, while the replicator compared her request to the rations she had on record. Then the door slid back to reveal the steaming cup. It wasn't very big—the serving sizes had been reprogrammed for nonessential items—but the aroma was more enticing than ever. Janeway took a careful sip, reveling in the bitter liquid. Much better than the Kirse food, she thought, and then laughed at her own chauvinism. The fruit and the pastry had both been delicious; it was less the taste than the provenance that she questioned.

Still holding her coffee, she turned back to her desk, flipped on her screen, and touched keys to call up her secretarial routine. "Computer. Any word from either Tuvok or Torres?"

"No, Captain. I have flagged any such transmission for priority interrupt. Do you wish to maintain that status?"

"Yes."

"Status confirmed."

Janeway nodded absently, her attention already caught by a report from sickbay. She skimmed through it, a frown deepening as she absorbed its significance. The scurvy was getting worse, and other deficiencies were beginning to make themselves felt as well. "Janeway to sickbay."

The deskscreen lit, and Kes's pointed face appeared in the monitor. "Sickbay here, Captain."

"I want to discuss his most recent report with the doctor. Is he—" Janeway paused. No, neither "in" nor "available" were quite the words she wanted. "—active?"

"He's with a patient," Kes answered. She glanced over her shoulder, then stepped slightly to the side, so that Janeway could see past her into the main diagnostic chamber. In it, the holographic doctor was bent over a young man—one of Chakotay's people, Janeway added, automatically, but couldn't match a name to the face—who was looking away, his face screwed up in visible pain. Janeway winced in sympathy, and Kes went on, "Mr. DeShay slipped in one of the Jeffries tubes, and cut his arm rather badly. The doctor has had a little trouble stopping the bleeding."

Beyond her shoulder, Janeway could see the hologram frowning over what looked like a twenty-centimeter gash in the young man's—DeShay's, she corrected herself, trying to fix face to name—forearm. DeShay's uniform was bloodied, and a second technician, a dark man a little older than DeShay, hovered in the background, holding a bloody towel. The doctor's hands were perfectly clean, however, the forcefields that created him repelling the organic molecules, but no one in sickbay seemed aware of the anomaly. As she watched, the doctor reached for a second probe, ran it slowly along the edges of the cut. In its wake, DeShay's arm showed a ragged pink scar, the skin around it hot and red where it wasn't bruised. The doctor nodded, apparently satisfied, and reached for a hypospray. He injected DeShay with it, saying something, and then turned to face the outer office.

"I'll be out in a minute, Captain."

Janeway nodded, as always not quite sure how to deal with the doctor's attitude. If nothing else, it was hard to think of effective sanctions against someone who did not have a physical existence. To her surprise, however, the doctor was as good as his word.

"You wanted to speak to me, Captain?"

"I've seen your report," Janeway said. Over the doctor's shoulder, she could see the two crewmen preparing to leave, DeShay grimacing as he tried to roll down his torn sleeve, the other man listening soberly to Kes as she handed him a hypospray, gesturing to DeShay as she spoke.

"Ah. Not good news, no. I hope conditions on the planet are half as good as they say."

"The situation looks promising," Janeway answered. "Certainly the Kirse have the food we need, at least according to the preliminary analysis. Whether we'll be able to trade for it still an open question, which is why I wanted to talk to you. Your report's clear, Doctor—things are getting worse—but I want to know why."

The doctor snorted. "Because deficiency diseases are progressive, that's why. Plus of course this crew is under abnormally high stress to begin with, which leaves them no reserves when things get worse. I'm not at all surprised to see it."

"So where does that leave us?" Janeway asked, though she suspected she already knew the answer.

"Exactly where we were before," the doctor answered. "Either we take on healthy food here, or we won't make it to the next source of supply."

Janeway sighed, and nodded. "Thank you, Doctor. Janeway out."

She stared at the empty screen for a moment longer, then reached for her datapadd to study the doctor's report again. She recalled it to the working screen, but couldn't seem to concentrate on the printed columns, the doctor's tidy reduction of possible death to a matter of mathematics. This was not what she had joined Starfleet for, to superintend an inevitable death: the thought had flickered through her mind more than once in the days after *Voyager* had encountered the Caretaker's Array, and once again she shoved it down. Eventually, she would find a solution, an answer that led to survival, even if it was the long-term survival defined by seeing their children bring *Voyager* back to the Federation.

"Captain." The computer's cool voice brought her attention back to the screen in front of her. "The information you requested has been transferred to your terminal."

"Thank you," Janeway said, glad of the distraction, and reached for the screen controls. As she had expected, the compiled files held little more information on Thilo Revek than Chakotay had already given her, but she read through them anyway, trying to get a sense of the feeling behind the baldly stated facts of birth and education. There wasn't much, but by the time she finished she was sure that at least some of the writers had disliked Revek. Chakotay had reported the same thing, and she leaned back in her chair to finish the last of her now-cold coffee, replaying her own brief encounter with the technician. He had been friendly enough, even helpful, but she had to admit that she didn't quite trust him. And that could be completely unfair, she admitted, a career Starfleet officer's instinctive dislike of someone who resisted authority, or it could be the sort of hunch she would be foolish to ignore. And right now, she added silently, she had no real evidence either way. She would have to wait and see how Revek behaved at their next meeting.

"Tuvok to Captain Janeway."

The familiar voice broke through her musing, and she snapped forward in her chair to answer. "Janeway here. Go ahead, Mr. Tuvok."

"Lieutenant Torres and I have our first report on the Kirse transporter," the Vulcan answered. "We would like to discuss it with you."

It wasn't like Tuvok to request a personal meeting before she'd had a chance to look over a report, Janeway thought, a sinking sensation growing in the pit of her stomach, and it was equally unlike him to overreact to anything. "Very well. Meet me in the ready room in—" She glanced at the chronometer, calculating times. "—half an hour."

She had given herself time to shower, and the hot water revitalized her, so that as she stepped into the ready room she felt ready to cope with whatever new crisis Tuvok and Torres had discovered. They were there ahead of her, heads bent together over Torres's datapadd, but Torres looked up quickly as the door opened.

"Captain. I'm glad you're here."

Tuvok lifted an eyebrow, and the half-Klingon engineer flushed, the color staining her skin.

"Um, would you like some *saaba* tea, Captain? I had Neelix brew us a pot."

Janeway hid her automatic grimace. As far as she was concerned, the only virtue of Neelix's brew was that there was an ample supply on board for those who could stomach it; to her, it tasted the way her dog had smelled when she came inside after a run in the rain. *And I'm still not sure whether I dislike it because it tastes bad,* she admitted, *or because that bad taste reminds me too much of home.* "No, but thank you, Lieutenant," she said aloud. "So. What have you got for us?"

Torres glanced at Tuvok, seemed to receive some silent signal, and plunged on. "I've run an analysis on the tricorder readings we took on the planet, particularly of the Kirse transporter in action. It's somewhat similar to our own transporter, but has some significant limitations."

She slid her datapadd across the tabletop, and Janeway glanced at the columns of figures filling the screen. "Give me a summary to start."

"It looks as though the Kirse beam is limited to molecular resolution," Torres began, "and it may only be able to transport metallic compounds, though my sim was less clear on that. However, that was the only way we saw it used on the planet."

"So the Kirse were literally beaming those doors into and out of existence?" Janeway asked. "Where does the displaced matter go, a buffer of some kind?"

Torres shook her head. "I don't know. Logically, it

should, but we didn't pick up that kind of energy level on the surface. Either the buffers were extremely well shielded, or the Kirse simply move the mass from one point to another." She glanced at her padd again. "I also ought to mention that I didn't see any sign of any protection or special characteristics of the doorway areas, either."

"So what you're telling me," Janeway said slowly, "is that the Kirse have something that functions halfway between our transporter and—what?" She looked at the numbers on the datapadd.

"I don't know," Torres said. "The really interesting thing is, the emission patterns, the configuration of the beam, the phase lengths—it looks as though the Kirse were working on a system of their own, based on principles I don't recognize, but then someone told them about our system. And that someone presumably is that human, Revek."

"I would have expected Revek to know more about the transporter system," Janeway said, though the protest was perfunctory.

"He's—he was," Torres corrected herself, "a computer technician, when he worked for us, for the Maquis, I mean. And he was never Starfleet. He wouldn't necessarily have learned more than the minimum, and that wouldn't be enough to let them duplicate the system."

It made sense, and Janeway nodded.

Tuvok said, "I felt those two factors were significant, Captain. And also that they had security implications."

That was a typical Vulcan understatement, and Janeway smiled. As always, Tuvok looked faintly puzzled by her expression, but dismissed it as another emotional factor that he would never understand.

"First, I think we should assume that Mr. Revek is working for the Kirse, and willingly so, unless we see other evidence to the contrary."

Janeway made a face at that, but nodded.

"Second, I think we should also be aware while we are on-planet that this transporter capability is a potential weapon, to which I have as yet been unable to devise an effective counter."

Janeway drew a slow breath at the picture the Vulcan's words conjured for her. The Kirse transporter could be an effective weapon, all right, if a crude one. She imagined tons of wall suddenly displaced onto an enemy, or a section of floor suddenly disappearing, doors that opened onto killing grounds and vanished once the victims had passed through, leaving them trapped. "Any thoughts so far?" she asked, and knew it was only her training that kept her voice steady.

"Nothing useful," Tuvok answered. "Lieutenant Torres and I are working on it." He paused. "There is a third factor that had occurred to me."

"Oh?"

"I could not help wondering if the Kirse's apparent interest in trade does not derive from our possession of a working transporter."

"Ah." Janeway leaned back in her chair. That would make sense, particularly with Revek there to tell them of the Federation's resources—and, if Torres was right, to whet their appetite for a more effective system. "Unfortunately, Tuvok, we don't have a lot of choice. You've seen the doctor's most recent report?"

"I have." The Vulcan gave a stiff nod of acknowledgment. "It appears to weaken our bargaining position somewhat."

Janeway grinned in spite of herself, and once again received Tuvok's quizzical glance in return. "We'll just have to do the best we can."

"Captain," Torres said. "Permission to join the away team tonight."

Janeway shook her head. "No—"

"But, Captain, if I go, I might be able to get another look at their transporter, take some readings. I know what I'm looking for now."

Janeway shook her head again. "Then program a tricorder with those questions, Lieutenant Torres, and one of us will carry it. I have no intention of risking my chief engineer as well as my first officer and security chief."

Torres opened her mouth, then closed it again, as though the reality of her own position had only just registered. "Oh," she said, feebly, and then, more strongly, "Very well, Captain. I'll have the tricorder ready for beam-down."

"Thank you, Lieutenant Torres." Janeway rose to her feet. "And, by the way. Nice work, both of you."

CHAPTER
5

THE AWAY TEAM, ACCOMPANIED BY TORRES, GATHERED IN one of the small staging rooms beside the transporter chamber for a final briefing. Janeway had insisted on dress uniforms even for the ex-Maquis of the away team, however quickly the latter had had to be created from stores, and now, looking at them, she was glad she had done so. The severe uniforms carried a promise of Federation power, however illusory; more than that, it reminded them all of the proper protocols and patterns, protocols that were vital to follow in meeting a new species. They were maybe especially important now, so far from home, from the Federation's support, and Janeway drew herself up a little in her stiff-collared coat. She was proud of her people, she admitted silently; they looked—they were—good, some of the best she'd ever served with. Even the ex-Maquis were some of the best, combining Starfleet training and practical experience; they had been lucky that it had been Chakotay's ship *Voyager* had followed into the Delta Quadrant.

"Gentlemen," she said, and the others looked at her, Tuvok and Chakotay cutting short their desultory, low-voiced conversation. Kim drew himself up to his full height—he looked older in his dress uniform, and the planes of his face seemed suddenly sharper, more mature—not quite coming to attention, but almost so. Janeway gave him a faint, approving nod, and went on. "You've all seen the briefing summary."

There was a murmur of agreement, and Chakotay said, "The medical report wasn't encouraging."

Janeway smiled, the expression wry. "No. We don't have much choice left, Chakotay, and that's the main reason I've agreed to this dinner." She took a deep breath. "The report should have been clear enough, but I'll say it again. We have to resupply here, gentlemen. We will not stay healthy enough to reach another planet even if we could identify one. Which means that we have to achieve good relations—trade relations—with the Kirse at all costs."

She saw Kim stir at that, but the ensign said nothing, and she went on steadily. "The other concern we have is with the Kirse transporter and its possible use as a weapon. Lieutenant Torres has done her best to give us a full analysis of the beam and the system behind it, but so far we've been unsuccessful. Mr. Kim, you have the tricorder Lieutenant Torres programmed?"

"Yes, Captain." Kim touched his belt in confirmation.

"It's set to passive monitor," Torres said. "I've programmed it to begin active recording if the Kirse beam passes within twenty meters of its sensors, but if it doesn't switch on, Harry, you can operate it manually by—"

"I know," Kim interrupted, and tempered his words with an embarrassed smile. "I understood it when you went over it before."

Torres's face darkened briefly, but then she nodded, controlling her temper. "Then get me some good readings."

"I'll do my best," Kim answered, and looked back at Janeway. "It's all set, Captain."

"Good." Janeway looked more closely, saw that the tricorder was largely concealed by the dress uniform's coat. "But don't let data gathering jeopardize our relations with the Kirse. As for security issues . . . we'll follow standard protocols."

"We'll be standing by," Torres said, fervently. She hesitated. "Captain, I really wish you would take me along instead of Chakotay."

"Denied." Janeway knew she sounded harsh, and realized it was at least in part because of her own uncertainty. Torres was inexperienced in a command role; worse than that, she was still disliked by a large minority among the Starfleet crew, people who resented her having been promoted to chief engineer over Lieutenant Carey, a Starfleet officer. However, if the Kirse attacked, if the away team was eliminated, *Voyager* would need its chief engineer on board, both to fight back and to figure out some way to keep the replicators and the engines running. She shoved aside the suspicion that she would be bequeathing Torres an all-but-impossible problem—the fact that she wouldn't be around to worry about it did nothing to alleviate the guilt—and went on more easily. "We've been over this already, Lieutenant Torres. I want you on the ship."

"Aye, Captain." The engineer rarely sounded more stiffly Klingon than when she was angry, but at least she had her temper well under control this time.

"Then let's go." Janeway paused in the door to the transporter chamber. "The Kirse are waiting."

Torres handled the beam-down herself, watched without jealousy by the transporter chief. He was Starfleet, and Janeway marked his attitude with approval. Torres seemed to be winning over at least some of the technical crew. Then the familiar whine of the transporter beam drowned her thoughts, and she opened her eyes on a twilit courtyard. Tuvok had been right, the open space was nearly three times as large as the room where they'd first met the Kirse, and it was full of plants as lush as any she had seen in the Kirse's outer gardens. White flowers the size of her spread hand were just uncurling from near-black pods, and even as she watched one opened fully, its petals quivering slightly in the faint breeze. She could hear water running, could smell its cool dampness in the fading light, and turned her head to see water rising from a circular fountain. The shallow basin was inlaid with more of the multicolored metals in a pattern that reminded her faintly of an old-fashioned compass rose.

"It's beautiful," Kim said, and she turned back in time to see him blush. "Sorry, Captain."

"Not at all." In the distance, between a stand of trees as slim and pale as candles, Janeway could see the Kirse—a larger party this time, four aliens plus Revek—approaching along the graveled walk. "It is beautiful."

"Thank you," Adamant said. "Thilo suggested that you might enjoy dining here."

Janeway nodded to the human, who hung back at Night-Whispers' side, still smiling faintly. "I appreciate the choice, Mr. Revek."

"My pleasure, Captain." Revek glanced at Adamant, seemed to receive some unspoken signal. "Let me introduce the rest of our party. Adamant and Night-Whispers you know, these others are Keyward and Fair-Watching."

Janeway nodded politely. The Kirse were very similar in features, and even the presence or absence of the great wings—something to investigate further later, she added silently—didn't help much in telling one from the other. Adamant and Keyward were distinguished only by Adamant's slightly greater height, while Fair-Watching and Night-Whispers seemed identical except for the color of their tunics. "And this is my first officer, Chakotay; my tactical officer, Tuvok; and my operations officer Harry Kim, whom you've already met."

Adamant bowed gracefully, the others copying him a heartbeat later, and cocked his head, studying Tuvok with frank curiosity. "You are not of the same pattern as these rest? Is it an issue of function?"

"I am a Vulcan," Tuvok said, with more than usual austerity. "This has nothing to do with my position on *Voyager*."

"I told you about Vulcans," Revek said, and Adamant gave him a quick glance.

"My apologies. I'm not familiar with your species, despite Thilo's briefings." He gestured toward the path the Kirse had arrived on, and lights sprang to life along its edges, small lights that quivered like flames and did little more than illuminate the actual walkway, so that the twilight pressed in unabated on all sides. The effect was startlingly beautiful, like a picture of some faerie kingdom from a children's storybook. "But I hope to remedy my ignorance over dinner. If you'd come with me?"

"Of course," Janeway answered, and fell into step at his side. She glanced back once, and saw the others pairing off, and Revek took his place at Adamant's right. The noise of the fountain receded as they made their way back down the path, the polished stones giving a musical, faintly metallic sound underfoot, as though they walked on muffled bells. More of the white flowers were springing into bloom all around them, and Janeway realized that most of the garden's plants, trees and shrubs and smaller species, were wound with the vines. Revek saw her looking and leaned forward around Adamant's shoulder.

"This is the night-garden—or rather, it's the night-garden now, when those flowers, moon-flowers, I call them, since I can't pronounce their proper name, are blooming. In daytime, it's the fountain-yard, and believe me, it looks completely different."

"I believe you," Janeway said, softly, and didn't particularly care if he heard. The moon-flowers were giving off a faint, clean scent, more like soap than any floral perfume, and the air was perfectly still and cool. She glanced up, and saw the sky vivid with stars, the ghostly band of the Milky Way still visible behind them, unaffected by the lights that guided their feet.

"A better translation might be milk-flowers," Adamant said. "Since they're related to the galaxy-shadow Revek says you call the Milky Way, and since Revek tells me 'milk' is always white."

"They bloom for one night," Revek said, "and then they die and another bloom replaces them the next night. In the morning, before the sweepers come, the fountain-yard is ankle deep in their petals."

Janeway looked at him, not knowing how to answer, but Revek was already talking to Adamant.

"Milk-flowers might be better, at that, but it's not as euphonious."

"Dinner is here," Adamant said.

The path ended in a circular area paved with the same compasslike pattern that had decorated the bottom of the fountain. Tables were walking toward them across that circle, followed by benches and a tall, thin column on wheels. Dishes were already on the table, but they were held motionless by more of the mechanical hands. As Janeway watched, the tables formed themselves into a rough semicircle, and the column moved to its center. Arms unfolded from the central spine, bent themselves into graceful arcs, then spat thin filaments that seemed to bury themselves in the pavement. More lights flared along those filaments, gossamer, ghostly sparks that somehow gave an astonishing amount of light. In spite of herself, Janeway gasped, and heard Chakotay murmur something under his breath.

"Captain," Adamant said, and gestured to the farthest table. "Let us eat."

Janeway followed him to the table, and seated herself gingerly on one of the benches. It seemed steady enough now, but she remembered its entrance, scuttling along behind the tables, and found herself bracing her body against any sudden movement. A metal hand heaved itself up from the table, the long, multi-jointed fingers glittering rose and gold in the light from the candelabrum, and lifted the lid from the nearest dish. The savory smell, surprisingly familiar, homey even, garlic and onions mixed with the subtler scents of earthy vegetables, made Janeway's mouth water. A second, almost invisible hand, this one little more than a curved scoop like the hands of the creatures in the gardens, pushed the dish toward her, and she reached eagerly for the spoon, but Adamant forestalled her.

"Allow me, Captain."

"Thank you." Janeway allowed him to ladle the thick stew onto her plate, wondering if she was expected to reciprocate. To her relief, Adamant served himself as well, and out of the corner of her eye she saw the same ritual being repeated at the other tables.

Adamant released the dish, and another scoop-hand slid it to Revek, who helped himself. Another dish, bright bronze banded with silver, suddenly rose from the tabletop, balancing on two remarkably human-looking feet, and trudged toward her. The contents of the bowl—coarse, dark red grains, like sea salt or peastone—slid from side to side, but stopped short of the edges.

"Thilo is fond of this," Adamant said, "though I'm not. But perhaps you will like it also."

"It's a dried tree gum," Revek said, "with a flavor between lemon and hot peppers. I found the food a little bland when I first landed."

"Thank you," Janeway said, and wondered if the serving bowl had been made for Revek. She took a spoonful, setting it beside the main stew, and the bowl rose again as she returned the spoon. It headed to Revek, who helped himself more liberally.

"There's wine as well," Revek went on, "but it's potent."

He nodded to a tall glass that stood by her place, filled with a pale gold liquid that released faint bubbles to the night air. Janeway took a careful sip, and couldn't keep her eyebrows from lifting. The—wine—looked innocuous enough, more like terrestrial champagne than anything, but it had the alcoholic bite of a well-aged whiskey. She set the glass down, resolving to drink very little, and a slim, vaguely bird-shaped machine tipped forward, replacing the small amount she had drunk. It tilted back with a soft click of metal on metal, and the legs retracted slightly, stabilizing it on the tabletop. It was an ingenious design, she thought, and a clever piece of engineering, but, if it kept refilling the glasses as they were emptied, it would also insure that the Kirse's guests were, if not actually drunk, at least suffering from diminished judgment by the end of the meal. Not a nice trick, she thought, all her earlier wariness rushing back, and she glanced at the other tables. Tuvok and Chakotay were both experienced officers, and Chakotay's service with the Maquis would only have reinforced the need for caution. Kim, on the other hand, was both young and inexperienced, fresh from the Academy, and she wondered if there was some way she could warn him without offending the Kirse. As she watched, the ensign tasted the wine, and in spite of herself she couldn't help smiling at the shocked expression on his face. He swallowed manfully, however, and managed to smile in response to the Kirse's—Night-Whispers, she thought—murmured question. He would be all right, she thought, and turned her attention back to her own table.

There were four more courses, all of a similar style, thick stews or what seemed to be sauteed vegetables served over a delicate, pearl-like grain that tasted a bit like homemade bread, and by the end she found herself agreeing with Revek. The flavors were a little bland to a human palate; the red grains did add a much-needed bite to the rich service. There was no meat, or nothing that she recognized as animal protein, though she guessed that some of the heavier-tasting vegetables would prove to be protein-rich legumes. The tree-cheese that Revek had mentioned earlier, and which reappeared at the center of another delicate pastry, would probably also be a good protein source, she added silently. The Kirse world seemed to have everything *Voyager* needed—if they could just strike a trade agreement.

She took another sip of the so-called wine, its

harshness something of a relief after the delicacy of the food, and glanced cautiously at Adamant. So far, the Kirse leader had proved unwilling to discuss trading, and she had not wanted to press the matter, unsure of Kirse etiquette. They had talked instead of star patterns—Adamant was apparently something of an amateur astronomer, if she had understood his elliptical references correctly—and he had pointed out both a brilliant blue-white point that was a nearby nebula, a star nursery, and the streak of light that was one of the orbiting stations. There was no moon, and when she expressed surprise, he had questioned her on the functions and appearance of lunar bodies. All the while, she had been aware of Revek watching her, and the other members of the away team, always with a look that said, smugly, that he knew more than he was telling.

"A very pleasant meal, Captain," Adamant said, and Janeway dragged her attention back to him. "Shall we walk a bit before the sweet?"

"Certainly." Janeway stood with him, aware that the rest of the away team was copying her, the other Kirse rising with Adamant, and Revek grinned at her. He had drunk more of the Kirse wine than any of the other humans, though he didn't seem to be much affected by it.

"I think you'll enjoy this."

"I'm sure." Privately, Janeway was much less certain, but she was not going to reveal that to either the Kirse or Revek.

Adamant gestured, and the tables lifted themselves, their dozens of hands rising in a flurry of movement to secure the dishes they carried. Slowly at first, then faster, the tables began to walk away, the benches scurrying after. Their legs made an odd metallic scuffling on the pebbled walkway. Adamant ignored them, and nodded to a different path. "If you'll come with me, Captain?"

Once again, Janeway fell into step at the Kirse's side as they started down the new path. She could hear the rest of the away team behind her, the sound of their feet on the stones and the occasional murmur of voices, guessed—hoped—that they were being as cautious as she herself was. Beside her feet, along the edges of the path, lights flickered to life, paler than the chains of light that had illuminated their dinner, and she glanced curiously at them. They looked almost like bioluminescence, had that peculiar blue tint to them, and she wondered just how much of the Kirse technology was organic. Certainly the tables seemed to follow an animal design, however mechanical they had looked.

They turned a bend in the path, and light flared ahead of them, blue-white and bright as a full moon. In the center of a sudden clearing stood a silver frame, shaped vaguely like a harp, though the metal was ridged and knobbed like bone or bamboo. In that frame hung a glowing mass, seeming in the darkness as bright as the warp core, and on its face crawled a thousand fainter lights. She caught her breath at the sight, and tasted honey in the wind.

"Our sweet," Adamant said, and she thought there was a distinct note of pride in his voice. "Please, Captain, help yourself."

Janeway hesitated, caught between diplomatic imperatives, but common sense won out this time. "I've never seen anything like this. Tell me about it."

Adamant blinked, looking faintly disconcerted, but answered without seeming to take offense. "These are—Thilo tells me it's called honey. The hive is here to finish the meals."

"On Earth," Janeway said carefully, "the insects

that make honey object to our taking it, and they have a fairly effective defense when annoyed. I take it that your honey-makers don't object?"

"They're bred both to make far more than their needs," Adamant answered, "and to be without aggressive defense." For an instant, his face seemed to cloud, but then the expression vanished. "It can be a problem, though more for them than for me. But please, help yourself." He stepped forward then, into the circle of light cast by—was it the insects, Janeway wondered, or the hive itself? Despite his assurances, she braced herself, more than half expecting to hear the angry drone of wings, but the insects seemed to ignore him. He extended a long finger, probed carefully, and then snapped a corner from the hive. He held it out to her, and Janeway took it, the glow fading even as she watched. A single insect still clung to the piece of comb, its blue-lit abdomen pulsing gently, and she peered curiously at it. It looked almost as silver as the hive frame—was it metal? she wondered suddenly—but before she could look more closely, it spread its wings and soared back to join the others.

The rest of the away team was helping itself, each coached by one of the Kirse, and Janeway took a cautious taste. The thick liquid wasn't as sweet as terrestrial honey, had a pleasantly bitter overtone, and Revek nodded to her.

"You can eat the comb, too."

"It's very good," Janeway answered, and Chakotay moved up to stand at her side.

"When I was a very young boy, we used to go on honey raids. This kind of bee would have been much easier to deal with."

The other wingless Kirse, Chakotay's dinner companion—Keyward, Janeway remembered—moved up with him, and gave her a nod of greeting before turning to Chakotay. "These bees were once much less friendly. But there's a trade-off for every step of progress."

"Oh?" Janeway looked at Keyward, but it was Adamant who answered.

"Yes. But I think this is part of our possible dealings together."

Then he was ready to start trading. Janeway suppressed a sudden, unworthy glee, and said, "Indeed?"

"I believe you said you were interested in foodstuffs," Adamant said.

"Yes." There was no point in going into more detail yet, Janeway thought, not until she knew what the Kirse might want in return. Out of the corner of her eye, she saw the rest of the away team gathering, Tuvok dependably austere despite the piece of comb that dripped blue light over his hand, Kim licking the last flecks of honey from his fingers, but focused her attention on Adamant.

"And there is much here that you might want," the Kirse leader went on. "And I have no objection to trade with people, as long as the trading is fair and open. I am certainly willing to offer both food itself and even rootstock if that is within your desire and if your ship can tend it properly, and my price in return is simple. I wish only the information I would need to re-create your transporter."

Janeway hesitated, aware of Tuvok's sudden, focused stare. The Vulcan had been right—no surprise there—but she still had not decided how she would answer.

Adamant tipped his head to one side. "It is an issue of security here. Thilo mentioned to you the Andirrim, who are the principal problem, though other animals have tried attacking from time to time. You have also seen our defense band."

"The platforms," Revek said, and Adamant gave him a sharp, unreadable look.

"They need regular and nearly constant maintenance," Adamant went on, "and, unfortunately, the Andirrim have discovered this. They lie in wait for the service shuttles, and attack them, and then use the weaknesses lack of maintenance creates in the band to attack the planet." He smiled, suddenly and briefly. "As you will have noticed—" He faltered then, made a whistling trill, and looked at Revek.

"Silver-Hammer," Revek said.

"So. As you will have noticed, Silver-Hammer has made a beam that can move some matter, but not all, and it is not sufficient to move a living object at all—not and have it remain living." Adamant tipped his head to the side again. "So I am more than willing to trade for the food you want, Captain, but that is the price I require."

"I see," Janeway said, and decided to delay. "Frankly, this wasn't something we expected—we assumed your transporter functioned according to your desired specifications."

"I am also surprised," Tuvok said, "that Mr. Revek was unable to provide the information you required."

Revek laughed. Adamant said, matching Tuvok's austerity, "Thilo's skill is in computers, not in the hardware and theoretical foundations of your transporter system. And his ship was badly damaged on landing."

"If I'd had a working transporter," Revek murmured, "I wouldn't have had to land it."

Adamant ignored the interruption. "He has done what he can, but our transporter has not progressed beyond this point."

"I see," Janeway said. "Certainly we're interested in pursuing an agreement—your food is excellent-tasting as well as nutritious for our people—and I can see that we might be able to offer, say, the technical specifications for our system in exchange for re-supply."

Adamant frowned slightly. "I would prefer to trade for actual hardware, as well as the specifications."

"I don't think that will be possible," Janeway answered. "At most, we might be able to replicate some of the crucial parts for you—and from what we've seen of your technology, you should have no trouble duplicating the rest of the system."

"Perhaps—" Adamant began, and Keyward leaned close to him, murmuring in the Kirse language. Adamant nodded, and looked back at Janeway. "Clearly the details will have to be worked out, but can I take it that we have an agreement in principal?"

Janeway nodded slowly. "We need to resupply our ship, you need the transporter. We should be able to work something out."

"Then let us say this for now," Adamant said. "Send one of your people down to examine what we have to offer—our fields are rich, the first harvest is ripe, and I think you will find what you need. Then tell me if it's not worth the components we want."

"The issue isn't one of worth," Janeway said, "but of our own situation. Our supplies are limited—you know from Mr. Revek how far we are from our home ports, from the Federation. Unless you could offer us a way back there, we literally cannot spare the parts from our own transporters."

"I regret that I don't have that to place on the table," Adamant answered, and smiled. "And I am—not unsympathetic—to your difficulties. But the Andirrim are a persistent and annoying problem that needs to be permanently resolved."

"With your permission, then," Janeway said, "I'll

send some of my people down tomorrow to examine the food that's available, as you offered. In the meantime, I and my officers will discuss how best we can meet your needs, and get back to you."

"Agreed," Adamant said, and looked over his shoulder. "Thilo can accompany them."

"Very well." Privately, Janeway was less sure that Revek's presence was desirable, but she saw no point in protesting. "Adamant, I thank you for a truly lovely dinner. We'll contact you in the morning regarding our survey."

"Captain, you are most welcome." Adamant bowed deeply over his folded hands.

Janeway touched her communicator. "Janeway to *Voyager*. Four to beam up."

Janeway did not sleep well that night, despite her very real exhaustion. A part of her dreaming mind was busy with *Voyager,* while another worried at the transporter question, so that in her dreams she chased or was chased down the corridors of the Kirse gardens, her way blocked at every turn by overstuffed furniture that chattered to her in inane upper-class British accents. Under the circumstances, she wasn't sorry when the computer sounded its preprogrammed alert, and took a certain pleasure in the drawn faces of the rest of the previous night's away team as her officers assembled in the briefing room. She had called a full meeting, wanting input from all of the ship's senior officers, and now, looking at the faces, she was glad she had done so.

"You look tired, Chakotay," she said. "How did you sleep?"

The first officer looked up at her as she took her place at the table, surprise at such a personal question fading to comprehension at the matching expression on her face.

"Not very well, Captain, actually."

Janeway nodded. "And you, Mr. Kim?"

The young ensign blushed. "Um, not very well, either, Captain. I, uh, had indigestion."

"He was sick as a dog," Paris said, not very much under his breath.

"Right," Janeway said, with deliberate ambiguity. "I want each of you to report to sickbay after this meeting. Let's just be sure there's nothing unexpected in the Kirse food, too."

"Yes, Captain," Kim said.

"We've been eating very badly for a while now," Chakotay said. "There's bound to be a reaction."

Janeway nodded. "I agree, that's probably it. But it's better to be sure."

"Very good, Captain." Chakotay leaned back in his chair.

"Now." Janeway steepled her fingers, wishing that it wouldn't look unreasonably self-indulgent to spend a replicator ration on coffee, and glanced around the table. All the department heads were there, with the exception of the holographic doctor, and she glanced at Kes, sitting as always at Neelix's side. Before she could ask, however, a wallscreen lit, and the doctor's dyspeptic features appeared in its frame. "Good," she said aloud. "We're all here."

The doctor stared back at her, visibly unabashed, and Janeway wondered, not for the first time, who had been the pattern for his social template.

"Our main concern," she said, "is the Kirse offer. As you know, they want to trade their food—which we need—for transporter components, the hardware they would need to build their own version of our transporter system. I have said that we need to check out the supplies on offer before making an offer of our own, and Mr. Paris and Mr. Kim will form that party. If you've recovered, that is, Mr. Kim."

"I'm fine now, Captain, thank you." Kim was still blushing, and Janeway curbed her own amusement.

"Excellent. Now. Comments, please, on the Kirse offer."

There was no answer immediately, and Neelix looked wildly from side to side. "Well, if nobody else will say it, I will. We should take their offer, immediately, and be glad they don't want anything more important."

Torres took a sharp breath, visibly controlling her temper, and Neelix spread his hands. "What did I say? You told me that you could lose the use of two or three transporters without it presenting a real problem."

"The transporter system is redundant," Torres said, through clenched teeth, "and in the course of normal operations, yes, we could temporarily do without one or more of them." She looked at Janeway. "But if we're going to spend the next seventy years getting back to the Alpha Quadrant, we can't afford to give away—sorry, to trade away—any of the hardware. To put it bluntly, there won't be any replacements—no nice Federation starbases to draw new parts from. Under the circumstances, I don't think we should give up anything that might be a potential spare part, even if that day is years down the road."

"I concur," Tuvok said. "But it may be possible to trade them something less than the full set of hardware."

Chakotay nodded. "Right. Their technology is already advanced enough to build something very close to our system, or we'd be facing a Prime Directive situation."

Janeway nodded. That was one of the few fortunate things about *Voyager*'s predicament: the Kirse were clearly an advanced people; there was little *Voyager* could do to change their culture.

"But," Chakotay went on, "it raises at least potential security issues. From what Neelix has said—and from what little Keyward said over dinner—the Kirse don't seem interested in off-planet exploration. Most of their focus is on the planet itself, and the gardens."

Neelix bounced slightly in his chair. "That's right. I've never heard of a Kirse leaving its planet. Never. Of course, they don't have to, everybody comes to them."

Tuvok looked at Chakotay. "I believe I take your point. Although the Kirse themselves may not travel, and therefore their possession of Federation transporter technology would be unlikely to erode our technological advantage, you are concerned that some other peoples might obtain the technology from them, and that over time the knowledge would spread sufficiently to threaten us."

"Exactly." Chakotay spread his hands. "It seems plausible to me."

"I suppose we could try to restrict their right to trade the transporter any further," Janeway began, but shook her head. "No, that would be unenforceable on every level. We'd have to sell them an entire chamber, and seal it, to make it work, and we'd have no guarantee that they couldn't figure it out anyway. Plus there's more than legitimate trade to worry about. These raiders, the Andirrim—they could steal technology as easily as they steal food."

"My dinner companion, Fair-Watching, dismissed the Andirrim as animals," Tuvok said. "However, he also admitted that they were 'clever animals' and a nuisance. And they are allied with the Kazon-Ogla. I do not think we can afford to allow the transporter to fall into their hands."

"I agree," Janeway said. "So that rules out selling the Kirse hardware, on a number of grounds, and the plans on security grounds. Where does that leave us?"

"Hungry," the doctor said, from the wallscreen, "and with an empty larder."

"Thank you, Doctor." Janeway controlled her annoyance with an effort. "I take it the medical situation hasn't changed?"

"Not for the better," the doctor answered. "To put it bluntly, if we don't resupply here, you'll be lucky to have enough well crew left to run the ship by the time we reach the next M-class planet."

"You're a real ray of sunshine, aren't you?" Paris muttered, loudly enough for the doctor to hear.

"One of us has to be realistic. And quite frankly I don't relish the idea of inhabiting a dead ship until the power runs out."

"Gentlemen," Janeway said.

Paris had the grace to look abashed, and the doctor sighed. "I'm sorry, Captain. But the medical situation borders on the critical."

"I am aware of it," Janeway said. She looked around the table. "So. We can't afford to trade the Kirse hardware, and I would prefer not to sell them the complete schematics for fear of their eventually falling into Kazon-Ogla hands. But we have to resupply here. Lieutenant Torres, what are our chances of selling them a deliberately weakened version of our transporter system?"

Torres frowned. "I could probably—definitely—put together a version with a shorter range, maybe a higher power cost, but first I'd need to know just what kind of limitations we would want to impose."

"There's no guarantee the Kirse would accept a limited system," Chakotay said, but his tone was less negative than his words.

"But if they want it badly enough, which they seem to do," Kim said, "since maintaining their orbital platforms is the issue, they might be willing to accept a system that would let them do that. . . ." His voice trailed off, but Janeway nodded.

"Mr. Kim's right, maintenance of the defense system sets the acceptable parameters for the Kirse."

"Even if they're willing to accept limits," Chakotay said, "there's no reason to think that they can't build a system comparable to our own from that starting point. And then we have the same problem as before."

"I agree," Janeway said. "It's fairly simple, really. If we trade the transporter technology in any form, we will have to assume that at some point down the road the Kirse will expand on what we give them until they have a system comparable to our own, and once that happens, we have to assume that other Delta Quadrant races, and eventually the Kazon-Ogla, will also acquire the system. What we can do—and I think we must do—is delay that point as long as possible."

Chakotay nodded. "I agree, Captain."

"Even assuming a worst-case scenario," Tuvok said, "one in which the Kirse are able to duplicate our system quickly, and in which the Kazon-Ogla acquire it quickly and directly from their own client race, a process I would expect to take between one and two years, we—*Voyager*—would be and would remain one to two years ahead of the dispersement of that technology. The Kazon-Ogla do not willingly share anything, least of all something that might give one faction an advantage." He paused. "Of course, these numbers are rough approximations. I will run a simulation to achieve a more precise estimate, but the situation seemed to warrant a quick result."

No Vulcan, Janeway thought, could ever bring himself to say "a guess." She said, "Very well. Lieutenant Torres, I want you and Mr. Tuvok to analyze the requirements of a transporter system that will be sufficient to service the orbital stations. Once that's done, Lieutenant Torres, you'll work out a version of our transporter that will achieve those goals, while Tuvok gets a more precise estimate of the minimum time it could take the Kazon-Ogla to get the transporter technology from the Kirse."

Torres nodded, her head already bent over her datapadd, and added, belatedly, "Yes, Captain."

"Very good, Captain," Tuvok said.

"In the meantime," Janeway went on, "Mr. Kim, once the doctor has given you a clean bill of health, you and Mr. Paris will contact the Kirse and beam down to examine the food they have on offer."

"Right away, Captain," Paris said, and Kim echoed him reluctantly.

Kim sat on the edge of the diagnostic table, uncomfortably aware of Kes and Paris deep in conversation in the next compartment, while the holographic doctor peered thoughtfully at the readouts on the wall displays.

"Well," he said at last, "I would say you're suffering from nothing more than a moderate case of indigestion."

"That's what I said it was," Kim said.

"Then I'm glad I could confirm your diagnosis." The doctor turned away to touch controls beside his work station. "Go ahead, you have your clean bill of health."

Kim nodded, and slid off the table. The doctor didn't speak again until he was in the doorway. "In fact, you're doing better than you were. Last night's dinner seems to have improved things."

"Thank you," Kim said, startled, but the doctor was bent over a computer screen, apparently oblivious. Kim shrugged, and rejoined the others.

"So, Harry, you ready for the adventure?" Paris asked. Kes gave them both an impartial, distracted smile, and slipped past him to rejoin the doctor.

"The doctor says I'm fine," Kim answered, and with difficulty suppressed his grievance. *I said I was fine, that it was nothing, but nobody listened to me.*

"Great. Tuvok's already spoken to the Kirse—to Keyward, he said it was—and they're expecting us. The captain said we're to report directly to the transporter room."

"Let's go," Kim answered.

The duty technician was waiting at the transporter console, and nodded to Kim as the doors opened. "Coordinates locked in and ready, Mr. Kim."

With difficulty, Kim kept himself from glancing at Paris. There were still a few people on *Voyager*—ex-Maquis as well as Starfleet—who refused to accept the pilot's presence, and who did their best to avoid treating him as the officer he was. Paris said the only thing to do was to ignore them, unless and until it interfered with duty, but Kim could tell it wasn't easy. *And it's not right, either,* he thought, but knew this wasn't the time or place to press it.

"Ready, Tom?" he said, and took his place on the transporter platform.

"Ready when you are," Paris answered, and gave him a quick, wry smile.

"Stand by," the technician said. "Coordinates confirmed. Energize."

Kim took a deep breath, and glanced quickly around. The Kirse had given coordinates for another of the open areas inside the citadel, this one deeply shadowed by the tower and windowless wall that soared easily a hundred meters against the bright sky. The other walls had windows and the arch of a Kirse door, but there was no one in sight. There were no plants, either, but paving underfoot was banded with a golden lattice, and each intersection was picked out with a dull blue glass cabochon. Kim started to examine one, but straightened hastily at the sound of a voice from the open doorway.

"So you're here." Thilo Revek strode out from the archway, flanked by two more of the winged Kirse. They were both female, distinctly so, the curve of breasts and hips clearly visible under the thin tunic, and Kim heard Paris's soft, almost soundless sigh of admiration.

"Behave," he said, under his breath, and stepped forward to meet Revek. "The captain made arrangements with Adamant for us to examine the food they're offering in trade."

"And I'm here to interpret," Revek answered. "Not that you should need my help. These are—" He stopped then, and glanced at the Kirse on his left, who answered the unspoken question with a chuckling trill. "Lord, Adamant's not giving me the easy ones. All right. This is Harp—" He gestured to the Kirse on his right. "—and that's Grayrose."

"I'm to assist you however I can," Harp said, to Kim. She started a trill, then corrected herself, shaking her head. "Grayrose has been assigned to Paris."

"Lucky me," Paris said, under his breath, and added, more loudly, "Pleased to meet you."

Grayrose gave an austere nod, but her eyes were bright with curiosity.

"There are a number of fields to examine," Harp went on, "as Captain Janeway expressed interest in variety first. I thought it would be easier if we were to split our efforts. You and I could look at the crops closest to the—" She hesitated for a fraction of a second over the word. "—to the citadel, and Grayrose and Paris could take one of the shuttles to the Lakeside area."

Kim hesitated, suspicion flaring. It was never a good idea to split an away team, especially when they knew so little about the Kirse—or, for that matter, about Revek. On the other hand, he couldn't see how to refuse gracefully—and besides, he told himself, they were trying to establish good relations with the Kirse. "All right," he said, and was uncomfortably aware of Revek's slight smile. "I'll just need to inform the ship of our change in plans."

"Of course," Harp answered, and sounded surprised that he would even ask.

Kim touched his communicator, a little reassured by her attitude. "Kim to *Voyager*."

"*Voyager* here." To his relief, it was Janeway herself who answered.

"Captain." Kim paused, trying to figure out the best way to convey what needed to be said without offending the listening Kirse. "I just wanted to apprise you of a slight change in plan. Mr. Paris will be going to—I believe you said the Lakeside fields?"

Harp nodded once.

"To the Lakeside fields," Kim went on, "and I'll be working in fields nearer to the citadel."

There was a little silence, and Kim would have crossed his fingers had he been able. "Very well, Mr. Kim," Janeway said at last. "We'll be keeping in contact with both of you. *Voyager* out."

Was there a slight emphasis on the word "both"?

Kim wondered. It certainly sounded as though the captain had gotten his message. "Then we're at your disposal," he said, to Harp, and only then wondered if it was a felicitous choice of words.

The Kirse seemed unaware of any double meaning. "Excellent," she said, and looked at Grayrose.

"I'll take a shuttle," Grayrose said, in answer to the unspoken question. "And Thilo."

Harp nodded. "This way, then, Kim."

She gestured, and Kim suppressed a start as the heavy note of the Kirse transporter sounded again. A gate, taller and narrower than the arches inside the citadel, appeared in the previously featureless wall, and through the new opening he could see the gentle slope that led down to the gardens.

"If you want," Harp said, apologetically, "I can get us a shuttle, but it isn't far to walk."

"Walking's fine," Kim said, and looked at Paris.

"Right," the pilot answered. "I'll see you back here in—how long is it likely to take us to look at these fields, Grayrose?"

"I think you should allow at least four hours for a proper survey," the second Kirse answered. Her voice was a little lighter than her—was Harp a sister, Kim wondered, or were the Kirse simply possessed of fewer physiotypes than most species?

"I'll see you back here in four hours, then, Harry," Paris said.

"Right," Kim answered, and Harp gestured toward the new-made door.

"If you'll come with me?"

It was hard to suppress his misgivings as he followed the Kirse through the long tunnel. Although she wasn't tall, the tips of her wings nearly brushed the ceiling, and he saw her relax visibly, the pearl-gray membranes shivering, as they left the tunnel. Behind him, the Kirse transporter whined again, and he looked back to see that the door had vanished. Harp followed his gaze, and said, apologetically, "I can't leave it open, or the gardeners will get in."

"Gardeners?" Kim asked, and Harp shrugged one shoulder, slanting a wingtip toward the first stand of trees at the foot of the low hill. Several of the creatures they had seen on landing were gathered around one heavily laden tree, some scrabbling in the dirt by its foot, the rest stretching for the fruit that hung from the upper branches. One jumped repeatedly toward a fruit so large that Kim could see its ripe roundness even at a distance, ignoring a rock that would have given him the height he needed to reach it. They didn't seem to be intelligent, Kim thought, if you defined intelligence as tool-using.

"They're a reasonable makeshift," Harp said, "but they can be a nuisance."

Before Kim could answer, or even think of which of his dozen questions to ask first, she had lifted her wings, brought them down with a dull clap of displaced air. The creatures looked up, little eyes suddenly wide and afraid, and then scrambled in a body over the low hedge that bounded the tree and vanished into the tall grass of the next field.

"Why'd you do that?" Kim asked. It wasn't the most intelligent question he'd ever come up with, he admitted an instant later, and wished he could recall it. The Kirse gave him a blank glance.

"They'd just be in the way."

"Oh." It was true, Kim supposed, but he couldn't help thinking there must have been an easier way to move them on. Harp started down the slope, her wings rising slightly to balance her weight, and Kim followed. "Tell me, the—gardeners, you called them. They've obviously been, well, modified." Harp gave him another blank look, and Kim stumbled on. "Um, they have metal parts, that look almost like prostheses, like replacements?"

"Oh, the adaptations." Harp's expression cleared, and she cocked her head. "What about them?"

Where to begin? Kim wondered. He said, "Well, for a start, why? Why do whatever it is you're doing if they're such a nuisance? And anyway, what are the parts for?"

"To keep them functioning properly," Harp answered. "One does what one can with the available materials."

"What do they do?" Kim asked.

Harp shrugged again, her wings shifting with a muted thump of air. "The cultivations are extensive, and it would be a waste of resources to send ones like me to manage them. These can be adapted, and they'd otherwise be useless, so it seemed the most efficient way to handle the situation."

They had reached the bottom of the hill and the graveled path that ran between the rows of trees. The air was very still, warm and heavy with the scent of the ripe fruit. Kim swallowed, and did his best to ignore the tantalizing smell. "So you mean the metal, the machine parts, are all there to make the animals act as caretakers in the fields? As gardeners?"

"Just so." Harp gave the stiff Kirse nod, and then stretched, reaching into the nearest tree, and brought down one of the pale, pink-skinned fruits. "Here, these should be of use to *Voyager,* and you seemed to enjoy them last night."

Kim gave her a sharp glance, but took the fruit. "You weren't at dinner."

"It's common knowledge."

To his horror, Kim felt himself blushing. He had known that he had eaten more than his share the night before, but he hadn't thought he had behaved so badly that it would be the subject of Kirse gossip. *Maybe they just kept track of our preferences so that they'd know what to sell us,* he told himself, and trained his tricorder on the fruit in his hand. As he had expected, the readings were positive, some of the vitamin content off the standard scale, but he extracted the probe anyway, took a core sample for later analysis.

"You can go ahead and eat the rest," Harp said.

Kim hesitated, but the smell was too good to resist, especially after the weeks of Neelix's cooking on *Voyager.* They would have to make sure that Neelix didn't try to do too much with the Kirse food, it was just the sort of thing he would spoil with too much seasoning. . . .

"A little farther on," Harp said, "there's a stand of—" She hesitated, groping for a word. "—Thilo calls it purple wheat, and you might find that useful. And then there is a sample-garden beyond that, it has a dozen or more plants from all over the planet. I expect you'll find something there that will be what you want."

"All right," Kim said, indistinctly, through the last mouthful of fruit. There was no pit, he realized abruptly, nothing that could serve as a seed, and he wondered how the tree reproduced itself. He had a good tissue sample that should answer that; better to save his questions for things that the samples couldn't resolve as easily, particularly since he had the distinct sense that Harp had deliberately changed the subject before.

"This way." Harp started down the wide path, turned back when he didn't follow at once. "It isn't far, just a hundred of your meters."

Kim ignored her for a moment longer, certain that

he'd seen something—one of the creatures?—watching from behind a thick-growing stand of bushes. Nothing moved there now, however, and he supposed he must have been mistaken. "Coming," he said, but couldn't quite shake the feeling that they were being watched.

CHAPTER 6

PARIS LEANED FORWARD AGAINST THE SAFETY STRAPS, peered past Grayrose's right wing at the green and gold patchwork that unreeled beneath the shuttle. By his best estimate, they were maybe thirty kilometers from the citadel, though the placement of the shuttle's windows made it impossible to see back the way they'd come. The lake that Grayrose had mentioned was clearly visible, a narrow arc that was either spring-fed and -drained or completely artificial, and even as he thought that, Grayrose threw the shuttle into a steep bank. She straightened only when they were flying parallel to the shore, and Paris released his grip on the edge of his chair. He had always counted himself a good pilot, but Grayrose was something else. *Either she's physically immune to g-force blackout,* he thought, *or I should be thinking about walking home.* He smiled at that. Before he'd joined *Voyager's* crew, the word "home" had had too many connotations, too many bad memories—too many reminders, if he was honest with himself, of all the ways he'd screwed up. But now, it had a relatively simple meaning: "home" was *Voyager,* nothing more, and nothing less. *Home is where your species is,* he thought, and let his grin widen. *But I do wonder where Revek thinks his home is.*

"Enjoying the ride?" Revek called, raising his voice to be heard over the noise of the shuttle's triple engines, and Paris nodded.

"Sure. Do we get a repeat performance on the way back?"

Grayrose's wings twitched at that, but she said nothing.

"What do you expect from a native flyer?" Revek asked in return, and Paris blinked. He hadn't thought of the winged Kirse as flying under their own power, had somehow assumed that the mass/wing ratio was too great—*and it still looks heavy to me,* he thought, slanting a wary glance at Grayrose. But if the Kirse were significantly lighter than she looked—hollow-boned, maybe, like terrestrial birds—and if the wing-span was larger than it seemed from the folded membranes, then he supposed it was possible.

"I didn't know you could fly," he said, to Grayrose, and felt instantly foolish. "I mean, yourself, without power," he added, and felt even less intelligent as the Kirse tilted her head to look back at him.

"It's a convenience of the form," she said. "I was designed for it."

"Designed?" Paris repeated, his attention sharpening, and Revek smiled.

"Bred for it, I think you mean, Gray."

"Bred for it, yes," Grayrose repeated, and turned her attention to her controls. Paris watched her, knowing better than to pursue the question, but unable to shake his conviction that the Kirse had meant what she had said. *Designed,* not *bred,* had been her first choice, and that could be important information later. Grayrose leaned comfortably against a padded cylinder that ran from floor to ceiling, her safety harness running around shoulders, hips, and thighs, leaving her wings and arms free. Looking more closely, Paris could see the wing membranes shiver faintly with each adjustment Grayrose made to her primary controls, and realized that she was flying the shuttle as much by inbred instinct, her sense of balance and placement, as by the instrumentation that flickered on the panels in front of her. It was a disconcerting realization, and he couldn't say whether it reassured or alarmed him.

Before he could decide, Revek leaned forward to touch Grayrose on the back of the neck, well above the massive muscles that powered her wings—the equivalent of a tap on the shoulder, Paris guessed, watching Grayrose's head tilt in response.

"Set down at the blue beach, why don't you?"

"Ah. A good idea." Grayrose touched her control yoke, and the shuttle yawed sharply, nearly throwing Revek back into his seat. He made a face, tightening his harness, and Paris was glad his own webbing was secure. He straightened cautiously, and Grayrose glanced over her shoulder, a faint smile on her face. Revek smiled back, the expression wry, and Paris realized that the Kirse had done it on purpose.

The shuttle was descending rapidly, a steep glide path that Paris guessed was right at the limit of the machine's tolerances. Out the nearer window, he could see a checkerboard of farmland, the rough squares alternately green and gold, rising toward a wooded hill. He caught a brief glimpse of a clearing on the crown of the hill, but then the shuttle banked again, lining up for its final approach. He could see the lake now, and the broad, blue-streaked sands that rose to meet them, and in spite of himself he braced for the crash. It couldn't be sand, he told himself, it had to be able to take the shuttle's weight; the Kirse might sacrifice one of their own, but not Revek, not so early in the negotiations, and then Grayrose lifted the shuttle's nose and dropped them neatly onto solid ground.

Paris gave a sigh of relief, and knew that Revek saw, but couldn't bring himself to care. Grayrose was a reckless pilot even by his estimation. *I wonder,* he thought, *if there's any way of getting her to let me fly us home?* Still, he had to admit that she was competent—the fact that they were down safely was proof enough of that.

The Kirse was already loosening herself from her safety harness, and Paris copied her. Grayrose opened the main hatch, a short ramp unrolling at the same time, and Paris followed her out onto the broad beach, Revek at his heels. The sand underfoot was solid, all right, and blue, streaked with every shade from the palest ice to near-black indigo, swirled together like frozen smoke. Paris shook his head, astonished yet again by the sheer beauty of the Kirse planet. *You'd think I'd get used to it,* he thought, *that I'd start to expect to find another gorgeous vista around every corner, would start yawning at even perfection, but I don't. I wonder if it still amazes Revek?*

"It is beautiful, isn't it?" Revek said, as if he'd read the other man's thoughts, and Paris gave him a startled glance.

"It is." Underfoot, the beach felt grainy, like sand, but his feet glided over the surface without displacing a single fragment of the color. He frowned, puzzled, and Grayrose lifted her wings, working the heavy shoulder muscle.

"The beach was primed as a landing zone after the last Andirrim raid. They're afraid to land on the sand—and well they should be, the ground won't be solid for them."

Paris stumbled, his foot sinking in sand that was suddenly unstable, and Grayrose caught him, balancing his weight with arched and lifted wings.

"Sorry," she said, "I should have warned you. The field only extends a few dozen meters from the shuttle."

"Field?" Paris straightened, and glanced back at the shuttle. The sand beneath it was still solid, but on all sides the gentle breeze stirred the loose grains, carving out a broad oval of stability. "You didn't land on that," he said, in spite of himself, and Grayrose blinked.

"But I did. Oh, I see. The field travels with the shuttle, is created by the shuttle projector. I don't need a full landing strip."

"Better you than me," Paris said. In fact, he thought, the idea was appalling—if anything went wrong with the field, or its placement in relation to the shuttle, and the shuttle's speed, there would be nothing the pilot could do to prevent a crash. The Kirse didn't seem to believe in safety margins, and he wondered again if there was any way to avoid the flight back to the citadel.

"The fields are up above," Grayrose went on, and began trudging up the slope, balancing herself with her wings. Paris followed, the sand crumbling underfoot, and looked back from the top to see the smooth swirls pitted by footprints. Revek pulled himself up next, and pointed toward the distant hill.

"And that's one of the hardpoints."

Grayrose gave him a sharp glance, but then seemed to relax.

"Hardpoints?" Paris asked. They were expecting the question, he knew—at least Revek had planned it—but there was no reason not to go along with him, at least for now.

Grayrose gave the hill a rather wistful look. "The shuttle launch sites for platform maintenance, or when the Andirrim or other animals attack. This one is where I launched from the last time they came."

"Really?" Paris's interest sharpened. Even if he was expected to ask—and could expect to get rehearsed answers—it would be very interesting to know more about the Kirse defense system. "Our sensors didn't pick up any buildings, no silos or anything like that."

"Oh, there aren't any," Grayrose answered. "The shuttles are either working or under the hills until there's an attack, and then the working ones go to their launch points. Each pilot collects them there." She paused, still staring at the hill. "In the old days, the repairs were all done from the ground, by remote control. But then the Andirrim developed their jamming system, and since then the platforms have had to be tended in person. They're clever, the Andirrim."

Paris nodded. The Kirse system was obviously highly efficient, or they wouldn't have lasted this long, and it was obviously designed to make use of a small population, but it was deeply vulnerable at several points. If you could somehow get past the orbital barrier, the Kirse would have to concentrate on defending the citadel itself, an obvious and unmistakable target. And with the Kirse busy there, the Andirrim would be able to steal as much as they wanted.

"But we should see the fields," Grayrose said,

regretfully, and turned toward the nearest stand of gold.

"And if you're thinking what you might be," Revek said, softly, "I wouldn't. The Andirrim tried attacking the citadel last time—right, Grayrose?"

The Kirse nodded. "It was difficult for a little. They sent down a thousand dronecraft—some stolen from here, I might add—and nearly a hundred crewed machines, all to attack the citadel, to keep the shuttles from lifting. But Adamant called the shuttles in and they were driven off planet and out of the system."

Paris blinked. Even allowing for the usual pilot's boasting, it was an impressive achievement, and somehow Grayrose didn't seem the kind to brag. But the Kirse remained vulnerable, as any remote system was vulnerable, and the idea bothered him more than he liked to admit. *And the worst of it is,* he added silently, *I don't know if it bothers me because I like them, or because I think we could make use of it.*

They spent the next three hours moving from field to field. Grayrose intoned the Kirse names for the plants, a series of trilling whistles that the Universal Translator rendered into long descriptive names and Revek corrected to shorter and inevitably more appropriate ones. Revek's names tended to be as amusing as they were descriptive—like the lily with three pink stamens that he called Patty, Maxine, and Laverne—and Paris found himself warming to the man. And to Grayrose, too, he acknowledged, watching the Kirse stretch to reach the leathery pod of a wallet-tree. She was a comfortable companion, and as beautiful in her own way as the planet that had reared her—and that, he told himself firmly, was no way to think. He took the pod that Grayrose held out to him, split along its seam to reveal vivid orange fruit, and trained the tricorder on it without really seeing the readings. The last thing he needed was to get too friendly with one of the Kirse, especially since they hadn't established trading rights yet.

He glanced up at the cloudless sky, and saw that the sun had declined below the meridian. He checked his chronometer, realizing that he was due back at the citadel in less than an hour, and touched his communicator. "Paris to Kim. You there, Harry?"

There was a little pause, and then Kim's voice came through clearly, sounding slightly out of breath. "Kim here. Everything all right, Tom?"

Paris's attention sharpened, and he glanced quickly over his shoulder. Revek was well out of earshot, sitting against the trunk of one of the low-growing fruit trees, a half-peeled tart-apple in his hand. Grayrose was closer, but her attention seemed to be focused on something on the ground at her feet. "We're all fine here, thanks. What's up with you?"

"We're finishing up the survey," Kim answered, his voice sounding more relaxed. "There's one more small field to go."

"And I'm just about done here, too," Paris answered. It was probably just Kim's inexperience that made him sound nervous, he told himself. Still, it was a good thing they were returning to the citadel. "It's about a twenty-minute flight for us, so we should return as scheduled. I'll inform you if there's any change in plans."

"Right," Kim said. "And I'll do the same. That should give me time to finish this field, though."

"Great," Paris said, and waited. If there was anything wrong, now was the time for Kim to say something, do something, that would signal a problem.

"I'll see you at the citadel," Kim said. "Kim out."

And that should mean there was nothing out of the

ordinary, Paris thought, turning his tricorder on the final stand of pale gold grain. The star-shaped heads were heavy with seed—edible seed, he corrected himself, watching the tricorder readings change, similar enough to terrestrial wheat to make it worth trying to make flour from them. The Kirse planet was almost unbelievably fertile, the plant life incredibly useful to humans. *And I would love to know why I don't trust it,* Paris thought, closing down his tricorder. *I like Grayrose, even if she's a maniac pilot, but there's something about this planet that I just don't feel right about.*

Something moved in the grain field, tossing the star-shaped heads like a nonexistent wind. Paris reached for his phaser, and Grayrose sprang to her full height, her wings rising to cup the still air. Revek, slower to respond, rolled to his knees, but Paris was not surprised to see a phaser in his hand as well.

"What is it?" Revek called.

Grayrose lifted her wings still further, and beat down hard, rising a few meters into the air. She hovered for an instant, wings working, and then let herself softly down again. "A gardener. Alone, I think, but I think we'd better get back to the shuttle."

The disturbance was moving off, but not far, the grain shivering into stillness less than fifty meters away. "Trouble?" Paris asked, and moved closer to Grayrose.

"Probably not," the Kirse answered. "But since we're nearly done—" She broke off, shaking her head.

"Better not to take chances," Revek muttered, joining them. He had not yet holstered his phaser, Paris saw, and checked his own instinctive movement. He returned his tricorder to his belt instead, and looked at Grayrose.

"I thought Adamant said the gardeners were harmless."

The Kirse didn't answer, started instead for the path that led back to the beach and the waiting shuttle. Paris glanced at Revek, but the other human studiously refused to meet his eye.

"If we're in danger," Paris said, "it would improve our chances if you told me what was going on."

Grayrose didn't seem to hear. Revek gave him a quick glance, but said nothing. *And that,* Paris thought, *is outside of enough.* He caught the other man by the shoulder, and swung him around so that they stood face-to-face. "I want an answer, Revek."

Revek jerked himself free, but not before Paris had seen genuine fear in his eyes.

"The gardeners by the citadel are—mostly—harmless," Grayrose said.

Paris jumped—he hadn't heard or seen her turn back to them—and then wondered if he'd hurt their chances of a deal by grabbing Revek. The Kirse seemed fond of him—*why,* he added silently, *I don't know*—but Grayrose made no comment, fixing him instead with her luminous pale-blue eyes.

"Because they are so close to the walls, to the citadel itself, they have been more extensively adapted than the rest," she went on. "Here, where there is little reason to interact with them, they are left mostly intact. Which means they are hostile even as they are useful."

"How do you mean, hostile?" Paris asked. He heard the grass rustle behind him, and glanced back quickly, his hand on his phaser. He could see nothing in the sea of grain, not even an unexplained movement of the seed heads, but out of the corner of his eye he could see Revek watching the field with an almost feral intensity.

"They aren't really dangerous," Grayrose said,

"but they will try to attack sometimes. I try to avoid them—I don't like killing them."

Paris gave her a quick glance, trying to divide his attention between her and the source of the strange sounds. "So why not just stun them? Revek's phaser is standard Federation issue, I can see that from here. Even if you didn't have the system before, you could have gotten it from him."

"Why?" Grayrose asked in return, and her voice was tinged with sadness. "They would just do it again and again until they pushed hard enough—got close enough, or posed enough of a danger—that I or another would have to kill them then. It's necessary—required."

"But they might not attack you again," Paris began, and heard something in the grass to his left. He spun, leveling his phaser by instinct, and caught the barest glimpse of something brown moving between the heavy stalks.

"Gardener," Revek said, shortly, and thumbed his phaser to a killing level.

Grayrose beat her wings again, lifting herself ponderously into the air, an odd-looking phaser suddenly visible in her hand. Paris hesitated, then touched his own controls, adjusting the phaser to heavy stun. He wouldn't kill, not if he could avoid it—Starfleet training was too strong—but he could easily believe that it would take significant power to bring down one of the creatures they had seen earlier.

"To your right," Grayrose cried, and fired. The bolt from her phaser dissipated harmlessly in the air above the field, but the streak of light was clearly visible. Paris focused along it, leveling his own weapon, and something burst from among the heavy stalks. He fired, knew he'd missed, but Revek fired an instant later, and the creature stumbled to its knees. Another one, bigger than any of the other creatures Paris had seen, loomed above it, and he fired again, brought it tumbling over the body of its companion.

"Clear?" Revek called, not taking his eyes from the field, and Grayrose's voice came fluting back.

"Clear. I see no others."

Revek gave a sigh of relief. "Come on, let's get back to the shuttle before any more of them show up."

Paris hesitated, looking at the piled bodies. One, the one he'd shot, was only stunned, but the other— He wrinkled his nose at the smell of scorched fur. It was definitely dead, but he should still examine it, take readings for the doctor to analyze later. He reached for his tricorder, but Revek caught his arm.

"Come on," he said. "We need to get back to the shuttle."

"But—" Paris broke off at the look on Revek's face.

"Do you want her to have to finish that one off? Don't make her notice it's still alive."

Paris glanced at Grayrose, back on the ground again, her face turned studiously away from the piled bodies. There was something about the way she was avoiding them, and him, that convinced him, and he started down the path after her.

They reached the beach without hearing any more sign of the creatures, and Revek gave a sigh of relief as they stepped awkwardly onto the shifting slope.

"We should be all right now," he said. "They don't generally follow beyond the fields."

"Really?" Paris said, involuntarily, and Grayrose gave him a curious glance.

"What do you mean?"

Paris hesitated, wishing he'd kept his mouth shut, but the Kirse was regarding him with a friendly intensity that was surprisingly compelling. "I would have thought that the creatures—gardeners—would try to get people on the beach." He slipped as he spoke, and Grayrose gave a silvery laugh.

"Oh, I see, to give them an advantage. But with phasers, it's less so."

"I suppose," Paris answered, and picked his way more carefully, scowling at the blue-swirled sand under his feet. Revek, he saw, with some bitterness, had already reached the area stabilized by the shuttle's fields, and was almost halfway to the hatch.

Grayrose touched his shoulder. "I appreciate what you did, back there," she said, softly, "and I am grateful."

Paris blinked, startled, and almost fell again as a stone twisted under his step. By the time he'd righted himself, Grayrose was out of earshot, and he had to hurry to catch up. Once he'd reached the stabilized sand, its patterns now blurred by sand that had drifted from the rest of the beach, it was easy to draw abreast of her, and they reached the shuttle together.

"Glad to help," he said, hoping to prolong the conversation, draw her out, but she shook her head slightly.

"No more." She tilted her head, a mere fraction of movement, pointing ahead of them up the ramp that led into the shuttle.

Revek had already opened the hatch, and was sitting at the top of the ramp, his head tipped to the side in a surprisingly Kirse gesture. Paris blinked, startled—until that moment, he had assumed that Revek's rapport with the Kirse extended to all of them—and Grayrose swept past him up the ramp.

"Have you started the check, Thilo?"

"Just the preliminaries," Revek answered.

"Then you can take your places," Grayrose answered, and took her place in front of the pilot's column. At her signal, the safety webbing snaked from its pods and fastened itself around her body. Paris stepped past her, and took his place in the row of passenger seats, fumbling his own harness into place against Grayrose's takeoff. He watched out of the corner of his eye as Revek did the same, wondering again just what the human's relationship was to the various Kirse. Certainly he seemed very close to Adamant, the Kirse leader—and was that why Grayrose wanted to keep her knowledge that one of the creatures had survived a secret? She had said that she was under orders to kill the creatures, rather than stun them—*at least I think that's what she meant when she said it was required*—and maybe she was worried Revek would tell Adamant, or one of the others in authority. It made sense, but he knew better than to rely too much on logical conjecture when dealing with nonhumans. He would work from that assumption for now, but keep an open mind.

The shuttle lurched as Grayrose began the launch run, and in spite of himself Paris dug his fingers into the padding of his couch. He could see Revek's eyes tightly closed as the shuttle bounded forward, seemed to bounce once, and then was airborne. Grayrose glanced over her shoulder, laughing.

"Sorry. But it's good to be flying again."

"Yes, well," Revek said. "I'd like to stay flying, Gray."

Grayrose laughed again, and Paris said, "I think Grayrose is an excellent pilot."

Revek gave him a quick glance, surprise turning to a knowing smile, and Paris felt his cheeks growing warm. "She's a very good pilot," Revek said. "But, like I said, I'd like to get home in one piece."

"And where is home these days, Revek?" Paris asked. He saw Grayrose's wings twitch, and damned himself for an idiot. *I should know better than to let him provoke me like that,* he thought. *I hope I haven't spoiled everything.*

To his surprise, however, Revek gave a snort of laughter. "Touché. I do think of the citadel as home these days—I have to say, I never expected to see another human face once I'd met your Caretaker."

"So you didn't even try to get back to the Federation," Paris said.

"I tried," Revek answered. "Though I'm not sure why I bothered. I mean, barring miracles, and they seem to be rather rare on the ground these days, at maximum speed it's a seventy-year trip back to the Alpha Quadrant. And even if I did live that long, I wouldn't have much time left once I got there. So I'd been keeping an eye out for likely places to settle even before I landed here." He gave the younger man a shrewd look. "Don't tell me Starfleet training keeps you from even thinking about settling. Provided you found the right world, of course."

"It doesn't," Paris said, and looked out the shuttle's window. Revek was unfortunately right, not even Starfleet training could keep people from thinking about other possibilities, from making the same calculations Revek had done and pondering the same answers. So far, none of the planets had appealed to him as much as the chance of reaching the Alpha Quadrant again, but he knew that other people had been tempted, and he'd heard whispered regrets from more than one friend as *Voyager* left the Brioni behind. He allowed himself a bitter smile. In a way, he was lucky: he had lost nothing by being thrown into the Delta Quadrant—prison had been no fun, and the years before it hadn't been that much better—and he had nothing much to gain by making it home again. He already had the best position he could reasonably hope for; there weren't many captains who'd trust him with their ships, not with his record. Home could well be a change for the worse for him. *Yeah,* he thought, with another bitter smile, *I understand you, Thilo Revek, or at least I can sympathize with your motives. From everything Chakotay said about you, from everything that's in the records, you weren't much better liked than I was among the Maquis. No wonder you jumped at the chance to stay. I wonder if I'd do the same.* He shoved that thought away, appalled and annoyed at his own descent into self-pity. *No, I wouldn't, not now. I have friends on* Voyager, *and a chance to do the work I love for a captain I genuinely respect. That doesn't change—I won't let it change.*

The rest of the flight back to the citadel was uneventful, and Grayrose set the shuttle down with demure skill, barely bouncing the heavy craft. Kim and his Kirse—Harp, Paris reminded himself—were waiting in one of the arched doors, but came out from its shelter as the shuttle rolled to a stop. Paris wrestled himself out of the safety harness, and was second out of the shuttle, almost stepping on Grayrose's heels. Kim gave him a friendly wave, and stepped forward.

"So how'd it go?"

"All right," Paris answered. "We got all the samples we needed, but we had a run-in with a couple of those gardener-creatures." *And we—well, Revek—killed one of them, but there's no need to mention that yet.* "How about you?"

"One of the gardeners attacked you?" Kim sounded genuinely shocked.

"Yeah. Grayrose says they're different from the ones around here," Paris answered.

"That's correct," Harp said. "Here they're more securely adapted."

And I don't think we ought to be discussing that in

any more detail, Paris thought. He said, "So, did you get your samples, Harry?"

"Um, yes." Kim nodded brightly. "Everything's recorded."

"Right." Paris looked at Grayrose. "Then we should get them back to the ship. Thank you very much for your help, all of you." He touched his communicator. "Paris to *Voyager.* Two to beam up."

Chakotay was waiting in the transporter chamber, unobtrusively watching over the technician's shoulder, but looked up as the away team materialized in the chamber.

"Gentlemen," he said. "The captain wants to see you."

What've I done this time? Paris suppressed that answer—Chakotay had never much cared for his sense of humor—and Kim spoke quickly, stepping off the platform.

"Shall we download the tricorder readings first?"

"Bring them along," Chakotay answered. "We can get a preliminary look at them in the ready room while you download."

And that settles that, Paris thought. He fell into step at the first officer's side, and was not surprised to find a turbolift waiting for them, doors open. "Is something wrong?"

Chakotay shook his head. "No more than there has been. But if we're going to trade, the captain wants to get negotiations under way as soon as possible."

"So that we have room to maneuver," Paris translated, and immediately wished he hadn't.

Chakotay lifted an eyebrow at him. "A position you should understand." The first officer sighed then, looking into the distance. "And we may need all the room we can get."

The rest of the senior officers were already waiting

in the ready room, and a viewscreen was lit as well, displaying the doctor's perpetually frowning visage. The captain looked up at their entrance, and Paris was startled to smell coffee, and to see a small cup in front of her. Either things were going better, he thought, or much worse.

"Gentlemen," Janeway said, and Paris dragged his attention back to the matter at hand. "I know you have quite a bit of data in your tricorders, but I want to get a verbal report as well."

"Right, Captain," Paris answered, and Kim cleared his throat.

"If it's all right with you, Captain, I'd like to go ahead and start the downloading now. That way, we'll have at least some of the data by the time we've finished."

"Proceed," Janeway answered, and Kim looked at Paris.

"Tom?"

Paris hastily unhooked his tricorder, and the younger man took it, crossed to the nearest console to begin the transfer.

"Now," Janeway said. "Mr. Paris. Let's hear from you. What did you find on the planet?"

Paris blinked, marshaling his thoughts. "Well, to begin with . . . the exact information's in the tricorder, of course, but pretty much everything they— they being Revek and a Kirse called Grayrose— showed me was not only edible and nutritious, but according to the sensors contained esters that would taste pleasantly similar to familiar foods. I took a number of molecular samples, too, which ought to prevent any nasty surprises like last time, but that will have to wait for a closer analysis."

Chakotay cleared his throat. "Sorry to interrupt,

Captain, but I should mention that the doctor has already set up a test protocol, and all molecular samples are being routed directly to that program."

Janeway nodded. "Excellent. Continue, Mr. Paris."

"That's pretty much it for the food." Paris hesitated, wondering exactly how to bring up the fight with the gardener-creatures. "We ended up flying to fields some distance from the citadel, and while we were there, our party was attacked by some of the creatures that we saw when we first landed."

Janeway's head lifted at that. "I want a full report, Mr. Paris. All the details."

Paris nodded. It didn't take long to tell the story, even putting in all his conjectures, and when he'd finished, he was all too conscious of how little he actually knew about the Kirse.

"So the creatures nearer to the citadel are—what did Grayrose call it, 'adapted'?—to make them docile, while the ones farther away are not," Janeway said thoughtfully.

"It would be interesting to determine the size of the Kirse safe area," Tuvok said. "It would give us some idea of their—the Kirse's—assessment of their own defensive capabilities."

Janeway nodded. "I concur. Mr. Tuvok, that's your department." She looked at Kim. "What about you, Mr. Kim? Let's hear your report."

Kim took a deep breath. "I don't have much to add to Tom—Paris's report, Captain. Everything that I scanned and sampled was edible and potentially something we'd be interested in trading for. I did see some of the gardeners, too, though my escort—Harp, her name was—didn't seem to think they were dangerous." He paused then, frowning. "All of them had the metal parts that we saw before, and Harp said those were the adaptations. And when I asked why they bothered, she said something about doing what they can with available materials."

"Can you remember exactly what she said?" Janeway asked.

Kim's frown deepened, but he shook his head. "I'm sorry, Captain. She said they used the creatures because they were available. She said it would be a waste of resources for the Kirse to farm the planet—to do the actual work themselves—and that the creatures would otherwise be useless. But that's all, and I can't swear to the words."

"That might explain why they kept cringing at our tricorders," Torres said. As always, it was hard to tell if she was angry, or merely intent on the job at hand.

Paris nodded. "It might also explain why they've got the roads booby-trapped the way they do—it's not to stop the Andirrim, but any unadapted gardeners. From what little Grayrose said, they're not intelligent."

"Would she say if they were?" Chakotay asked. His face was drawn into a frown of distaste. "Captain, I have to say that the Kirse show a great disrespect for these animals—even if they are a lesser one, they're still another life-form. I'm not sure it bodes well for our dealing with them."

"Grayrose didn't want to kill that one," Paris said, and knew he sounded defensive. "And she was glad I only stunned the other one."

Kim said, "I agree with Mr. Chakotay, the whole idea makes me uncomfortable. But I also have to say I didn't see any signs of real intelligence when I was on the planet. I was looking for it, too—specifically, to see if any of them used tools—but it never happened. And they had opportunities."

"It's not a great solution," Paris said, "but from

what Grayrose said, the Kirse have a fairly small population relative to what they control. I can see where they might not think they had any other choice. Particularly if they're metal-poor, like Neelix said." He braced himself for a cutting response from Chakotay, but the first officer said nothing. Paris glanced warily at him, but the other man's face was expressionless, unreadable. *All right,* Paris thought, *so I've put myself outside the pale one more time. But you didn't think much of me to begin with.*

In the viewscreen, the doctor cleared his throat. "I think the health of this crew—"

"Yes, Doctor, I know." Janeway laid her hands flat on the table. "All right. Mr. Chakotay, I recognize and respect your concerns, but the safety of our crew has to come first even if this weren't potentially a Prime Directive matter. We'll continue negotiating for now. Lieutenant Torres, have you finished the modifications to the transporter system?"

The engineer nodded. "I have a couple of templates to work from, all of which should give the Kirse what they need without compromising our security. I'm just waiting for Tuvok to review them."

"Good. Then, Tuvok, you'll finish that, and I'll set up another meeting with the Kirse." Janeway pushed herself to her feet, and the others rose with her. Glancing sideways, Paris thought he saw anger, or perhaps disappointment, flicker across Chakotay's face, but then the first officer had himself under control again. "Dismissed."

Janeway looked up in surprise at the sound of her door buzzer. She had expected to have some time alone, at least an hour or two before she had to return to the bridge and the anticipated transmission from Adamant responding to her first offer. "Who is it?"

"Chakotay." There was a little pause. "Captain, may I talk to you?"

"Of course." *What's gone wrong this time?* Janeway wondered, and hit the door release. As the panel slid back, she glanced instinctively at the status display on the side console. Everything showed green, all ship's functions well within the new limits established since their arrival in the Delta Quadrant. Of course, if they had been back in the Alpha Quadrant, some of those lights would be glowing orange, the readings unacceptable by Starfleet standards, but they had all had to make adjustments. "What is it?" she asked, and motioned the first officer to a seat.

Chakotay made a face, but seated himself. "Nothing serious—nothing to do with the ship," he said. "But I am—concerned—about the Kirse."

Janeway nodded, and sat down opposite him. "You know the situation as well as I do. If we don't get supplies here, we won't make it to another system."

"Assuming, of course, that M-class planets continue to be as rare as they have been," Chakotay answered.

"Would you take that chance with your ship?" Janeway asked, and the first officer looked away.

"I've never liked no-win situations," he said, after a moment.

Janeway allowed herself a smile, knowing it came out wry, and Chakotay matched it, reluctantly.

"What the Kirse are doing to those creatures—it goes against everything I was brought up to believe," he said. "No one, no being, has the right to make use of another like that."

"Your own people used draft animals," Janeway said. "The traditionalists among them still do, for all that machines are available to do the same work."

"It's not the same." Chakotay shook his head, more in frustration, Janeway guessed, than in denial. "We treat animals, all living things, with respect, we ask permission to make use of them and give thanks for their labor."

"Do you think it makes much practical difference to the animal in question?" Janeway asked.

Chakotay frowned. "Of course it does. Even if an animal can't answer, can't understand, our asking, the act of asking, makes us behave in humane fashion—" He broke off, his frown deepening. "And you know that as well as I do."

Janeway sighed, and abandoned the position. She hadn't had much hope of convincing Chakotay anyway, not with his background, his deeply held beliefs—*and I have to admit,* she added silently, *I'm just as glad I can't. But I also can't give up what I've been taught is my duty.* "Chakotay," she said, and groped for the right words, the ones that would build a bridge between them, allow her to acknowledge his beliefs without compromising her own. "I agree with you that the Kirse's treatment of these creatures is highly questionable—it made me queasy to see it, and Paris's story didn't make me feel any better. I also know that you know how desperate we are for food." Chakotay started to say something, and she held up her hand. "No, let me finish. But even if we weren't in need, even if we had a dozen other planets to chose from, we could not do anything here. We have no right to interfere in the Kirse culture—not only do we not understand, we cannot understand, their culture, their problems and their assets, in sufficient depth to decree what they should and shouldn't do, we have no right to even think of doing so. We are too much on the outside, and nothing can be truly resolved by outside fiat, no matter how well-intentioned that interference might be. That's the Prime Directive, and it's been proved to be a good and a just—even a vital—principle over the entire course of the Federation. And I swore, when I joined Starfleet, to follow the Prime Directive no matter how difficult it was or how wrong it might seem in the short run. I will not break that oath."

She stopped then, unsure of her own words, hearing them pompous, even foolish when spoken aloud, in her cabin orbiting this world that had never heard of the Federation.

She looked back at Chakotay, wondering if she'd said enough, or said too much, if it was wise to try to reach a Maquis renegade with talk of Starfleet, and saw him nodding slightly. She bit her tongue, choking back the other things she might have said, and waited.

"You're right," Chakotay said at last. "And I think I knew you were right. But what they're doing isn't good. It isn't right."

"No." Janeway hesitated, wondering if she'd said too much, betrayed too much of her own feelings.

"So what do I do to live with myself?" Chakotay asked, and Janeway heard the echo of her own anguish from decades before, however much he tried to hide it.

"You live with yourself." She managed another wry smile at the surprise on Chakotay's face. "I asked the same question of someone once, and that's what he told me. I didn't think it was much help at the time, but it ended up making sense. You go on."

"I can't imagine that was what you were looking for," Chakotay said, but he was smiling, too.

"No." There had been a song as well, slow and sad, a woman singer whom she'd long ago forgotten, except for the sweet falling phrase: *some days you just do anything you can and get by.* She put the memory aside, and Chakotay pushed himself to his feet.

"I appreciate your time, Captain."

The words were formal, but there was a warmth behind them that prompted her next question. "Chakotay."

"Captain?" He paused in the doorway.

"Before you knew this, what did you think of the Kirse?"

"Ah." Chakotay gave her a lopsided grin. "Before—I liked Keyward. I liked them all. Which I guess is part of the problem."

He let the door close behind him. Janeway stood for a moment, staring after him. He was right, a large part of the problem was that the Kirse had seemed likable, and it had hurt to have to see what they were doing to the gardening creatures, especially when there was no way to interfere with their system. "I know what you mean, Chakotay," she said, softly. "I like them, too."

There was really no choice—as Chakotay had said, *Voyager* was in a no-win situation. Still, Janeway found it hard to suppress the sense of uncertainty as she faced the viewscreen, waiting for the Kirse to complete contact. *I have my crew to think about,* she told herself, they have to be my first responsibility, but the words were cold comfort.

"The connection is established, Captain," Kim announced, and Janeway nodded, drawing herself up to her full height.

"Thank you, Mr. Kim."

The image solidified quickly out of the multicolored static of the Kirse communication system, and Adamant's sculpted face looked out at her. "Captain Janeway."

"Adamant."

"Have you had a chance to look over the samples yet?" the Kirse leader went on.

"Yes." In spite of herself, Janeway's eyes strayed to the datapadd balanced on the arm of her chair. The doctor's tests had left no doubts at all: the samples had met, even exceeded, every requirement he could make; if *Voyager* resupplied here, even the most pessimistic projections allowed them to reach the next M-class planet with stores to spare. "And we are interested," she went on, "but there are some technical matters that will have to be cleared up first."

"It has been my experience, from working with Thilo, that our technologies are compatible," Adamant said.

"Apparently," Janeway answered. "But we cannot spare any of the transporter hardware. We're willing to trade information about the system but that's all."

Adamant frowned. "There are—limits—on the technical resources here. Particularly hardware that requires a great deal of metal in its manufacture. At the very least, I would need the raw materials for such hardware before I could consider this bargain."

"That might be possible," Janeway answered. They had expected that answer, had planned for it, but it was all she could do to suppress the feeling of desperation. The longer they had to wait to get supplies, the more likely it was that more of the crew would fall ill, and the harder it would be to hold out for the bargain *Voyager* needed. She made herself continue as though there was nothing wrong, no hurry in the world. "Perhaps my chief engineer could meet with some of your technical staff and discuss the matter—see how much metal, or other raw materials, you might need, and whether that can be made to fit with our supply situation."

Adamant blinked, then nodded slowly. "An excellent suggestion. Send your engineer, I'll be waiting."

The screen went dark before Janeway could respond. She looked over her shoulder, and Kim gave an embarrassed shrug.

"They've stopped transmitting, Captain."

"Right." Janeway stared at the screen—once again filled with the green-and-white disk of the Kirse planet, all artificial features obscured by clouds and distance—for a moment longer, then shook her head. "Very well, Lieutenant Torres, it's up to you."

B'Elanna Torres glanced around the courtyard. The Kirse seemed to have an aversion to people beaming down into the citadel itself, but she couldn't be sure why, or even if, it was significant. Underfoot, the sun-warmed stones had been laid out in a checkerboard pattern, alternating squares of deep purple and warm gold, the same material as the road that had first brought her to the citadel, but otherwise the courtyard was completely empty. Even the walls that defined it were without doors or windows, and the nearest tower, rising up over the wall to her right, was equally blind on her side. From everything Kim and Paris had said, this was normal—the Kirse would create a door when they needed one—but it took every bit of self-control not to treat this as a hostile reception. She touched her communicator instead.

"Torres to *Voyager.*"

"*Voyager* here." It was Chakotay's voice, and Torres was startled by her own disappointment. *Still,* she told herself, *you can't expect the captain to hang around monitoring an away team's conversations.*

"I've arrived, but there's no one here yet." Even as she spoke, she heard the rumble of the Kirse transporter, and turned to see a door materialize in the wall below the tower. "No, scratch that, the door just opened. I think my party's here."

"Carry on, B'Elanna," Chakotay answered. "And keep in touch. *Voyager* out."

A Kirse, not one of the winged ones, stepped out from the new door's shadow, his—no, her, Torres realized, though this one was so thin as to make gender almost impossible to guess—*her* bare feet almost soundless on the stones. She stopped a few meters from Torres, brought her hands together in what Torres guessed was meant for polite greeting.

"B'Elanna Torres? I'm called Silver-Hammer. I'm sent to show you our system, and to discuss trading raw materials."

Torres nodded. "Glad to meet you," she said, knowing she sounded gruff, but didn't know what else would be appropriate. The Kirse seemed unmoved.

"If you'd come this way?"

Torres followed, wondering where Revek was. Every other team had reported his presence—but then, they'd all been fully human. *Maybe they don't think he'd get along well with a half-Klingon,* she thought, and didn't know whether she should be offended or not. The truth of the matter was that she hadn't liked him much on their first and only meeting, but it irritated her that the Kirse had noticed—*no*, she corrected, with her usual rigid honesty, *it irritates me that I showed it. I have to be more careful.*

Silver-Hammer stopped at the center of the courtyard, so abruptly that Torres almost walked into her. Before she could say anything, however, either question or apology, the Kirse extended her hand, and the transporter sounded again. At their feet, the purple square disappeared, revealing a set of stairs spiraling down into darkness. The edges of the gold squares to either side seemed perceptibly paler, too, and Torres wondered if they had been that pale before the transporter operation.

"Down here," Silver-Hammer said.

Torres followed, cautiously, and was glad when light faded on at their approach. There was no rail on the stairs, only a central core that the treads coiled around, and that core was the only source of light, a ball of blue radiance glowing through the stone. It moved with them, never illuminating more than a few meters in any direction, and after one quick glance Torres was careful to keep her eyes fixed on the stair in front of her. As far as she could see, they were descending through empty space, and the light from the courtyard didn't penetrate nearly far enough to show her anything.

"Stop a minute," Silver-Hammer said.

Torres did as she was told, repressing the desire to tap her communicator, signal the ship, and Silver-Hammer raised her hand again, pointing her palm at the opening above them. The transporter sounded, and the square of light blinked out, but not before Torres had caught a glimpse of something bright and silver cupped in her hand. The controller for the transporter? she wondered, but the Kirse was already continuing down the stairs.

The stairway seemed endless, an empty spiral through the dark, but the rational part of Torres's brain guessed they had only descended about twenty meters before the light from the core picked out the end of the stairs and the dark surface of pavement below them. Silver-Hammer's fist clenched, fingers working, and another string of lights appeared, running along the top of a wall. They grew rapidly brighter, and Torres realized that they were standing at the bottom of what looked like a deep and artificial canyon—so much like one, in fact, that she caught herself looking for signs of damp, and listening for the sound of rushing water. Instead, the transporter sounded, and a new door appeared, spilling light across the dark-gray stones.

"This is the workshop," Silver-Hammer said, and paused inside the door.

Torres followed, and jumped as the wall sealed itself again behind her. "Do you always do that?"

"The doors?" Silver-Hammer blinked. "It's safer— or maybe I mean wiser? The work here is delicate, I wouldn't want anyone to interfere with it. Or for anyone to get hurt by it."

And that was a distinct possibility, Torres thought, looking around the room. It was an enormous space, a good fifteen meters on each side, but every available space was crammed with machinery, the same gleaming, attenuated shapes she had seen when they first arrived, and the moving parts were as strangely exposed as they had been in the hall. It seemed impossible that anything could function without interfering with all of its neighbors, and in spite of herself she stepped closer, only to see the faint glow of the fields that separated each component. It seemed like an incredible waste of power, and totally at odds with the readings they had gotten from the planet, and she turned to Silver-Hammer, speaking before she thought.

"How do you keep all those forcefields lit? We don't read enough power to run a light source, much less something like this."

Silver-Hammer smiled. "You can't expect me to answer that, surely."

Torres felt herself blush—the question had been naive—but decided to bluff it through. "Well, I'll need to know about your power capability to give you a proper analysis of the transporter system. Obviously you have more to spare than I would have thought."

"True." Silver-Hammer nodded, grave, the smile abruptly gone. "The planet's core is the primary source. The world is young and hot enough to give power to spare."

"But you shield it."

Silver-Hammer nodded again. "Otherwise it might become vulnerable. The Andirrim are certainly clever enough to make that a focus of their attacks."

Torres felt a sudden chill at the thought. Core taps were an excellent source of heat and therefore of power, but they were also inherently vulnerable, and an accident at one could be devastating. "You have a lot of trouble with the Andirrim."

"Enough," Silver-Hammer answered. "Sometimes they come to trade, and bring enough metal that there's no choice but to do business, but that's only when they need supplies themselves. Mostly they come to raid."

"I hope they don't show up any time soon," Torres said.

"If they do, it will probably be to trade," Silver-Hammer answered. "They were driven back last time, and took little with them."

"Good." Torres suppressed the rest of what she would have said—Starfleet training was right, you had to be very careful taking sides in local disputes—and reached for her tricorder. "Will you show me your system?"

Silver-Hammer hesitated for a fraction of a second, and then pointed to a block in the center of the room. "There."

Torres moved cautiously toward it, unslinging her tricorder as she went. The block had the massy, dull look of lead, but metal tubing—gold and silver, rose and pink and every shade of red as well—coiled across its surface, emerging from the sides and corners to knot around each other, passing through spheres with strange, multi-petaled surfaces, and then diving again below the surface. There was an oddly organic look to it all, a wet slickness to the surface, but when she trained her tricorder on it, the readings were definitely mechanical. Or at least nonorganic she amended. The entire assembly was enclosed in a powerful forcefield. She adjusted the tricorder's sensors to penetrate it, and saw that the contained radiation was almost off the scale: a self-contained power source, she wondered, or just Kirse engineering?

"This is the power source?" she asked, and Silver-Hammer moved to join her, peering curiously at the tricorder's screen. Torres repressed the instinctive desire to snatch it away, and instead pressed the control that blanked the screen. The Kirse gave her a startled, disapproving look, and Torres met it with her most stolid stare.

"This is the heart of it, yes," Silver-Hammer answered, after an instant's pause, and Torres switched the tricorder back on, taking a few carefully casual steps toward the shielded block as she did so. To her relief, Silver-Hammer didn't follow, and she made herself concentrate on the displays. The waveforms were only vaguely familiar, the usual patterns overlaid with a complicated harmonic, and she scowled at the screen, trying to work out the implications. From the look of things, Revek had told the Kirse as much as he knew about the Federation's system, but that knowledge had been superimposed on an entirely different kind of transporter. The resulting hybrid was powerful, even overpowered, capable of reaching beyond the planet's atmosphere, but it was unable to achieve more than molecular resolution. And that meant that the beam couldn't handle living matter—or at least, she added silently, not and keep it living. Of course, it would work perfectly well on the inert matter of the walls and floors, but to use it for that, essentially opening and closing doors—the Kirse would have to draw on the power of a core tap to be able to use their transporter so extravagantly.

"Originally," Silver-Hammer said, "before Thilo, that is, the beam would only reconstitute the matter that now makes up the walls. And break it down, too, of course." She paused. "It would break down almost anything, actually, but would only re-create certain compounds."

"Which you then used in the walls?" Torres asked. In spite of herself, she felt a slight chill at the thought of experimenting with the Kirse proto-transporter—no, not a transporter, she corrected herself, the thing must have functioned like the destructor ray of bad fiction—imagining the experimental mass disappearing never to return. "You must have had a tremendous energy release, if you couldn't reconstruct the material."

Silver-Hammer nodded. "It feeds back into the beam, and then into the system. It's highly efficient."

And highly dangerous, Torres thought, and eyed the forcefield enclosing the machine with new respect. The amount of energy released in such a transaction was enormous; for the system—and presumably that was the hardware as well as the fields and software—to absorb it as controlled feedback was an amazing feat of engineering. It was also something no Federation engineer or scientist would ever be prepared to tolerate: the consequences of a system failure would be disastrously high. Of course, she hadn't seen any other Kirse in the area—maybe that was the function of the canyonlike hallway, she thought, to keep outsiders at a safe distance in case of trouble. "Your forcefields must be very efficient, too," she said, and Silver-Hammer gave an almost shy smile.

"You mean if the transporter fails?"

"I mean to keep it from failing," Torres answered.

"All of this complex can be isolated if necessary," Silver-Hammer answered. "Forcefields are set to seal the corridors—which are isolated anyway, both by double-thick walls and simple distance—or if the forcefields are the problem, the transporter will be used to block the tunnels physically. If there's enough, I can fill the corridor outside meters-thick with solid stone, enough to contain and smother any reaction."

"Killing you or any other operator," Torres said. "Is there always someone on duty, then?"

"Oh, no." Silver-Hammer shook her head for emphasis. "Everything is on a—what Thilo named a deadman switch. If there is a certain pattern of failure, then the safeties are engaged and the section is sealed."

"I see." Torres suppressed the desire to shake her head in disapproval—the deadman switch was the only sensible idea in the lot; everything else was either ridiculously overpowered, like the original transporter, or depended on the willingness of the Kirse to sacrifice themselves to save the rest of their people—and glanced again at her tricorder. "Now I'll need to take a look at the control system."

"Of course." Silver-Hammer held out her hand. A gleaming disk, bright as a mirror, bright as silver, was cupped in her palm, and Torres reached for it. Her fingers slipped on ridged scars, a bezel of flesh holding the control centered in the Kirse's palm. For an instant, Torres didn't realize what she was touching, but then she understood, and removed her hand as though she'd been burned. The control was somehow embedded in Silver-Hammer's hand—like a cyborg, like the Borg—and possibly connected to the Kirse's nervous system, a machine that could no longer be released or removed, a responsibility made permanent by the fusion of skin and metal. She shuddered, and Silver-Hammer tipped her head to one side.

"Is something wrong?"

"Wrong?" Torres did her best to swallow the word, bite back her anger, but the sight of the gleaming disk waved so casually beneath her eyes was too much to stomach. "Yes, there's something wrong. How can you do that to yourself—?" She broke off then, seeing the Kirse frown.

"I don't understand."

"To link yourself to a machine—" Torres stopped again, at once appalled and steadied by the blank look on Silver-Hammer's face. The Kirse genuinely didn't understand, was truly confused by her response.

"But why not?" Silver-Hammer's voice was plaintive, a child rebuked by a parent for an infringement it didn't truly understand. Torres had heard that note in her own voice too many times as a child, asking why she was different from her peers, why she felt different, was treated differently, and shoved that knowledge away as too painful, retreating again into the familiar Klingon anger.

"There's so much to do, and I can't do it all," Silver-Hammer went on. "If I'm not part of the system—literally so, by the links—the system will fail. It's the most efficient way to make use of all the resources."

"But it makes you a machine yourself," Torres cried, "and you're a person. It's just wrong." She stopped, too late remembering the lectures at the Academy—even in her brief tenure there, she had heard all the reasons for the Prime Directive, the ethical debates as well as the practical causes. And to lose her temper now, when *Voyager* was in such desperate need, only proved again that she had never been Starfleet material. Silver-Hammer was still looking at her, not quite alarmed, not yet, but on the verge of it, and Torres made herself take a slow, deep breath, and then another. "I'm—sorry," she said at last. "It's an issue of some importance in the Federation, and my people—my mother's people, the Klingons—are prone to expressing our emotions somewhat violently."

She was quoting Tuvok, she realized, an overheard explanation for one of her rages, and could feel the color rising under her skin. Silver-Hammer seemed unaware of her response, however, and made the slow Kirse nod. "Ah. Thilo has mentioned some cultural taboos, but not this one. I also apologize for having offended you. Please accept that it was not intentional."

"Of course." Torres nodded back, the adrenaline still pulsing in her blood, and Silver-Hammer tipped her head to one side.

"I—you're still upset."

"It'll pass."

"This is a thing I understand," Silver-Hammer said. "There are people, and animals like the gardeners, that are too aggressive—that were bred for aggression, some of them, and are not always under control. There are systems that will regulate the hormone flows, that they can use to damp their instincts."

"Not more machines," Torres said, and couldn't hide her revulsion.

"Implants, yes," Silver-Hammer answered, "but under their own control. Not for the gardeners, of course, but for people, certainly. An assistant, you might call it. I could show you how it's done."

Torres stopped, silenced by the sudden possibility. Freedom from the Klingon anger, the rough aggression that was the first answer blood and upbringing gave her, a freedom that was under her control, available at her choice. . . . Silver-Hammer was offering only the plans, not the device, no obligation to do more than look. *But the price of that solution is that I'd be relying on something that isn't me*, she thought, *that is a machine that could be broken or be removed, that could become too much a crutch. More than that, it would erase a part of me, however much I may dislike it.* "No," she said, and to her own surprise the anger was gone from her voice. "But thank you, Silver-Hammer."

"As you wish." Silver-Hammer looked again at the disk in the palm of her hand, extended it toward the other woman. "Shall we continue?"

Torres nodded, and did her best to avoid touching the scarred interface between Kirse and machine. Maybe her response was unreasonable, but at least Silver-Hammer was the only Kirse she'd seen who resorted to the implants.

It took her another three hours to finish her analysis of the Kirse transporter, even drawing on the resources of *Voyager's* computer, but at the end of that time she had a fairly complete picture of the system, and a shrewd idea of what the Kirse would need to adapt their system. The Kirse world was clearly metal-poor—many of the apparently metal parts were actually ceramics and sophisticated composites, light and sturdy, with true metals used only where nothing else would serve. *Voyager* would certainly have to include some metal parts to make the revised system work, but Torres could already see how to rearrange her carefully hoarded stores to allow the bargain. In fact, she thought, glancing at the wall-mounted condensor system, the seashell-spiral chambers gleaming copper-pink—a false color, each one formed from ceramic rather than metal—there was a good chance that the Kirse could duplicate some of *Voyager*'s spare parts in the ceramic or in one of the composites, thus making up for anything she traded away. She smiled, imagining the possibilities, and Silver-Hammer stirred, wings twitching in what looked like a suppressed stretch.

"Have you come to a decision, then?"

"I've finished my assessment," Torres corrected, cautiously, and then relented. "My recommendation will be that we proceed with the trade."

Silver-Hammer lifted her wings and hands, a gesture at once as alien and as familiar as the delighted hand-clap of a human child. "Excellent news. You'll want to contact your ship, I presume? And of course privately."

"Please," Torres said.

Silver-Hammer lifted her left hand, directed the control disk at the only section of wall not covered with machinery. The transporter sounded, and Torres looked sideways to see light pulsing behind the protecting forcefield, a blue-white glare deep in the core of the machinery.

"Through there is private," Silver-Hammer went on, and Torres dragged her attention back to the Kirse. "I'll remain here—there are a number of routine tasks that need my attention."

"Thanks," Torres said, and started for the new door, threading her way through the crowding machinery. Once through the door—the wall was well over a meter thick, she noted—she found herself in a room like a domed cylinder, light diffusing through the pale-gray walls. She glanced around, not quite sure she should believe in Silver-Hammer's promise of privacy, but decided not to scan for observers. Starfleet training stressed the importance of at least the appearance of trust, and besides, she added silently, she wouldn't exactly be telling the Kirse anything they couldn't already figure out. She tapped her communicator. "Torres to *Voyager.*"

"*Voyager* here," Chakotay answered.

"I've finished my analysis," Commander Torres answered.

Chakotay's voice changed instantly. "Good news. Stand by, I'll inform the captain."

"Standing by." Torres glanced around the room again. It was very empty, without even a scattering of dust on any of the shining surfaces, and she wondered what it was used for. Or had it been created just for her? she wondered suddenly. The Kirse transporter seemed powerful enough to do that, particularly if it used the templates Silver-Hammer had showed her—

"Janeway here." The brisk voice cut through Torres's musing. "What do you have for us, B'Elanna?"

"Good news, I think, Captain. The Kirse transporter system can be adapted to use Federation technology with only a minimum of transferred hardware."

There was a momentary pause, and Torres could almost see Janeway's frown. "We don't have much hardware to spare—as you keep telling me."

"No, Captain." Torres took a deep breath, trying to decide how much to say. "I think I've worked out a solution, something that'll work for both of us."

"All right," Janeway said. "Beam back aboard, and let's go over the details."

"Aye, Captain," Torres answered, and cut the connection.

One good thing about the Kirse, she thought, materializing on *Voyager* less than fifteen minutes after her conversation with the ship, they didn't believe in unnecessary social amenities. Silver-Hammer had accepted her departure with equanimity, and without the niceties that would surround, say, a Klingon departure. Torres grinned at the thought, then smoothed her expression as she approached the ready-room door. "Captain? It's Torres."

"Come in."

The door slid open on Janeway's words, and Torres stepped into the room, not surprised to see both Chakotay and Tuvok sitting at the table as well as the captain.

"So," Janeway continued, "you think you've found us a way to have our cake and eat it, too?"

Torres blinked, then remembered the human metaphor. "I think so," she answered. "My data's already in the computer, undergoing final analysis, but I'm pretty sure I have the answer. The Kirse transporter isn't that different from ours—the primary problems are ones of resolution—and I can see at least two ways to adapt our system to their ends. However, because the Kirse don't have much metal—a lot of what I thought was metal is metallic ceramic or composite—we will have to provide them with some components from our supplies." She grinned then, unable to suppress her own pleasure at the tidy solution.

Janeway lifted an eyebrow. "I take it you've worked out a way around the problem you yourself pointed out?"

Torres nodded. "It's actually really simple." She reached for her datapadd, triggered the file of notes and sketches she had made on the planet, and swung it to face Janeway. "All right, the transporter components can't be made of ceramic or composite, given the field resonances involved—that's one of the problems the Kirse have been having getting their system up and running. And we can't afford to sell them our only spare parts, the only spare parts in the whole Delta Quadrant. But—" She touched the datapadd's screen again, bringing up the final sketch. "—if we cannibalize some of our isolinear optical chips, we can convert them to transporter components for the Kirse, and replace them with composite copies. Kirse technology is more than capable of doing that. So we don't lose any spare parts."

"Will the composites function as well as the originals?" Janeway asked.

"That's what I'm testing now," Torres answered. "But the preliminary calculations indicate that they will—maybe even better."

Janeway looked at Tuvok. "Do you see any objections?"

"From a security standpoint, no," the Vulcan answered. "Nor from any other. May I say I think Lieutenant Torres has found an elegantly practical solution?"

"I agree," Chakotay said.

Janeway smiled. "As it happens, gentlemen, so do I. But I appreciate your testimonials. Very well, Lt. Torres, let's see what the final analysis says, but unless it turns up something very much unexpected, consider yourself commended."

"Thank you, Captain," Torres said. She paused. "There is one thing, though."

The smile faded from Janeway's face, and Torres hid a grimace. "Oh?"

Torres nodded. "The Kirse seem to make substantial use of implanted technology to control their system. Almost to the extent of making them part of it."

There was a little silence, and then Janeway said, "Go on."

Torres took a deep breath, and launched into a description of what she had seen, of the transporter controlled from the silver disk embedded in the flesh of Silver-Hammer's hand. She kept her voice steady, pleased that she managed to finish without betraying too much of the visceral revulsion she had felt at the sight. "I'm mentioning this because it's something we didn't know before," she said at last. "I don't know if it makes a difference."

"Are you saying they're like the Borg?" Chakotay asked.

"No." Torres shook her head emphatically, surprised at her own certainty. "But not like us, either."

"We use implants," Janeway observed. "Medical prostheses, implanted communicators, the Universal Translator . . ."

"It's not the same," Torres said. "We don't—we don't control *Voyager*'s systems that way." She sighed. "I suppose it's only a matter of degree, but—well, Captain, I found it disturbing."

Janeway nodded, looked at the other officers. "Comments?"

"There is no logical reason not to use such an implanted system," Tuvok said. "Particularly among as small a population, as the Kirse seem to have. I have never been able to track more than a hundred Kirse life signs at any one time, and I frequently see fewer. The Federation's choice of technologies has been shaped by a much larger population, as well as aesthetic choices."

"I can't say the idea appeals much to me," Chakotay said, slowly, "but I think Tuvok's probably right. And, Captain, as you've been saying all along, we don't have much choice."

"No." Janeway smiled ruefully, softening the abrupt negative. "But I think it's a good thing to know about. Make sure all of the away teams know about this development, and make sure they observe any effects." Her smile widened. "Well done, B'Elanna."

It was dismissal, and Torres rose to her feet, collecting her datapadd. The captain was right, the implants were only a degree more intrusive than ones that the Federation used all the time; was right, too, to remind everyone how badly they needed the supplies. *But still,* she thought, *I wish I hadn't seen it.*

CHAPTER
7

JANEWAY CONSIDERED THE REPORTS ON HER SCREEN, weighing her limited options. *No options at all, really,* she thought—as the holographic doctor had reminded her less than two hours before—*but at least I think I can live with the choices.* She glanced again at the datapadd on which Torres's final report was displayed in its unedited form, and the sketches and equations, rough as they were, were even more clear. They could spare the metal parts, assuming that the Kirse were willing to duplicate them in composite, and that meant that *Voyager* could buy the food it needed to survive. The oddities, the uncomfortable aspects of the Kirse, were irrelevant compared to that simple fact, and that knowledge had sustained her when she had made her final bargain with Adamant less than three hours before. *Voyager* would get its food at a price they could afford: that had to be her first priority. She took a deep breath, and touched her communicator to contact the surface.

To her surprise, it didn't take long to establish a basic agreement. The Kirse were more than willing to copy the isolinear optical chips in the most suitable of their composites, and to accept the components that *Voyager* could spare for use in the new transporter system. Adamant was even willing to allow a team to begin harvesting the first load of food, and Janeway, with a private sigh of relief, dispatched an away team under Paris's command to handle that chore. A second, smaller team, headed by Tuvok and Torres, beamed down to the citadel to help the Kirse establish their new system.

All that, however, had been some hours ago, and she glanced at her screen with some impatience. The first step had been to find out if the Kirse could indeed copy the isolinear chips, and so far there had been no reports from the surface. She reached for her communicator. "Janeway to bridge. Any word from Tuvok yet?"

Chakotay's face appeared in the screen in almost instant response, hiding several of the open files. "Nothing yet, Captain. But he's scheduled to make a check report in another hour."

"Thank you. Janeway out." She closed the connection and leaned back in her chair, frowning at the viewscreen without really seeing the layered reports. She hadn't expected anything—Chakotay had his orders, would inform her as soon as Tuvok and his team finished examining the sample ceramic anti-stabilizer—and she knew that he knew perfectly well that this was just a way of occupying herself until the reports did come in. It was better, however, than spending the time on the bridge. She could still remember her own years as a first officer well enough to conjure up the sense of frustration she had felt when the captain wouldn't go away and let her get on with her work. She had sworn then that when she got command she would never inflict that on her people, and to a great extent she had kept her word. *Of course,* she added silently, a smile stealing across her face, *I understand what my captains were doing there now.*

"Chakotay to Captain Janeway."

The sound of his voice broke her reverie, and Janeway allowed her smile to widen. Tuvok must have finished his survey ahead of schedule. "Janeway here."

"Captain, we're reading an unexplained subspace wave just at the edge of our sensor range. I don't think it's a ship, but we can't be certain—and we don't have a definite identification." ·

"I'm on my way," Janeway answered, all thoughts of the past, even of Tuvok's mission, swept away in the sudden adrenaline rush.

The waveform analysis was spread across the main viewscreen when she arrived, and she frowned at it as she took her place in the command chair, already sure she didn't recognize the pattern. "Long-range sensors?"

"It's still too far away to show up on either visual or nonenergetic sensors. All we can expect to get is the waveform," Kim answered. His hands played across his controls, but Janeway guessed it was nervousness, the desire to recheck his readings, rather than any real hope of getting new information.

Janeway stared at the wave, shook her head as the screen vanished, replaced by the now-familiar starscape. "Any thoughts, gentlemen?"

Chakotay made a soft sound through his teeth. "It's not really the same thing," he said, "but it reminds me of—imagine you held the displacement echo of a Romulan cloaking device up to a mirror. That's what that pattern reminds me of."

Janeway looked down at her personal screen, touched keys to call up the various files on the cloaking device. The similarities were there, all right, but, as Chakotay had said, the picture in her screen was a mirror image of that pattern, peaks and valleys reversed. "Very interesting, Mr. Chakotay," she said. "And I think you're right. Go to yellow alert. Mr. Kim, hail the surface—Tuvok first, Adamant if you can't reach him."

"Captain, Mr. Tuvok is hailing us," Kim answered, and Janeway lifted an eyebrow.

"Put him on the screen."

"Captain." The Vulcan's expression was as deceptively serene as ever. "The Kirse report that one, maybe as many as five, ships have entered the system. They are cloaked, and therefore according to Adamant probably Andirrim."

"The location?" Janeway asked.

"Transmitting the sighting coordinates now." Tuvok pressed a button out of range of the viewer, and Kim looked up.

"The coordinates match the spot where we picked up the waveform, captain."

Janeway nodded. "Keep scanning, Mr. Kim. Report any change immediately. Mr. Tuvok, what are the Kirse plans?"

Tuvok looked over his shoulder. "You will have to ask Adamant that yourself, Captain." For an instant, Janeway could have sworn she heard disapproval in his voice.

"I beg your pardon, Adamant," she said. "I didn't realize you were there."

"I am here," the Kirse answered, and the image

swung sideways to bring him into focus. "If it is the Andirrim—and it most probably is; theirs is the most sophisticated cloaking device of all the attackers'— they may well want to trade. If so, I will let them land." He shrugged slightly, as though anticipating her response. And he probably could, she realized; Tuvok was bound to have made the objections that trembled on her tongue. "As you know, the shortage of metals is acute. I cannot afford revenge, or spite."

"Captain," Kim said, and Janeway glanced at him. "We're getting something on the visual scanners now."

"Put it on the main screen."

Instantly, Adamant's pale face was replaced by an image of stars. Five points of light shone brighter than the others: the approaching ships, Janeway knew, and looked at her own sensor board. "Any chance of an enhanced view, Mr. Kim?"

"Working on that now, Captain."

A moment later, the picture swam and then re-formed to show a massive, slab-sided battleship. It was shaped like a rhombohedron, a slanted rectangle balanced on its narrow edge, and Janeway repressed a sudden grin. It looked very much like the flying brick of Starfleet gossip—but then, no brick she had ever heard of had been studded with quite so much weaponry.

"The size is a little deceptive," Kim said. "Overall, it's only about as long as one of our nacelles, and maybe three, four times as deep."

Janeway nodded absently, her attention focused on the surface of the Andirrim craft. It wasn't finished, unlike Federation craft, or even the Kazon-Ogla; instead, the hardpoints—weapons, certainly, many of them, but also sensors and things she couldn't even begin to identify—sprang directly from a dull brown surface like rusted iron. Which of course it couldn't be, she told herself, but it was hard to shake the association. In contrast, the hardpoints were multi-colored, some sealed in white reflective coatings, others painted red or black, still more made of polished silver or gold metal, so that the entire ship had the haphazard look of a child's first exuberant attempt at modeling.

"They're all like that," Kim said, and sounded as surprised as she felt.

"Power readings?" she asked, and was not surprised when the young man shook his head.

"They're shielding, Captain. I can't break through at this distance." Something beeped on his console, and he adjusted his controls. "Adamant is hailing us again."

"Put him on," Janeway ordered. "Split the screen."

"Captain Janeway." Adamant's face, and the cool grace of the machines on the wall behind him, were an odd contrast to the Andirrim ship. "I am receiving a transmission from the approaching ships. Do you wish to be part of the conversation?"

"I'd be glad of it," Janeway said.

"Very well." Adamant did something out of sight, and the screen divided yet again, revealing a very different face. It was humanoid in the gross details, the two eyes, single narrow nose, wide mouth placed as they were in humans, but the eyes were vivid red and slit-pupiled like a cat's, and the gold skin had a distinct pattern of scales, darker patches forming a delicate lace over the Andirrim's face and hands. A thick waving mane of hair as red as its eyes framed its face and streamed over shoulders and back, a weird combination of mammal and reptile.

"Adamant," the Andirrim said, and the Kirse lifted his chin.

"Nal Sii'an. You've been here before, you know the possibilities."

The Andirrim—he had to be a captain or even the fleet leader, Janeway thought—blinked, thick membranes briefly shuttering his glowing eyes. "We are aware of the—possibilities. We acknowledge our recent defeat, and are here to offer trade instead."

"I can hardly be expected to take that on trust," Adamant answered.

"We have a thousand tons of ingot on my ship alone," Nal Sii'an said. "And half again as much on each of my companions. We need food, Adamant, and the fruit of the deia tree."

Janeway frowned at that, curious, and saw her expression mirrored on Adamant's face.

"You know as well as anyone that deia does no good to you and yours. I do not wish to sell it."

Nal Sii'an made a hissing noise that could only be read as contempt. "And there I am in agreement with you, Kirse-*Ĕme*. But it is required of me as the price of doing business on the homeworld. So without that, I may not trade. And there are three thousand tons of ingot ready for sale."

"I wonder what deia is to them," Chakotay said, quietly, muting the viewscreen pickup with a gesture. "Sounds almost like a drug of some kind."

Janeway nodded, still watching the screen, and saw Adamant sigh. "If you wish to poison yourself, that's your own business. Very well, I accept the proposition. You may enter orbit."

"There is another ship there before us," Nal Sii'an said. "Stranger-ship, what brings you here?"

Janeway nodded to Chakotay, who reopened the pickup. "My name is Kathryn Janeway. I'm captain of the Federation starship *Voyager*."

"*Voyager?*" Nal Sii'an repeated. "Federation?"

"We're from—quite a distance away," Janeway answered. "You would not have heard of us."

"We hear many things," Nal Sii'an said, "but, no, we have not heard of you. I ask again, what brings you here, and to the Kirse?"

"Like you," Janeway said, "we came to trade. In peace."

There was a little silence, and then the Andirrim nodded jerkily. "Then we will come into orbit, Adamant. Will you tell your stations to let us pass?"

"They will not fire," Adamant answered. "Come ahead."

"We're on our way," Nal Sii'an said, and his image disappeared from the screen.

"The Andirrim ships are under way," Kim announced. "They're following a course that will take them into a parking orbit just inside the limits of the orbital stations."

"How long will it take them to reach orbit?" Janeway asked.

"If they maintain their current speed, they should be in position in six hours," the ensign answered.

Six hours. Janeway frowned again, considering her next move. Her main concern had to be the safety of the ship, of course, but securing their supplies ran a close second. "Mr. Tuvok," she said, and the Vulcan stepped into the camera's range. "What's the away team's status?"

"My security personnel and Lieutenant Torres are at the citadel," Tuvok answered. "Mr. Paris's party is harvesting our first load of food under the direction of a Kirse guide. The fields are some distance from here, four hours' flight at their shuttle's top speed."

"I see." Janeway paused, wondering how she could phrase her question without risking offense to the listening Kirse. "Mr. Tuvok, what's your assessment of your mission in light of this development?"

There was a brief silence, and she wondered if the Vulcan was going to choose this moment to express his displeasure with human circumlocutions. "I am somewhat concerned about Mr. Paris's distance from the citadel should the Andirrim prove hostile," he said at last, "but otherwise I am confident of our hosts' security."

"Captain Janeway," Adamant said, "I should warn you that the Andirrim may be lying to us. I don't think they are—they need too much from here, since their last raid failed miserably, and it's the wrong season for the testing of their youth—but it remains a possibility. You should be aware of it."

"Thank you," Janeway said. "I'll certainly bear that in mind. But tell me, what is it that they need so desperately?"

An odd expression, something between guilt and disapproval, passed across Adamant's face. "They will trade for food," he said, "as you wish to do, but they also want the deia fruit. And here I own a certain part of the guilt, because I didn't know what the deia was to them. It is a beautiful plant, and harmless, even beneficial, to you and me. But it is addictive to the Andirrim—the dream-sweet, they call it—and though they have managed to eliminate it on their own worlds, there are still those who want it, and they know deia still grows here. I sold it once, before I knew, and now I am torn. I was responsible for the creation of some of those who now demand the deia, and I know they will suffer without it, yet I don't want any more such addicts on my conscience."

"You mean these Andirrim are—in essence—drug dealers?" Janeway asked.

Adamant tipped his head from side to side. "Not

exactly. Nal Sii'an is known to me, and he is an officer of the Andirrim navy—it's their government who deal in the deia."

"Sounds like something the Kazon-Ogla might think of," Chakotay said quietly. "Keep a client population sedated or at the very least distracted, so that they can run things."

Janeway nodded. The possibilities were indeed appalling, but all too plausible. "If that's the case, Adamant," she said, "you might want to consider guarding the plants as well as the fruit. The Andirrim might want to rebuild their original source of supply."

"That which has grown here is rarely as fertile elsewhere," Adamant answered, with a distinct note of pride in his voice. "But I shall take your advice. Thank you."

"And I appreciate your openness," Janeway answered. "Mr. Tuvok, keep me informed of any changes in your status, and be ready to beam back to the ship at the first sign of trouble."

"Yes, Captain."

"Good. Janeway out." She looked around the bridge, checking the familiar play of lights that signaled the ship's status, and Chakotay cleared his throat.

"Do you think we can trust the Andirrim, Captain?"

That was the prize question, Janeway thought, the one on which *Voyager*'s very survival could depend. And that, of course, gave her her answer. "We'll maintain yellow alert for now," she said. "Mr. Kim, I want continuous monitoring of the incoming ships. Go to red alert at the slightest sign of hostility."

"Yes, Captain," Kim answered.

"Mr. Chakotay," Janeway went on, "I want you to inform Mr. Paris of the situation. Tell him to collect as much food as he can, but to beam himself and his crew back up here at the first sign of trouble."

"Very good, Captain." Chakotay turned to his own console, and Janeway stared at the image on her personal screen. The pale shapes that were the Andirrim ships crept slowly across the schematic of the Kirse system, drawing inexorably closer to the planet where *Voyager* hung in orbit. The orbital stations filled space around them, a thousand tiny lights that would protect the planet, but could all too easily endanger the ship. But that, at least, was something she could remedy, she thought. She reached for her datapadd and began calculating a safer orbit, grateful for a job to occupy her mind.

The beep of the communicator was loud over the quiet of the Kirse field. Tom Paris straightened from the skid of piled grain and the quiescent harvester-robot that pulled it, and reached for the communicator pinned to his chest. "Paris here."

To his surprise, it was Chakotay, not Tuvok, who answered. "Paris, this is *Voyager*. A fleet of Andirrim ships have just arrived in the system."

"Andirrim?" Paris repeated, involuntarily, and grimaced. "Sorry, sir, go on."

"Andirrim," Chakotay said, and his voice was grim. "Five ships. They say they've come to trade, and the Kirse are letting them take orbit, but we—neither Adamant nor the captain—are fully convinced it isn't a trick. We're at yellow alert just in case. The captain's orders are for you and your party to continue collecting as much food as possible, but stand by to beam up at the first sign of trouble. We're monitoring the ships' approach, and we'll keep you informed."

Paris glanced up at the sky, knowing the pointlessness of the gesture, seeing only the thin streaks of cloud that crossed the deeper blue. It was late afternoon, and the sky to the west was white with haze, turning the sun to a smear of light too painful to observe directly. "What about Tuvok's team?"

"They've been informed, of course," Chakotay answered. "Tuvok's with Adamant now, monitoring the approach from their control room, and will inform you and us of any changes, too."

Paris nodded, and turned to look across the field. His team was scattered, distant points of red and blue and black vivid against the pale breadcrust-brown of the waist-high grain; near each one, a rustling among the stalks marked the presence of one of the Kirse's harvester-robots. The first skids were almost filled, he guessed—at least, they should be, if his own was any indication. "Do you want us to start beaming the grain up now?" he asked. "We've got a lot collected already." It wasn't much, really, certainly not enough to feed all of *Voyager*'s crew, but at least it would be a vitamin source they had not had before.

"Good idea," Chakotay said, and not for the first time Paris heard a hint of reluctance in the other man's voice. It wasn't so much that the ex-Maquis didn't respect the idea, Paris knew, but purely that Chakotay still hated admitting that he, Paris, could be of service to the ship. *Not that I blame him, entirely,* Paris thought, *but I wish he'd let it go.* He pushed the thought aside, knowing how pointless it was, and concentrated on Chakotay's words. "Go ahead and get as much up as you can, but the team's safety is your first priority."

I know that. Paris suppressed the words, said, "Acknowledged. Paris out."

He stood for an instant, getting a grip on his anger—an anger only increased by the certain knowledge that a good part of it was guilt—then put two fingers in his mouth and whistled. Old-fashioned, low-tech, and effective, he added silently, as heads turned all across the field, and he raised a hand to wave them over to him. The robots' movements stilled—Grayrose had given each of them a controller for one of the machines—and the dots of color began moving closer. Renehan was the first to reach the little clearing, but Grayrose and the other humans weren't far behind.

"What's up, Tom?" Renehan asked, and one of the others, a gangly ensign named Laek who had proved himself an expert at the remote controls, echoed her.

"Word from the ship," Paris answered, and raised his voice to be heard by the others. "Andirrim ships have entered the system—they say they've come to trade, but the captain wants us ready for trouble."

Grayrose's wings rose and fell with a crack of displaced air, and several of the humans jumped at the sharp sound. "How many ships?" Grayrose asked, and Paris collected his straying thoughts.

"Five of them, Chakotay said. Does it make a difference?"

Grayrose shook her head, another gesture she had copied from the humans. "Probably not. Even when they come to trade, now, they come in force, just in case they find something unguarded."

A dozen questions trembled on Paris's tongue, but he knew his first duty was to get the food on board. "Right. The captain wants the stores we've collected beamed back to the ship now—to get as much as possible on board, just in case there's a problem. How're we doing?"

The rest of the team exchanged glances, and then Laek shrugged. "All right, I guess. My sled's just about full."

Two of the others nodded with him, and Renehan said, "Mine's full, but I could fit more into it."

Paris repressed another pointless glance at the empty sky. "How long to fill yours, Laek?"

"Twenty, maybe thirty minutes."

Paris glanced back at his own sled, nearly full itself. Thirty minutes more would let him cut the last section of this field, maybe even make a start on harvesting the silverine orchard that was next on their list, and thirty minutes shouldn't make that much difference to the Andirrim approach. "Right," he said aloud, "Rennie, finish filling your sled and then take the robot over to the orchard, get what you can out of there. The rest of you, finish your sections of the field, and then contact me. Let's get as much up to the ship as we possibly can."

"Right," Renehan said, briskly, and the others echoed her. Paris reached for his own control box, ready to set the robot moving again, but Grayrose laid a hand on his arm.

"Five ships?"

"That's what our first officer said."

"Did he name the commander?"

Paris shook his head. "Does it matter?"

"It could make a difference," the Kirse answered. "Paris—Tom. Even if they mean to trade, they may be dangerous."

"Thanks," Paris said, and knew he sounded less than gracious. To his surprise, however, Grayrose ignored him, her face blank, eyes focused in the middle distance. Paris frowned, and then she blinked, smiled, and was present again.

"Are you all right?" Paris asked.

"Of course. Why?"

Because you looked like— He stopped there, not sure what he should answer. *I don't know what you looked like, but I don't think you were here for that instant. And that makes no sense at all.* He shook his head. "Nothing, no reason."

"If you'll give me that," Grayrose said, and nodded to the control box, "I can probably get it done faster."

It was true, too, but nonetheless humbling. *Still,* Paris thought, *that's one thing I've learned in my checkered career: pride's irrelevant when food is the issue.* He held out the box, and the Kirse took it, long fingers curling expertly around the controls. It had been built to fit her hands, or at least Kirse hands; the toggles and sliders that had been so awkward to his touch were perfectly positioned for her use. The robot slid smoothly into motion, the tether that connected the skid to the end of the harvester tightening gently, without the clash of metal. Paris sighed, impressed and a little jealous, and the combined machines moved off into the last stand of grain. They weren't much like the robots he'd worked with in the Federation, were oddly—unnecessarily—humanoid in their construction, a roughly Kirse-shaped torso rising above the harvester's maw, the multiple arms at each shoulder looking like an afterthought. Most of the robots he'd seen in the Federation were boxy, distinctly mechanical shapes, formed by their jobs rather than any sense of aesthetics. *And I'm really just trying to distract myself from the problem at hand,* he thought, and turned to Grayrose.

"Do you think the Andirrim are really here to trade, or are they planning a sneak attack?"

Grayrose shrugged with her wings, never taking her eyes from the robot in the field. "They have attacked before, when they said they wanted trade. But I can't read their minds."

"Sorry," Paris said, startled, and Grayrose gave him an apologetic glance in turn.

"No, I'm sorry. I meant that it's hard to judge their intentions—the customs of animals are hard to comprehend."

In the field in front of them, the harvester pivoted at the touch of paired toggles, began its next pass. Paris said, "So you tested the Andirrim like you tested us?"

"Yes." Grayrose was again intent on the harvester, her eyes narrowed as she maneuvered it into a second turn.

"And they—ate the food you'd put out?" Paris went on. "The banquet in the hall?"

"They ravaged the gardens," Grayrose said, and there was no mistaking the bitterness in her voice. "They didn't even get as far as the citadel." She controlled herself with an effort. "But that was a long time ago."

The harvester had finished, was trundling back toward them, and Paris glanced again at his tricorder. Another twenty minutes, if Laek had estimated right, and then they could begin transporting supplies up to the ship. He squinted at the other harvesters, trying to judge how much they'd done, and his communicator beeped again.

"Chakotay to Paris."

"Paris here." Out of the corner of his eye, he saw Grayrose take a step away, not quite out of earshot, but a polite gesture.

"We've run an analysis of the Andirrim approach vectors, and their intention is, well, ambiguous. The captain wants the away team back on board before the ships reach orbit."

"How much time do we have?" Paris asked.

"Two hours. Three at the outside."

Two hours. Paris grinned, swiveling on his heels to take in the fields he had marked for harvest. In two hours, they could cut most of the plants he'd selected—already he knew which crops to leave out to make the best use of the time left, the berries that took time to shake from their branches without damaging the parent plant, the tubers that had to be cut free of their roots and stalks and then dug out of the ground. They could be left for later—assuming there was a later, of course, but the Kirse were friendly, and they had already survived attack by the Andirrim— He shook himself, made himself answer calmly, "Very good, Commander, but I want to go on harvesting up to the last minute."

"The captain says two hours," Chakotay answered. "And she means it, Mr. Paris."

"Acknowledged. Paris out." Paris stared for a moment at the fields, plotting the most efficient use of the machines.

"Is it good news?" Grayrose asked, and he started.

"Not exactly, I guess, but not bad, either. The captain's given us two hours to finish this before we have to beam up."

"It's a sensible thought," Grayrose agreed. "Shall I begin the orchard?"

Sensible, Paris thought. *This from a person who lands shuttlecraft on a moving runway.* He said, "If you would, that would be great. I'll join you in a minute."

The Kirse nodded, and started for the stand of trees. The harvester rumbled after, the sides of the sled twice as tall as she, the Kirse-shaped projection at the front of the main machine adjusting arm length and overall height to match the new crop. Paris shook his head, still amazed at the Kirse's skills, and touched his communicator. "Paris to away team. News from the ship. Check in, please."

The voices came back almost instantly, calling their

names, and Paris counted them off one by one. When the last one had answered—Joie Sakhlova, no surprise there—he touched the communicator again. "All right. We've had an update on the Andirrim approach, and the captain wants us back on board in two hours with as much of the harvest as we can manage. So this is the plan for now. Sakhlova, you and Laek finish the grain field, and then join me in the orchard. Renehan, you and McCabe move on to the next field—the one that we called two-A—see how much you can get from there. Maceda and Yoshiko, take two-B."

"We're not going to try for three?" That was Maceda, his voice almost obscured by a sudden burst of static.

"Say again?" Paris scowled, wondering what had caused the interference, and looked up at the now cloudless sky.

"We're not going to try to get field three harvested, as well?"

The static was gone as quickly as it had appeared. Paris filed it in the back of his brain, one more thing to worry about later, and answered, "No, not unless the two fields go a lot faster than I expect. We want quantity right now, not variety."

"Confirmed," Maceda said.

"Speaking of which," Paris went on, and heard choked laughter from someone, "I want to beam up what we've got. The ship should be able to do it on the fly."

There was a chorus of agreement, and Paris touched his communicator again. "Paris to *Voyager*."

"Voyager here."

Not Chakotay, this time, Paris realized, but Harry Kim, and in spite of himself felt a certain relief. "Harry. What's the situation?"

"No change." Kim sounded constrained, and Paris guessed that either the captain or the first officer was still on the bridge. "The Andirrim are still moving in—they've got their shields at standby, and so do we, but Adamant doesn't seem to think it's anything unusual."

"We have the first load of grain ready for transport," Paris said. "Tell the transporter chief she can take her coordinates from our communicators, and scan for the grain from that mark."

"Acknowledged," Kim answered. *"Voyager* out."

Paris turned back to the orchard, wishing Kim were on-planet with him—he liked the ensign, was closer to him than he was to anyone else on the ship, and if they were going to be in danger, he would rather they were facing it together—but then shoved that thought away. He heard the familiar, high-pitched whine of a Starfleet transporter, and the piled grain vanished from the back of his sled. The sound same again, more faintly, and he turned to see that Maceda's harvester had been emptied, too. At least *Voyager* would have some supplies, whatever happened, maybe even enough to make a difference, he thought, and looked back at his own harvester. It was moving delicately through the crowded orchard, the eight mechanical arms now fully deployed, glittering in the dappled sunlight as it reached for, tested, and picked the ripe fruit. The bright green ovoids made a hollow sound as they fell into the sled, and he hoisted himself up onto its edge to check their progress. The brown floor was already completely covered by the fruit, bright even in the shade, and he allowed himself a smile of satisfaction. It might not be as much as they'd been hoping to get, not a full resupply for the ship, but at least the science staff should be able to extract enough ascorbic acid from this load to keep the crew healthy.

"Voyager to Paris."

Paris let himself drop back off the sled, and touched his communicator. "Paris here. What's up, *Voyager?"*

"Are there any signs of electrical disturbance—storm clouds, anything like that—in your area? We're getting unusual interference in the transporter beam."

Paris looked up at the cloudless sky visible between the branches of the fruiting trees, and felt the sunlight warm on his shoulders as he stepped out of their intermittent shade. "Not a thing, Harry. It's a beautiful day."

"We weren't seeing anything either," Kim answered. "But it seemed worth asking."

"What kind of interference?"

"We don't know yet," Kim said. "It looked like a weather problem—high electrical activity in the upper layers of the atmosphere—but there isn't anything like that on our screens."

"Is it a problem?" Paris asked, and there was a pause.

"We don't know that either," Kim said at last. "The transporter chief's working on it. But the captain says you should be prepared for a quick beam-up if it worsens."

"I'll pass that along," Paris answered. "Paris out." He touched his communicator again, and made the announcement, listening hard for the static he had heard before. This time, the channel was as clear as the sky, the answering acknowledgments coming through without distortion, and he shook his head as he moved back into the shadow of the trees. "Grayrose?"

The Kirse answered without taking her eyes from the harvester. "Yes?"

"Voyager is reporting interference—weather interference, they think—with the transporter. Do you have any idea what might be causing it?"

"Weather interference?" Grayrose repeated. This time, her hands did slow on the controls, and out of the corner of his eye, Paris saw the harvester grind to a halt, one arm frozen with its fingers just touching a ripe fruit.

"Yeah. Like an electrical storm, something like that?" Paris gave a rueful smile, and pointed to the sky. "Not that there's any sign of anything."

Grayrose's mouth rounded, eyes widening. "The ion field," she said. "It could be that. The low-orbit stations release it when a hostile ship approaches, to confuse their sensors once they enter atmosphere. Would that interfere with your transporter?"

"It could," Paris answered, grimly, and touched his communicator again. "Paris to *Voyager.* I just might have an answer on that interference, Harry."

"Go ahead." It was Chakotay who answered, and Paris suppressed a grimace.

"Grayrose here says that the defense stations in low orbit release an ion field to confuse hostile craft in atmosphere. That could be the source of the problem."

"It sure could be," Chakotay answered, and his voice in turn was grim. "The interference seems to be building. Can Grayrose give us an estimate of its peak frequencies?"

Paris looked at the Kirse, who shook her head. "I'm sorry, I'm not part of that system. But Silver-Hammer would know. Or of course Adamant."

"She doesn't know," Paris repeated. "She suggests you ask Adamant, or Silver-Hammer."

"Right." There was a little pause. Paris imagined Chakotay consulting his console, and wished abruptly that he was back on the ship himself, sitting at the conn. The intensity of his desire startled him—the last thing he'd expected was to develop an attachment to *Voyager* or its crew—and he tried to shove it aside. But the fact remained: he wanted to be back on the ship, where he could do some good, where he belonged. He was glad when Chakotay spoke again. "It seems to be settling into a regular pattern, and there are valleys that shouldn't cause any problems for the transporter, so the captain says you should stay down there a little longer, see if we can't get the harvest finished."

"This part of it, anyway," Paris said, in spite of himself.

"We need everything we can get, Mr. Paris," Chakotay said flatly. "You know that as well as I do."

And in fact I don't think you're deliberately putting me in danger, Paris thought. *I just suspect you might not realize what you're doing. The debt I put you under by saving your life was bigger than I understood.* "Understood, Mr. Chakotay," he said, and forced a cheerfulness he didn't feel.

"Mr. Kim is contacting Adamant," Chakotay went on. "We'll contact you if there's any change in the situation."

"Thanks," Paris answered, and this time couldn't keep the irony from his voice.

If Chakotay heard, he gave no sign. *"Voyager* out."

"I wouldn't have thought our field would pose a problem to you," Grayrose said, and her fingers moved again on the control box. The robot came to life at the touch, its fingers closing gently on the fruit and plucking it with a smooth continuity of suspended motion.

"Complex systems are always vulnerable to disruption," Paris said, and knew he sounded bitter. It was one thing to have to rely on them in Federation space, where there were always other ships, other humans, and most of all the entire Federation itself to back them up, but it was entirely different here, where they, *Voyager* itself, had only the ingenuity of its own crew to bolster its machines and programs. He shook himself, managed to smile at Grayrose then. "But at least we know what the problem is. I'll inform the others."

Janeway frowned at the rhythmic pulse of the ion field reduced on her screen to a series of spikes and valleys. Below it, the transporter chief's analysis reduced it still further to a deceptively simple equation. If the energy level built beyond four thousand megajoules, the transporters would no longer be able to compensate—and the power was building, slowly but steadily.

"Captain," Kim said, from his post behind her. "I've reached Adamant."

"Put him on the main screen," Janeway answered, and straightened to face him. "Adamant."

"Captain Janeway. I understand there is a problem?" In the screen, the Kirse looked genuinely concerned.

"Yes," Janeway said. "I understand from Grayrose that your orbiting stations create an ion field in your upper atmosphere as part of your defenses. This is interfering with our transporter, and, while right now it's manageable, we need to know what the maximum strength will be, and whether the rate of change will remain constant."

"My apologies, Captain," Adamant answered. "I had no idea this would cause difficulties for your system—though I'm glad we found out this weakness now ourselves." He glanced down at something out of sight—probably a display console of his own, Janeway thought—and then looked back at the screen. "Our projections—assuming that the Andirrim make no hostile move, the rate of charge will remain constant, and will peak at a twenty-eight-percent increase over the present strength."

Janeway reached for her datapadd, plugged the percentage into the transporter chief's equations. The Kirse projected maximum came to 3989 megajoules—entirely too close, she thought, to the point where it becomes a barrier. "Thank you, Adamant," she said, and the Kirse held up a slim hand.

"There is one thing you should know. If the Andirrim offer hostilities, the low-orbit stations will discharge at full power, which will briefly double the field strength. It's effective against their landing craft."

And will render the transporter completely nonfunctional, Janeway thought. She said, "You said briefly. How long does the effect last?"

"It begins to fade almost at once," Adamant answered. "But it takes time for the field to disperse."

We can calculate it ourselves, Janeway thought. "Thank you, Adamant. *Voyager* out."

She sat for a moment, staring at the numbers in her datapadd screen, and heard Chakotay give a soft sigh that was almost a whistle of disbelief. A part of her was annoyed, but she knew perfectly well it was because she agreed with him: this was an impossible position, *Voyager* desperate for the food still being harvested, the away team at growing risk of abandonment as the ion field strengthened. "How much food do we have aboard so far?" she asked, and Chakotay glanced at his console.

"So far, six tons. But the team has just signaled for another pickup, which should bring it to seven."

Seven tons. Not nearly enough to feed the crew if

they were driven out of the Kirse system, forced to flee the Andirrim for any length of time, but it might be enough, rendered down to its component parts, to provide the vitamins they so desperately needed. Assuming, of course, she added silently, that the power cost remained reasonable. The replicators were still too much of a drain on the ships' systems to be used for long even in this emergency. "Janeway to sickbay," she said. "Doctor, do we have enough raw materials in this supply to keep the crew healthy?"

There was a little pause, and the doctor's face looked out at her. "Just barely. I can extract a concentrated form from what we have, but no one will like the taste."

"That's hardly the point," Janeway said, and the doctor shrugged.

"I would agree, but I didn't want it said I didn't warn you."

"Thank you, Doctor." Janeway flipped through her screens, searching for the figures on current power consumption. If they used manual or chemical extractions, they would stay within the safe parameters, but risked wasting some of the precious vitamins; the more efficient methods—all variations on the replicator or the transporters—all used too much power to be wise. She shook her head, wishing that Torres wasn't down on the planet. The engineer was a near-genius at the kind of improvisation that had become routine on *Voyager*. But there was no reason to think that, even if the Andirrim were hostile, the ship couldn't withstand their attack long enough to retrieve their crew, or, at worst, couldn't escape and return later to rescue the away teams. The Kirse were friendly, and would protect them, if it came to that.

"Do we recall the away teams?" Chakotay asked, and Janeway shook her head.

"No. We need food, Chakotay, not just vitamins, not if we're going to conserve enough power to get us home. The Andirrim may not attack, and even if they do, they'll be concentrating on the Kirse. We should be able to defend ourselves."

"Very good," Chakotay began, but Kim interrupted him.

"Captain! The first of the Andirrim ships has achieved orbit."

"Put it on the main screen," Janeway ordered. "What's the ion field doing?"

"Still rising." Kim answered.

"Right." Janeway stared at the image on the screen, the narrow rhomboid hanging apparently motionless against the planetary disk, its rusty colors even uglier in contrast to the lush world behind it. "Any sign of weaponry?"

"The shields are at standby," Kim said, "but the phasers are cold. Captain, they're hailing the surface."

"See if you can pick up the transmission," Janeway ordered, and an instant later a second image blossomed on the screen, Nal Sii'an's gold face framed by his scarlet mane.

"The Kirse are routing their response to us as well," Kim reported.

"Excellent."

"We are here, Adamant," the Andirrim said. "As promised. My shuttle is loaded with the ingot, also as agreed. Will you let us land?"

"Scan them," Janeway ordered. "Can you see the shuttle?"

"Their screens are blocking our sensors," Kim said. "There's a vehicle in what seems to be a launch bay, but I can't pick up anything more."

"I am prepared to allow your shuttle to land at the

following coordinates," Adamant said. "You will be met there by one who will speak to trade."

"That location is here," Chakotay said, and a small globe appeared in a corner of the screen, rotating to display a bright red cross. "Well away from the citadel."

And from the landing parties, too, Janeway thought. She nodded her approval, and Nal Sii'an said, "Will you vouch for the neutrality of the stranger ship?"

"They are here to trade, as you are," Adamant answered. "I can speak for that."

"Then we are launching our shuttle," Nal Sii'an said.

"I'll be waiting," Adamant said, and his image vanished from the screen.

"The shuttle's away," Kim reported.

Janeway nodded, seeing the small dot brighten against the planet's surface as the steering engines fired. "Course and speed, Mr. Kim?"

"Still working on it, Captain."

Janeway stared at the dot now falling toward the edge of the atmosphere, trying to match its position to the charts she had studied over the last week. Surely the approach angle was wrong, would bring the Andir-rim shuttle in too sharply—unless their shuttle was designed for higher tolerances than the Federation's, or, she added, her frown deepening, unless they weren't planning to land at the designated point. "Get that course worked out, Mr. Kim," she snapped, and Kim answered quickly.

"Just coming through." The line appeared on the main screen, curving over the surface of Chakotay's globe toward the cross that marked the rendezvous site. "It'll take them there," Kim went on, "but it's not the most efficient use of power. They're coming in too high in the atmosphere, they'll have to brake dynamically to make the landing."

"But it lets them change course up until the last seconds," Janeway said, and saw Chakotay nod, the same knowledge reflected in his eyes. "Chakotay, get our people back on board. Mr. Kim, raise Adamant."

"No response from the citadel," Kim answered. "They've gone to full shields there, and I can't even get a transmission through."

"Work on it," Janeway said. She wished, suddenly and violently, that her security officer and her best pilot weren't still on the surface, but shoved the thought aside.

"The transporter chief reports that the ion field has strengthened," Chakotay said. "She's having to bring Paris's party up two at a time."

"Right." Janeway stared at the screen, watching the red wedge of the Andirrim shuttle crawl along the course line. "Keep trying to raise Adamant, or Tuvok."

"I'm sorry, Captain," Kim said, "but I can't break through their shield."

"Try an overfocused beam," Chakotay suggested, moving to look over the younger man's shoulder. "We'll lose visual, but maybe voice can get through."

"Captain!" Kim said. "The Andirrim ship is hailing us."

"Put it on the main screen," Janeway said, "and keep trying to reach the surface."

The other images, planet and globe and the bright lines of the shuttle's projected course, disappeared, replaced by Nal Sii'an's scaled face. Behind him, another Andirrim, darker-skinned, with a rich purple mane, bent over a display table filled with fuzzy shapes, but the transmission blurred them beyond recognition.

"Captain," Nal Sii'an said. "I have a proposition for you and your ship."

"Captain," Kim said, his voice urgent, and Janeway risked a glance over her shoulder.

"What?"

"The Andirrim are blanketing all transmissions from *Voyager*. We've lost all contact with the surface."

"The transporter chief reports that she's retrieved everyone except Paris and Renehan," Chakotay announced. "And of course Tuvok's party."

Janeway looked back at the screen. "And what's the meaning of this?"

Nal Sii'an smiled, showing white and pointed teeth. The Andirrim had clearly evolved from a carnivore species, Janeway thought, and then was annoyed at its irrelevance. "As I said, we have a proposition for you, Captain Janeway. You came here to trade—you are trading, it seems, so you know the habits of the Kirse, and the prices Adamant charges. I propose an alternative."

"Such as?" Janeway's mouth was dry, but she made herself meet the Andirrim's gaze with what she hoped was regal indifference.

"Join us as we raid." Nal Sii'an leaned forward slightly, red eyes bright. "Together we can take far more than either of us could alone, and you will save whatever outrageous price the Kirse has charged you. We will divide the spoils evenly, ship by ship, and together we can deal the Kirse a defeat they won't soon forget."

"We keep our bargains," Janeway answered. "The answer is no."

"Then we will treat you as one of the Kirse," Nal Sii'an said.

"You'll regret any attack on this vessel," Janeway

said. There was no harm in bluffing, not at this point, and every second's delay meant that Kim might resolve the transmission problem and be able to warn the Kirse. "We are a Federation starship, we've come unimaginable distances to trade here. After that, do you think we'd stand for any interference with our affairs?"

She saw Nal Sii'an blink, the white membranes momentarily obscuring his eyes, but then the Andirrim shook his head. "No. You are known to the Kazon-Ogla, and they call you solitary."

"Would they tell you if we weren't?" Janeway asked, and smiled. For a moment, she thought she'd won, that Nal Sii'an would back down, but then the Andirrim shook his head, more violently than before.

"It doesn't matter. Either you are with us, or against us. And if you stand against us, we will destroy you."

"We won't help you," Janeway answered.

"Then prepare to die." Nal Sii'an drew his hand across the screen, and his image vanished.

So much for bluff. "Go to red alert," Janeway said, and the whooping alarm almost drowned Kim's voice.

"The Andirrim ships have gone to full shield, and have activated phasers and photon torpedoes. The shuttle is breaking off—it's left its course, and is heading for the citadel."

"Take the helm, Mr. Chakotay. Get us room to maneuver," Janeway said. It was a pity Paris was still on the planet, but Chakotay was almost as good a pilot, even if it wasn't properly the first officer's job.

"Aye, Captain." The duty pilot stepped aside, and Chakotay took his place at the controls, hands moving as he freed the great ship from its orbit.

"The Kirse defense system is activated," Kim announced. "The ion field is in place, but the shuttle is below it already."

"Let the Kirse deal with it," Janeway said, and forced it from her mind. She would need all her concentration to fight the Andirrim ships still in orbit. "Full tactical array on the main screen."

"Full tactical," Kim confirmed, and the main viewscreen was suddenly filled with a web of lines and symbols, *Voyager's* and the Andirrim ships' positions and courses, the mesh of the Kirse defense system, the orbital stations glowing red and angry.

"The Kirse stations are at full power," one of Chakotay's people—Pao—reported from her place at Tuvok's security station. "They're firing on the Andirrim flagship."

Even as she spoke, the screen went momentarily white. Janeway looked away, blinking hard to clear her vision, and saw the Andirrim flagship apparently untouched.

"Their shields absorbed most of it," Kim reported, "but it has to have weakened them."

"Andirrim ship bearing one-nine-zero mark four," Pao reported. "It's firing torpedoes."

"Evasive action," Janeway ordered, and a moment later the ship rocked slightly as the shock waves hit the outer screens.

"No damage," Kim said.

"Right." Janeway released her hold on the arms of her chair, a sudden unholy glee filling her. She was a Starfleet captain, and these Andirrim were going to get an object lesson in just what that meant. "Fire at will, Mr. Pao. Let's show them what we're made of."

CHAPTER
8

PARIS BLINKED AS THE LAST OF THE TRANSPORTER DAZZLE
faded from the air in front of him, and glanced at
Grayrose and Renehan, still waiting at the edge of the
orchard. "Four down, two to go," he said, and Renehan matched his grin.

"Keep your fingers crossed, then, Tom."

"Voyager to Paris." The transporter chief's voice
was distorted by the static that had been growing
worse since the ion field formed. "Maceda and Laek
are safe aboard. Stand by while we try to get a fix on
you—"

Her words were cut off by a soundless flash of light
that turned the sky to blinding white. Paris swore,
shielding his eyes, and heard the crack of air as
Grayrose's wings flapped in surprise.

"Chief, are you there?" There was no answer, and
he tapped his communicator. "Paris to *Voyager*. Are
you there, Chief?"

Static hissed, and for an instant he imagined he caught the shape of garbled words, but then even that vanished. Renehan looked at him, her eyes wide, but then forced a grin, hiding her fear.

"Looks like it's you and me, Tom."

"The Andirrim," Grayrose said. "They must have attacked."

"That was the ion field, then?" Paris asked. Overhead, the sky was still white, as though the sudden charge had condensed all moisture to a solid sheet of cloud.

Grayrose nodded, her expression remote, as though she was listening to something only she could hear. "They are calling the shuttle fleet," she said, and Paris realized that his image was literally true: the Kirse was receiving transmissions from somewhere. Probably from the citadel, he thought, and Grayrose looked at him. "The Andirrim have launched drones, plus a main attack shuttle. We must hurry."

She lifted the control box, summoning the nearest harvester, and it rolled toward them, shedding the sled and several pairs of arms as it did so.

"Where are we going?" Renehan asked, but followed the Kirse onto the narrow platform behind the harvester's head.

"To the nearest launch point. It isn't far." Grayrose squinted up at the white sky, then tilted her head as though to listen.

"What is it?" Paris said.

"The drones. They're designed to destroy the shuttles before they lift. I thought I heard them." Grayrose touched the control box again, and the harvester shed its last pair of arms. It looked like a completely different machine now, Paris thought, capable of speed.

"If they've got drones out, I don't want to be caught

in the open," Renehan said, and Paris nodded, pulling himself up next to her on the little platform.

"You must come with me," Grayrose said. "The gardeners, and anything else adapted, for that matter—the attack will upset them, you'd be in danger from them if you stayed."

"Not to mention the Andirrim," Renehan said.

"And them also," Grayrose agreed, with perfect seriousness.

"Right," Paris said. "Let's go."

Grayrose touched the control box a final time, pushing all the toggles fully forward, and the harvester jolted into motion. Paris tightened his grip on the protruding frame as the cumbersome machine lurched across a shallow ditch, but then they had reached one of the golden roads that crisscrossed the planet, and the harvester steadied again. It began picking up speed, power plant humming more strongly now, and Grayrose glanced again at the sky.

"The main body will be heading for the citadel, of course, but there will be raiders—"

Even as she spoke, something flashed against the sky, low on the horizon. Paris swore again, scanning the clouds, but whatever it was had vanished.

"Did you see something?" Renehan asked, and Grayrose pointed beyond the harvester's head.

"There's the launch site."

It was at least two hundred meters away, a low, unremarkable hill, except for the half-moon opening, too regular to be a natural cave, just below the summit. Paris could just see the nose of a shuttle like the one he had flown in protruding from the opening. More Kirse, at least three of them, all winged, were busy with something beneath the left wing.

"Great," he began, and his words were drowned in a sudden shriek of displaced air. Something small and brilliant silver skimmed past a meter or so above his head, followed by two more similar objects.

"Drones," Grayrose cried, and reached for the phaser she carried at her waist. She braced herself against the harvester's head and fired twice after them—less in any real hope of hitting them, Paris realized, than to warn the Kirse at the launch site.

"More behind us," Renehan said sharply, and drew her own phaser. Paris copied her, thumbing the setting to high, and aimed at the triple points of light that swept up the road toward them. He fired twice himself, heard Renehan's shots echoing his own, and then the first drone was on them. It spat fire, the bolts scorching the pavement alongside the harvester, and Grayrose fired once, aiming directly for its nose. The drone wobbled, then recovered itself, curving up and away to position itself for another run.

"Get down," Paris called, and flung himself off the harvester. He hit the ground hard and rolled out of it, distantly aware that he would be bruised in the morning if he lived that long. The second drone dove after him, firing, and he dove for the shelter of a shallow ditch, flinging himself onto his back to fire back at it. His shots came nowhere near, but the machine swooped away, and he rolled to his knees, searching for the third drone. For a second, he couldn't see where it had gone, but then he saw it, coming low and fast along the line of the road, bolts scarring the pavement as it came. Renehan, crouched in the harvester's uncertain shelter, fired once, and then again. The drone rocked, but kept coming. Paris took careful aim, and fired when he thought the angles were right. For a second, he thought he'd missed, that the drone would keep coming, would destroy the harvester and the two people with it, but then the drone exploded in a ball of flame, and he covered his head instinctively against the rain of debris. It fell short, mercifully, and a moment later Renehan was in the ditch beside him.

"Nice shot," she said.

By the harvester Grayrose raised her phaser, fired twice, and a second drone exploded, its remains careening into a nearby field. The third drone turned to attack again, still wobbling from Grayrose's first shot, and Paris fired hastily. The drone seemed to stop in midair, as though it had run into a brick wall, and then exploded like the others.

"Come on," Grayrose called. "We have to get to the launch site."

Paris scrambled out of the ditch, feeling the bruises and wrenched muscles, and started back to the harvester, Renehan at his heels. In the distance, he saw a flash of light, and then the smoke and flare as yet another drone was destroyed, but one was still circling, bolts raining from its phasers, while the Kirse fired back ineffectually.

"Hurry," Grayrose cried again, and shoved the harvester into motion. Renehan swung herself aboard, and Paris was grateful for her hand as he dragged himself up after her. At least one of the Kirse had been hit, he thought, or at least he thought he saw a gray body huddled beneath the shuttle's wing, and he lifted his phaser.

Renehan caught his arm. "We're too far off. And if they're drones, you're not going to draw fire."

Paris nodded, knowing she was right, and braced himself against the harvester's head, leaning forward as though that could somehow urge the machine to go faster. Grayrose's wings were lifted, shivering with leashed tension, and glancing down Paris could see her fingers almost white on the controls, locking them at their maximums.

Then the final drone exploded, tumbling out of the sky to scatter its remains across the road. Grayrose swerved to avoid the smoking fragments, and pulled the harvester to a stop against the hillside, making sure not to block the cave mouth. Two of the Kirse lay sprawled on the ground beside the shuttle, unmistakably dead, and Paris winced at the sight.

"The shuttles?" Grayrose called, and the third Kirse rose from beside the bodies.

"Undamaged. But without copilots—"

Grayrose made a sound that had to be a curse. Paris, knowing he would regret it, said, "Are these like the one I was in?"

Grayrose looked at him curiously. "Similar enough."

Renehan was looking at him, too, but her expression was one of wry knowledge. "You're out of your mind, Tom."

"Got a better idea?"

"Not really." Renehan glanced over her shoulder, scanning the white sky for more drones, and Paris looked back at Grayrose.

"I know I can fly those shuttles. I saw you do it, I saw the controls, I can handle it."

Grayrose and the other Kirse exchanged looks, and then Grayrose said, "It's not pilots that are needed, but—copilots? Gunners and watchers."

"Watchers?" Renehan asked.

"The field, and the Andirrim counterscreens, they blind most of our sensors," the second Kirse answered. "It takes two to fly the shuttles, one actually to fly, the other to act as eyes. And of course for the guns."

"That's even easier," Paris said. "We can do it, Grayrose." Out of the corner of his eye, he saw

Renehan nod in agreement, and gave her a quick smile.

"It—you would probably be safer here." Grayrose sounded reluctant to make the point, and Paris shook his head.

"I don't know, the drones might come back. Or the gardeners, like you said." She was wavering, he knew, and he pressed on. "And you said before, your people needed all their shuttles in the air to fight the Andir-rim last time. We're wasting time."

The Kirse exchanged glances again, and then Grayrose nodded. "Very well. You will fly with me, and Renehan with Seafire."

"Great!" Paris exclaimed, and Renehan laughed.

"You're out of your mind, Paris."

"And you're not?"

Renehan waved the words away, and turned to follow Seafire. Grayrose said, "Quickly, then. Let's go."

They left the bodies where they had fallen—no time to bury them, certainly, and not much else that could be done, but it still gave Paris a strange feeling to step around the huddled corpses to climb into the shuttle's cockpit. The interior was configured differently from the shuttle he had flown in before; the pilot's post was much the same, but the passenger seats had been replaced by a domed bubble enclosing an acceleration couch set in a ring of control panels.

"Your place is there," Grayrose said, and Paris strapped himself into the couch. The dome was clear—a heads-up display, he thought, for an instant, and then realized that it was not a projection, but armorglass or something similar. "The red boards are guns, green is sensors, all kinds. You don't need to adjust any settings, just tell me if you get orange or red lights."

"All right." Paris swung the chair, and found he could easily reach the four control yokes for the guns. They looked like systems he'd handled during his brief tenure with the Maquis, right down to the spotting lights, and even the oddly offset trigger couldn't shake his confidence. He noticed a band of dark gray keys running along the edge of the consoles—no, he realized, not just dark gray, but every shade of gray, running from absolute black to pure white. He frowned, and Grayrose touched one of the medium-gray keys.

"This is the spotter's call," she said. "If I call for it, or if there's a ship in either the white or the black range—" She swept a hand over the keys, indicating the two sections lying side by side. "—press the keys to give me a heading. I have a repeater at my station and I'll see where the trouble is."

Paris nodded, and Grayrose turned back to her station, began fastening her own harness.

"Why in the black or white?" Paris called after her.

"That indicates something directly behind me," Grayrose answered, and Paris could have sworn there was laughter in her voice. "I want to know that."

"Makes sense to me," Paris murmured, but his words were drowned in the sudden howl of engines.

"Stand by to lift," Grayrose called, and Paris raised his voice to carry over the noise around them.

"Ready when you are."

"Lifting," Grayrose answered, and the shuttle bounded forward. Paris braced himself against the sudden lift, and saw the ground fall away behind him. The second shuttle rose as quickly, and he thought he caught a glimpse of Renehan in her dome before the armor darkened.

"The other shuttle's away," he called, and Grayrose lifted a hand.

"The main fight is in orbit," she said. "Only one Andirrim shuttle got through before the field went up, but they're trying to break through the defense system."

At least that was something familiar, Paris thought, swinging automatically to check his weapons. All the checklights glowed green—and at least the Kirse used that same convention, he thought—though he had no idea what each one meant. *And it doesn't really matter,* he added silently. *I know the main things— trigger and aiming mechanism—and that's all that counts.* A part of him, the part that always sat back and analyzed his own actions, wondered how much he was doing this to make up for his failures as Starfleet and as a Maquis, but he shoved that knowledge aside. All that was past; what mattered now was this fight.

"Orbit it is," he said aloud, and overhead saw the white of the field darken toward the edge of space.

B'Elanna Torres frowned thoughtfully at the Kirse schematic displayed on the main screen, then glanced again at the image on her tricorder screen. Even with Revek's help, it had taken some hours to translate the Kirse symbols into their Starfleet equivalents, and even now she wasn't completely sure of all the congruencies. Oh, the various components matched, and she understood what parts had to go where to preserve the integrity of the various circuits, but she still couldn't be certain if the Kirse tolerances would match her own. Revek had laughed when she mentioned that worry, and said that she had nothing to worry about as long as all she was worrying about was whether the Kirse components were as high powered as her own. He had added that the Kirse were more willing to take risks than anyone else he'd ever known, but she couldn't find that entirely comforting. *After all,* she thought, *I want this system to work, not blow up in their faces.* All around her, the machinery-covered walls hummed gently, a soft harmony that filled the air just at the edge of hearing.

She checked her tricorder again, then extended the little pink-gold wand that the Kirse used to adjust the screen models, and touched the series of tiny blue triangles that should correspond to the phase transition matrix. A string of text sprang to life, unfamiliar, curling Kirse letters, and she glanced at her tricorder for the translation. This was the transition matrix, all right, and she shifted her grip on the wand to tug them into their new position. A warning light flashed on the tricorder's screen—she was exceeding the recommended link distance by almost thirty centimeters—but she ignored it, and returned to the palette to select the dynamic modulator. She set it into the circuit between the phase transition matrix primary energizing coils, and painstakingly redrew the lines that represented the circuits. A red light flashed—unbalanced output, indicating an unstable phase-in—and she swore under her breath, and touched controls to run a virtual diagnostic. An instant later, the trouble spot fluoresced orange, pointing to a misconnected microfilament, and she swore again as she reached to correct it. If they were back in the Federation, there would be machines to do this sort of work, she thought. If they were back in the Federation, there would be no need to do this kind of work in the first place, mating Starfleet technology to unfamiliar, incompatible alien systems—

She shook her head, watching the warning lights fade. It wasn't true, of course, or at least it had never been true for Starfleet—or, for that matter, for her time with the Maquis. It sometimes seemed, in fact, as though she had spent most of her adult life trying to make two incompatible systems fit together.

"Tuvok to Torres."

The words were loud in the humming quiet of the engineering chamber, and Torres made a face, setting her wand carefully aside before she answered. The wand was on whenever fingers touched its surface, and didn't need to touch the screen to function; she had already discovered how easy it was to accidentally erase a component with a misplaced gesture.

"Torres here." She knew she sounded gruff, but didn't care. She had been supposed to be left alone for at least the next four hours, needed that time if she was to modify the Kirse schematics—

"Report at once to the citadel's control chamber," Tuvok said. "The planet is under attack."

"What?" Torres heard her voice rise.

"The planet is under attack from the Andirrim so-called trading fleet," Tuvok said. "The away team is to assemble in the control chamber."

"I don't know where that is," Torres snapped, frantically gathering her tricorder and the various datablocks she had brought with her. As far underground as this room was, it seemed unlikely that the Andirrim could reach it without destroying the Kirse, but there was no point in taking even remote chances.

"Silver-Hammer is on her way to join you," Tuvok answered. "She will escort you here."

"Right," Torres said. Even as she spoke, the door slid back, and Silver-Hammer's now-familiar figure stood silhouetted against the darkness. "She's here now, Tuvok. I'm on my way."

"I will expect you. Tuvok out."

And that, Torres thought, *is Vulcans for you.* She

stuffed the last cartridge into the case, and Silver-Hammer said, "Good, you're ready. They're still a good way out, but this won't be a safe place to be if they reach the citadel."

Torres glanced at the walls, noting increased lights and movement among the plates of machinery, and there was a new edge to the sound that filled the air. "Where are they?"

"I thought Tuvok said you'd been informed," Silver-Hammer said, startled, and Torres made a face. She could remember hearing Tuvok's voice half a dozen times through the long day—warning her that an Andirrim had entered the system, she remembered, and then that the Kirse had agreed to let them trade, but after than, nothing more. *Which either means that I wasn't paying attention—possible, but not likely—or things moved a lot faster than the captain expected.*

She said, "The last thing I heard was that the Andirrim were here to trade, and that Adamant was letting them land. What happened?"

Silver-Hammer made a face. "What one might expect. Instead of proceeding to the rendezvous, the shuttle dropped a drone cloud and is heading here." She glanced at the walls again, eyes moving rapidly as she read the patterns of motion. "And we should hurry."

"Right." Torres took a step toward the door, but Silver-Hammer lifted her hand.

"This way. It's safer should the drones reach us."

The Kirse transporter sounded, and a new door opened in the far wall, its upper edge barely a finger's width from the lowest copper-bronze coil of tubing. Torres eyed it warily as she passed through the arch, judging tolerances, and shook her head. *Entirely too close for comfort,* she thought, *but so far, at least, they don't seem to miss. Though I would hate to be there when they do.*

Another door opened in front of them, and beyond it a short flight of stairs rose to a wider hall. The light was brighter there, and more focused, emanating from crystal strips set into the ceiling. Torres squinted at them—the first actual lights she had seen since she'd entered the citadel—but looked away quickly, dazzled, unable to see any details against the brilliance. She expected to reach one of the courtyards soon, but instead Silver-Hammer led her along the corridor, following the bands of crystal until they reached a second, wider corridor. They turned into it, but before they had gone more than twenty meters, the lights began to flash. Torres glanced up, and Silver-Hammer caught her by the arm.

"Quick, this way." She tugged the Starfleet engineer toward an alcove set into the steel-gray walls. Torres let herself be drawn, and heard a distant drumming, matching the rhythm of the flashing lights.

"What is it?" she called, but Silver-Hammer didn't answer until she had dragged the other into the shelter of the alcove. The sound was louder now, not a single drum, but thousands, the noise of a thousand hand-drummers, all keeping the same beat. She started to lean forward, to peer out of the alcove, but the Kirse pulled her back.

"You mustn't," she shouted, her voice barely audible over the approaching roar.

"Why not?" Torres screamed back, and Silver-Hammer shook her head, mouthing something the other could no longer hear.

Torres put her hands over her ears, and saw Silver-Hammer do the same. And then the wave of sound broke over them, and the corridor in front of the alcove was suddenly jammed with running figures.

They were all identical, squat and gray, all carrying phaser rifles at port-arms against armored chests, and no one of them was taller than Torres's shoulder. They were like the *gwarhai* of childhood story, she thought, dazed by the flashing lights and the noise, or the dwarf-armies of human legend. Then the last rank of them was past, and the lights steadied to normal.

"What was that?" Torres asked, and had to clear her throat before she could speak aloud.

"The third line—third line of defense," Silver-Hammer answered. "Come on, we have to hurry now."

Torres followed obediently, but the image, the running dwarfs, stayed with her, and she asked, "Third line?"

"The first is the orbital system," Silver-Hammer answered, and lifted her hand to create another door. This one gave onto still more stairs, and she started down, lights fading on as she moved into the darkness. She motioned for Torres to step past her, and raised her hand to seal the wall again behind them. "The second is the fields—"

"The gas—pollen," Torres corrected herself. "And the pods and all the rest." *And I was right about them,* she added silently, though the thought wasn't as satisfying as it might have been under other circumstances.

"Just so." They had reached the bottom of the stairs, and stood in a narrow blue-walled well. Torres glanced back the way they'd came but could see no sign of the door. The transporter sounded again, and she followed Silver-Hammer through the arch into another, narrower corridor.

"The gardeners, too?" Torres asked, and Silver-Hammer gave her a sharp, almost startled glance.

"No, not them."

A door opened in the wall ahead of them—a real door, Torres thought, amazed by the sight, the first real door she'd seen since she entered the citadel. She closed her mouth, and stepped into what was obviously the Kirse command chamber. Massive viewscreens filled each of the eight walls, filling the air with a flicker of confused and contrasting shadows, and, looking back, Torres saw the door slide closed to become once again part of its image. Silver-Hammer had not followed, and she was startled by the depth of her disappointment. An octagonal console—no, she thought, it was bigger than a console, more like a kiosk, with its raised sides and the transparent umbrella that formed a domed roof—filled the center of the room, and Adamant stood in its center, long hands splayed on the control boards. Multicolored light played in the dome above his head, and now and then he glanced up at it, but Torres couldn't recognize any of the patterns. The rest of the away team, Tuvok, his lieutenant Karlock and the two technicians Quarante and Jenar, were standing in a tight knot at the nearest corner of the octagon, and Tuvok nodded to the engineer.

"Lieutenant Torres. We are now all accounted for."

"Yes," Torres answered vaguely, her eyes riveted on the screen behind him. In it, an ungainly shape, angular and graceless and brown as old iron, moved slowly toward the image source, forcefields distorting the air around it as they held the ugly craft ten meters or so above the surface of the golden road. To either side, trees bent and tossed as though caught in a hurricane, and the air outside the supporting forcefields was hazed with pollen or dust. Or smoke, she added, seeing something hit the forcefield with a puff of flame, but whatever it was, it didn't seem to have much effect on the oncoming craft.

"The Andirrim shuttle?" she asked, softly, and Karlock nodded.

"The automatic defenses don't seem to be working," he answered, as softly, but broke off at a reproving look from Tuvok.

"There is still the river."

Even as he spoke, the shuttle reached one of the aqueduct bridges—*if it isn't the one we crossed*, Torres thought, *it's virtually identical*. Out of the corner of her eye, she saw Adamant's hands convulse on some control, and water rose abruptly from the riverbed, forming itself into an impossible tidal wave. The shuttle reeled sideways, but its pilot seemed to have been expecting the attack, and turned it into a controlled roll that brought the shuttle up and out of the onslaught. The wave crashed onto the bridge, momentarily immersing it, and when it passed, there were great gaps in the pavement. The Andirrim shuttle aligned itself with the road, and came on.

Tuvok shook his head, and Torres heard Quarante sigh.

"Impressive flying."

Jenar looked at him warily. "Yeah, but I'd've hated to be inside it."

"Presumably they have internal gravity to prevent injury," Tuvok said. There was something in the Vulcan's tone that silenced further comment, and Torres looked at Adamant. The Kirse was looking up again, reading something from the dome above his head—monitoring the space battle? Torres wondered suddenly. The Andirrim fleet was still in orbit.

"What about *Voyager?*" she said, and ignored Tuvok's repressive frown. "Is the ship all right?"

"We have lost contact with *Voyager* as of the Andirrim attack," Tuvok answered, "due to the ion field in the upper atmosphere and the shields here. But we have reason to believe that *Voyager* is holding its own."

Against five ships, Torres thought, and then shook herself. First of all, *Voyager* wouldn't be fighting five ships at once, because at least some of the Andirrim would have to be dealing with the orbital stations. And, second, *Voyager*'s weaponry had been consistently superior to anything they'd seen in the Delta Quadrant—it was demonstrably more powerful than the Kazon-Ogla's, and the Kazon-Ogla dominated the Andirrim. The odds were— She stopped then, and shook her head. No matter what she did, she couldn't quite convince herself that those odds were in *Voyager*'s favor.

Janeway stared at the main tactical display, relegating the constant murmur of command and confirmation to the back of her mind at least until someone addressed her directly. In the main screen, the Andirrim ships circled against the planet's face, the orbital stations a net of white light, brighter light rippling across it as the powerful cannons fired. The secondary display repeated the image in schema, with *Voyager*'s symbol at its center, and she frowned at the sight of one of the Andirrim ships turning toward them.

"Ship two firing," Kim announced, his voice unnaturally calm. "Shields at maximum."

"Returning fire," Pao added, from the security station, and a moment later *Voyager* shuddered under the impact.

"No damage," Kim said. "Shields still at ninety-eight percent."

"Their phasers are about eighty-five percent of ours," Chakotay said, quietly, "but that doesn't mean they can't hurt us. Or that it's necessarily their maximum strength."

Janeway nodded. So far, the Andirrim ships had concentrated on the defense barrier, firing at *Voyager* only sporadically, but any offense action from *Voyager* was likely to change that—and she wasn't sure the ship could handle five enemies at once. "Keep us out of engagement, Mr. Chakotay. This isn't our fight—"

"Captain!" Kim called. "The Andirrim have disabled one, no, two of the satellites."

"Have they breached the barrier?" Janeway asked. Two of the pale dots had vanished from the tactical display; she could see others moving, the pattern shifting to compensate for the missing pieces, but couldn't tell if the shift would be adequate.

"Not yet," Kim answered. "But it's putting a serious strain on the system."

"Right." Janeway studied the screen a final time, noting the positions of the Andirrim ships, and smiled at Chakotay. "It wasn't our fight, I should say. Take us in, Mr. Chakotay. We have our away teams to protect."

"Aye, Captain." There was a grim pleasure in Chakotay's voice. He touched the controls, and the image in the main screen swung wildly for an instant as *Voyager* moved into the attack.

"Engage the flagship if you can," Janeway said. "Stand by phasers, Mr. Pao."

"Standing by. Ready to fire."

In the screen, the nearest ship—ship four, in their hasty numbering—had seen their move, and was turning to face the new attack. Janeway smiled to herself, imagining the sudden burst of communication on board the Andirrim ships, and nodded to Pao. "Fire when ready, Mr. Pao."

Pao's hands moved quickly across her console, setting the final parameters, and in the screen Janeway saw the target codes shift and re-form. "Firing. Hits on their screens, but the shields are holding."

"Ship four is firing," Kim said, and Janeway saw the bolt of light flare on the screen, rapidly blanking the rest of the image. She braced herself, and the ship shuddered under its impact.

"No damage," Kim said, "but engineering reports that we're starting to see energy fluctuations."

"What's the range?" Janeway asked.

"Point-zero-two to point-one megajoules."

Janeway frowned. It was a large fluctuation, but at the lowest end of the spectrum. "We can live with that," she said. "Let me know if it reaches point-three."

Light flared in the main viewscreen, flat flashes bracketing the Andirrim flagship, but when the image cleared Janeway could see no damage on the rough surface.

"No hits," Pao reported. "Their screens absorbed the impact."

"Captain," Kim said. "Ship two is moving to engage us."

Janeway could see the movement for herself now, doubly reflected in the main viewscreen and in the tactical display beneath it, and blinked as phaser light flared from the newcomer as well. *Voyager* rocked under the doubled blast, and she heard Pao give a smothered exclamation.

"They're targeting the same spot on our shields, or at least they're trying to."

Not bad tactics, Janeway acknowledged silently, still

staring at the patterns on the screen, *given that their phasers are weaker than ours, but ineffective—at least as long as our shields hold.*

"Returning fire," Pao went on, "but their shields are still holding."

"Engineering reports that the fluctuation is between point-one-nine-eight and point-two-seven-nine," Kim said. "A spike reached three, but they've got it back down again."

"Keep us in position," Janeway said. "And keep firing, Mr. Pao."

"Aye, Captain," Pao answered. "Target?"

Janeway studied the tactical display. The Andirrim flagship and two of its fellows were still concentrating on the orbital stations, and under their onslaught four more of the dots that represented the satellites were flashing red, warning of shields stressed almost to failure. Even as she watched, another one winked out, and this time the satellites did not move to compensate. "Concentrate on the flagship," she ordered. "Treat the others as secondary targets. Shield status, Mr. Kim?"

Even as she spoke, the ship rocked again under Andirrim fire. Kim said, "Holding. But we're down to ninety-five percent on the forward screens, and engineering says we're going to lose more if we're not careful."

"Captain," Chakotay said. "Look!"

"Multiple launches from the surface," Pao reported, in almost the same instant, and in the screen the planet's disk was dotted with light, a dozen, maybe more, pinpoints rising toward orbit. "Tracking," Pao went on, her voice unnaturally calm. "Captain, they're definitely Kirse ships, and they seem to be heading to the satellites."

Before Janeway could answer, another one of the

orbital stations flashed red and vanished from the screen. The gap it left was obvious, a breach in the defense screen, and the Andirrim flagship swung toward it, maneuver engines flaring without sound. If it got inside the screen, Janeway realized, it could pick off still more stations, open a gap in the screen that the entire fleet could enter, and then they could turn on the surface with impunity.

"Target the flagship, Mr. Pao," she snapped. "Chakotay, see if you can get between it and the screen."

"Firing phasers," Pao answered, and the ship rocked again from a glancing hit. The other ships were closing in, swinging around to get behind *Voyager*, blocking their best retreat, but Janeway ignored them, her attention focused on the flagship.

"Keep firing," she ordered. The shuttles were still rising, but none of them were close enough yet to support *Voyager*'s effort; the rest of the Andirrim ships were still closing, and *Voyager* rocked under a concerted salvo, throwing her against the side of her chair. Their own phaser fire sparked and flared, its energies absorbed or repulsed by the flagship's shields, but the Andirrim ship bored on, heading for the gap in the screen. "Keep firing, damn it!"

"Shields down to eighty percent," Kim reported, and the ship lurched again. "Seventy-three percent. And the power fluctuations have steadied but mean stress is approaching point-nine."

Janeway didn't answer, all her attention focused on the flagship. If they could force it to turn, force it to return fire, break off from the barrier, then there was a good chance the shuttles would reach orbit in time to reinforce the stations, plugging the gap in the system. The phasers were ineffective, so far, but the combination of phaser fire and the explosion of a photon torpedo close at hand might well breach the shield. *Classic tactics,* she thought, *but can I spare the torpedo?*

"Rear shields down to sixty percent," Kim announced, "and falling rapidly. Captain, they're not going to stand much more."

Janeway smiled in spite of herself. *Whether or not I can afford the torpedo,* she thought, *I certainly can't afford to put it off any longer.* "Mr. Pao, prepare a photon torpedo."

"Aye, Captain," Pao answered, automatically, and Janeway saw Chakotay glance at her, frowning.

"Target the flagship," Janeway went on. "Keep the phasers on them. I want their shields stressed when the torpedo strikes."

She saw Chakotay's frown vanish, to be replaced by a smile of comprehension, and Pao answered again, "Aye, Captain. Torpedo ready."

"Fire," Janeway said, and the ship shuddered slightly with the release.

"Rear shields still dropping, Captain," Kim said. "They're not going to last much longer."

"Hold our position," Janeway answered. They had to remain here, drawing the Andirrim ships' attention as well as their fire, just a little longer, just long enough to keep them from gaining a position where they could do real damage to the shuttles.

"Torpedo running," Pao said. "Twelve seconds to impact."

Voyager staggered again, and Janeway heard a duty technician swear as he was flung against his console.

"Rear shields are down to twenty percent," Kim said. "The next hit'll breach them for sure."

"Captain," Chakotay began, and Janeway silenced him with a look.

"Just a little longer," she said, and didn't know if

she was talking to him or to the ship. And then fire bloomed in the viewscreen, a silent and momentary sun that briefly hid the Andirrim flagship.

"Direct hit!" Pao cried. "Shields are down—no, they've got them up again, but they're definitely at lower strength. And the Kirse shuttles have achieved orbit, they're coming after them."

In the tactical display, Janeway could see the points of light clustering, several of the shuttles moving into the places of the missing stations, the rest coming on toward the flagship, falling into a classic wedge formation.

"Captain," Kim said. "Transmission from the shuttle."

"Put it through," Janeway answered, and the speaker crackled to life, the voice distorted by the energy residue of the fighting.

"Paris to *Voyager*. Come in, *Voyager*."

"*Voyager* here," Janeway said, and allowed herself another smile. Trust Paris to find a way to put himself into the thick of things, for all his pretense of world-weariness.

"Nice shooting, Captain, but I suggest *Voyager* might be more effective elsewhere. Not to mention safer."

Cheeky bastard, Janeway thought. She said, "The thought had crossed my mind, Mr. Paris, but do you think you're up to replacing us?"

"There're a lot more of us," Paris answered, and this time Janeway laughed.

"Thank you, Mr. Paris. Mr. Chakotay, evasive action. Put some distance between us and the Andirrim, then let's see what more we can do."

"Aye, Captain," Chakotay answered, and the image in the viewscreen swung sharply as the ship heeled out of the plane of its orbit. Janeway allowed herself a sigh of relief that she knew was echoed throughout the ship. As long as they had room to maneuver, *Voyager* was in no danger; she just wished she could say as much for Paris and the rest of the Kirse shuttles.

Paris was still grinning as he released his communicator, and glanced again at the display flickering against the underside of his armored dome. The other shuttles—at least two dozen of them, now, closing in from all across the planet—showed as pink wedges, bright against the starscape and the face of the planet. The Andirrim ships were larger, electric blue rectangles—*but then*, he thought, *I hardly need the display to see them.* He could see them well enough with his own eyes, the rusty-looking rhomboids outlined by the flare of phaser fire, their own and *Voyager*'s, and now the first of the shuttles was moving to engage as well. *Voyager* was moving away, though, breaking free of the close contact to gain clear space where Janeway could use its superior size and maneuverability to advantage, and he turned his attention to the shapes around him. Two—no, he corrected himself, checking the positions again, three of the shuttles had moved to block the gaps in the barrier left by the destruction of the satellites, and a fourth was rising to join them. The rest of the shuttles were heading for the Andirrim craft, but so far their phaser fire sparked harmlessly from the Andirrim shields.

"What's our next move?" he called, not taking his eyes from the displays.

"What your captain did," Grayrose answered. "We have torpedoes, but we must weaken the shields first. Though she has damaged the flagship for us."

Paris nodded, seeing the way the Andirrim craft seemed to lurch against the starscape. The shuttles' fire was concentrated on the lower stern, brighter along the edges, the flare-back paling where the shields were weaker. Then new lights sparked in the sensor display, dots as blue as the Andirrim ships, and an instant later a silver of metal caught the reflected light of a phaser blast, outlining a needle-shaped orbiter against the starscape. "Grayrose! The Andirrim have launched fighters of their own."

"To be expected," the Kirse answered, but Paris thought her voice was grim. "I'm increasing shields."

An indicator moved on one of the circular boards, a green column sliding up to meet a yellow line. "You're on a yellow line," Paris reported, and wished he knew more about the Kirse systems. Most of it he could guess from Federation analogues, but their color use went against human convention.

"At maximum, then," Grayrose said.

"Right," Paris swung in his chair, scanning the display and the stars beyond it, and then grabbed for the weapon's controller as the first pair of Andirrim fighters swung toward them. With his free hand, he stabbed the tracking indicator keys—another Kirse system that had no human analogue—and then thumbed the tracking device to its highest setting. The bright orange crosshairs popped onto the screen, and he swung the assemblage, trying to line them up on the nearest blue dot. For an instant he had it, and depressed the firing stud, but the Andirrim slipped sideways, turning on its leading edge, and the bolt barely clipped the edge of its screen. He swore under his breath, and heard a whistling trill from somewhere in Grayrose's section of the ship.

"We are to go after the main—the flagship," Grayrose called. "Hold off the fighters if you can, but our main goal is the big ships."

"Right," Paris answered, and hastily checked his

boards again. Luckily, the torpedo release was close to the main phaser controls, and easily recognized. "Arming torpedoes," he said, and shoved each switch forward.

A chime sounded, and a musical phrase echoed from the speakers. "Torpedoes armed," Grayrose translated.

Paris nodded, scanning the dome, and hit the tracking keys again as another pair of fighters swept into range. The shuttle tipped sideways, and he felt the seat under him shudder at the near-miss, but concentrated on the pattern of the blue dots all around him. He fired once, then a second time, and this time saw the Andirrim fighter shatter to flame and debris. Grayrose gave a crowing call, pure and unmistakable delight, and another pink wedge swept past in the dome, followed an instant later by the bright shape of a Kirse shuttle. For an instant, he thought he saw Renehan crouched beneath the dome, but couldn't be sure.

A blue light flared in the corner of his eye, and he swung to face it, automatically bringing the weapon to bear. An Andirrim fighter, a dark diamond against the stars, filled the dome, the blue dot and the ranging crosshairs centered together on its shape, and he fired by instinct, holding the stud down for a long three seconds. Light flared, and then vanished as the Andirrim shields failed, and then the fighter exploded in a great cloud of flame. The shuttle shivered as bits of debris pelted the shields, and then they were out of its range, and Paris swung to confront the next fighter. He fired again, couldn't seem to hold it in his sights, but the fighter swooped away, vanishing in the shadow of one of the Andirrim main ships. Paris trained his weapon on it experimentally, and Grayrose called, "No."

Paris risked a glance at her, and saw her gesture, pointing to another shape in her screen.

"That one, the flagship. We're going for it."

"Right," Paris answered, and the shuttle seemed to fall away beneath him. Fire streaked overhead, dazzling him in the fractional instant before the dome darkened to compensate, and then they were past the Andirrim craft. To his surprise, there were no more blasts, and he swung his couch to look back along their path, to see it and the other Andirrim ships caught in a cloud of lights. Kirse shuttles and Andirrim fighters wove a net around each other and the Andirrim ships, fully engaged with each other; ahead, there was only the flagship and a pair of fighters.

"Good odds," he called, but Grayrose said nothing, her hands moving constantly on the banked controls.

The flagship fired, light blossoming beneath the point of its upper edge, but Grayrose swung the shuttle easily aside, and the bolt passed harmlessly. She evaded the next two with equal ease, but the third came close enough for the field corona to strike the shuttle's shields, and yellow lights flared across Paris's boards. Most of them flickered out again almost at once, but two remained, flashing slow but steady beneath the section of the controls that Grayrose had told him was reserved for the main computer.

"Trouble," he called, and Grayrose answered instantly.

"I see it. Nothing I can't handle."

I hope so, Paris thought, and shoved the words aside as the starscape spun outside the dome and suddenly they were alongside the flagship, close enough to see the protrusions and alien installations that covered its dulled surface. The firing stopped—either they were out of range, inside the system's limits, Paris thought, or they were clearing the way for their fighters. Or both. He spun his couch again, scanning the stars and the flagship's side, and two blue dots popped into sight, spinning down over the flagship's upper edge. He slapped the tracking keys, felt the shuttle turn in response, and brought the phasers to bear, firing as the dots crossed the crosshairs. His first shot missed, and the shuttle rocked as the fighters' phasers slammed into the shields. They held, but one of the yellow lights began to flash more quickly.

"That one," Grayrose called. "That light. When it steadies, we have no more shields."

"Great," Paris said, and fired again. He hit the second fighter head-on, but it came on through the cloud of fire, possibly damaged, but still firing.

"I'm taking us to the stern," Grayrose went on. "The flagship's shields are weaker there—see."

Paris fired yet again, more to keep the fighters at bay than in any real hope of hitting them, and glanced sideways to see a patch of pale yellow light superimposed on the flagship's flank. It pulsed with the same ominous beat as the light on his own console, and Paris instantly swung the control yoke to fire at it. The light seemed to strengthen, but warning chimes sounded from behind him, and he swung back to fire wildly at the diving fighters. He missed, but spoiled their aim, and the shuttle rocked only from the impact of the bolt corona. He fired again, more carefully, as the second fighter dove past, and had the satisfaction of seeing something fly loose from its warty surface. It disappeared behind the flagship, but an instant later its symbol vanished from his display.

"Concentrate on the flagship," Grayrose cried. "We can stand the fighter. Break the shield and launch the torpedo."

Obediently, Paris swung his controls, centering the crosshairs on the weakened patch on the Andirrim's shields. He fired, holding the stud down for what seemed an interminable time, and felt the shuttle rock under him. The yellow light on his board was flashing faster now, but the patch in the screen was throbbing even harder, and he kept the phasers on it, firing steadily. The yellow light strengthened, became almost solid, and the shuttle bucked again. Grayrose gave an exclamation in her own language, sounding at once angry and afraid, and Paris triggered the torpedoes. He saw them drop away from the ship, twin points of light brilliant as diamonds against the flagship's hull, and then the shuttle seemed to stagger in its tracks. The yellow light flared red for an instant, and Paris swung his couch to face the final Andirrim fighter. It was at point-blank range, clearly visible through the dome, and he fired more by instinct than plan. The fighter seemed to shudder, its image distorted for a fraction of a second by the failing shield, and then the entire ship vanished in a ball of flame. Paris covered his head, an unstoppable, reflex action, as debris bombarded the shuttle, chunks of flaming metal soaring past the dome. A second explosion rocked the shuttle, and he swung back to see the flagship falling away, trailing a debris cloud of its own. He caught a brief glimpse of a hole in the side hull, and then the shuttle was falling away, spiraling down toward the planet.

"Grayrose! We did it, Grayrose!"

There was no answer, and Paris frowned, risked a glance over his shoulder. The Kirse pilot hung slumped against her pillar, hands limp on the controls. Even as he watched, one hand slipped free, to dangle at her side. Paris swore under his breath, and glanced a final time at his display. The Andirrim were definitely breaking off the engagement, the fighters pulling free of the tangled fight, the bigger ships moving away under power, and Paris wrenched himself out of his harness.

"Grayrose?" Lights were flashing yellow all over the pilot's boards, but he ignored them, crouched at the Kirse's side. Her eyes were closed, the great wings drooping, uncontrolled, but there was no sign of external injury. He tore frantically at the straps that held her against the post, got them all loose at last, and laid her gently on the deck, turning her cautiously to check for injury. There was still no sign of one, but a thick cable trailed from a socket at the base of her spine. He touched it, unable quite to believe what he was seeing, and snatched his hand away from the too-warm casing. She had been plugged into the shuttle's system, part of the ship—and that, he thought, was probably what had hurt her. Hastily, he ripped up a strip of the deck covering, used it to protect his hand as he tugged the cable out of her back. He caught a quick glimpse of a socket, blackened metal and scorched ceramic, but a flap of skin rolled smoothly down over it, like an eye closing. He swallowed hard, tasting bile, and reached for her neck, feeling for what would be a pulse point on a human. He thought he felt something, the sluggish beat of blood, and slapped his communicator.

"Paris to *Voyager*. For God's sake, come in, *Voyager.*"

There was an instant's pause that seemed to last an eternity, and then Janeway's voice answered. *"Voyager* here, Mr. Paris."

Paris swallowed a sob, bending close to Grayrose's unresponsive body. "Medical emergency. Grayrose is hurt, badly hurt, she needs help—"

"Beaming you directly to sickbay," Janeway interrupted, her voice firm. "Are you injured, Mr. Paris?"

"No—"

The shuttle dissolved in midword, and Paris found himself crouching on the sickbay floor, Grayrose still in his arms. Kes bent over him, the holographic doctor directly behind him.

"Get her up on the table," the doctor ordered. "Quickly now."

Paris swallowed again, fighting tears and his own disorientation, and disentangled himself from the Kirse's body. He lifted her, awkwardly, Grayrose all dangling limbs and wings, and laid her as gently as he could on the nearest diagnostic table. The holographic doctor moved in, and Kes took Paris's arm, urging him away. For an instant, he resisted, wanting to see, to help, simply to be there, but then common sense reasserted itself, and he let himself be drawn into the next room. Through the glass, he could see the doctor working, capable, unreal hands busy on Grayrose's sprawled form, but then the hologram straightened, shaking his head.

"No—" Paris bit off the word as though not saying it, not acknowledging what he had seen, could keep it from being true, but the doctor came inexorably on.

"I'm sorry." The voice was tinny through the speakers. "There's nothing I can do."

"No," Paris said again, but even he could hear the admission in his voice. Kes touched his arm again, soft, wordless sympathy, but he pulled away, pressing his hand against the wall to keep himself from hitting something. *Not Grayrose,* he thought, *not her, I liked her, she was a friend, and I don't have enough friends to be able to lose any of them—*

"Janeway to sickbay." The voice came from the intercom next to his hand, but Paris ignored it, trying to force back the tears. "Mr. Paris, report."

The crack of command reached him at last, and he straightened, not caring if Kes or anyone saw him weep. "Paris here, Captain. Grayrose is dead."

"The Kirse?" Janeway's voice softened. "I'm sorry, Mr. Paris. For what it's worth, she didn't die in vain. The Andirrim are on their way out of the system. We've picked up Renehan, and are reestablishing contact with the other away team."

For what it's worth. Paris's mouth twisted in a bitter grimace, but training and the cold logic he'd learned with the Maquis and in prison reasserted itself. It wasn't worth anything, was no consolation, but you had to pretend it was, or you'd go mad yourself. He took a deep breath, and was remotely proud that his voice was steady as he answered. "Glad to hear it, Captain." He hesitated, then added, "Unless you need me, I'd like to stay here a little longer."

There was a little pause before Janeway answered, and when she spoke, her voice matched his own. "Go ahead, Mr. Paris. We'll let you know if you're needed. Janeway out."

Paris turned away from the intercom, went to stand by the window, watching the holographic doctor spreading a bodysheet over Grayrose. Her wings protruded above the edges, and Paris looked away. She had done her duty; he only hoped it would have been a consolation to her.

CHAPTER
9

TORRES LOOKED FROM WALLSCREEN TO WALLSCREEN, dizzied by the enormous, rapidly changing images in their depths. The fact that they were silent only added to the disorientation—or maybe, she thought, fighting for some sense of perspective, maybe it would be worse if the sound were in proportion to the picture. In the center of his console, Adamant moved fluidly from one set of controls to the next, now letting his hands play over rows of unseen controls, now glancing up at the lights that flickered in the transparent dome above his head, now fixing all his attention on something that only he understood in one of the massive screens. The rest of the away team stood close together, as though they were afraid of blocking Adamant's view of the huge screens, but the Kirse ignored them, all his attention devoted to the pattern he was weaving at his controls. Only Tuvok seemed able to follow that dance, or at least, Torres thought, he made a better show of it than any of the others.

She turned away from the central consoles, and stared at the screens, trying to make sense of the massive images. On one side of the room, behind Adamant, the screens were empty except for the trees and shrubs of the elaborate gardens, and the heads of a few of the dwarf-soldiers, crouching behind a low wall. On the other, the Andirrim shuttle moved up the road toward the citadel, surrounded by a cloud of drones, its own and the Kirse's tangled in a swirling mass, while more of the dwarf-soldiers sniped at it from the uncertain shelter of the gardens. The gardeners seemed to have fled, but even as she watched one, less metallic than the rest, leaped from behind a bush to grapple with one of the dwarfs. A second dwarf-soldier swung around, phaser leveled, and blasted the creature, but another sprang from hiding, and the soldiers drew into a tight knot, standing back to back against the gardeners. Behind them, the shuttle slid ponderously past.

Torres opened her mouth to say something, warn Adamant, anything, but before she could speak, the Kirse leader seemed to notice the fighting, and touched a control. Behind the struggling fighters, first one tree and then another bent sideways, limbs twisting around themselves to reveal the bright red fruit cradled in the cuplike caps at the end of each branch. Then the branches snapped forward, flinging the fruit in a ragged volley. They struck among the gardeners, releasing a cloud of glittering dust, and the creatures collapsed. So did two of the dwarf-soldiers, but the rest of them had hands cupped over their mouths and noses—presumably holding masks of some kind, Torres thought—and they dragged their fellows out of danger.

The image changed then, the screen refocusing on the Andirrim shuttle. It had gained another hundred meters, Torres realized, and was in parts of the garden than she herself had traversed on first landing. Even as she thought that, she saw more of the trees convulse, and release another volley of fruit. Some of them fell short, smashing into paving and ground with brief puffs of smoke, but most of them struck the shuttle's shields, releasing gouts of flame. The explosions were triggered by contact with the shield, Torres guessed, and shook her head again, admiring the Kirse ingenuity. The shuttle lifted slightly, rising out of range, but kept on. The drones fell away slightly, caught off balance by the changing altitude, and a hatch opened on the back of the shuttle.

"Look out," Torres called, and pointed. Out of the corner of her eye, she saw Adamant spin to face this new threat, but her attention was focused on the smaller craft rising from the shuttle's back.

"Attack squad," Adamant said, his voice grim.

The smaller ship—a brighter, more streamlined version of the larger shuttle—lifted away from its parent, jets blazing blue-white as it adjusted its course. Another group of trees flung their fruit at it, but they fell short, crashing harmlessly on the paving in front of the larger shuttle.

"Where the hell is it going?" Jenar muttered, and Torres was suddenly certain she knew.

"The citadel," she answered. "And they're coming in on the back side, where there aren't so many *Gwarhai*—sorry, soldiers."

She saw Tuvok look at her, his frown fading to agreement, and Adamant looked up from his controls. "I agree, that's where they're heading."

"Reinforcements," Torres snapped. "You have to get reinforcements in there."

"I am at my limit," Adamant answered, and for the first time since the attack began he sounded strained. "There are no more."

No more. Torres stared at him for a moment, then swung to face the screen that showed the undefended wall. There were only a few dozen of the dwarf-soldiers; even if there were twice as many out of range of the cameras, she thought, they would never be able to hold off a determined attack, especially not from those positions. "How many Andirrim are there likely to be in the little ship?" she demanded, and to her surprise it was Tuvok who answered.

"A craft that size should be capable of carrying at least a hundred Andirrim, possibly half again as many if they accept stressed systems."

"A hundred and fifty," Torres repeated, and shook herself. "You'll never hold them there," she said, to Adamant. "You have to pull back, take them inside the citadel."

"No!" Adamant's eyes widened with horror, but then he had himself under control, glancing from his controls to the screens and back again.

"There's no other way you can stop them," Torres said, and Tuvok nodded.

"I concur, Adamant. Given the transporter system within the citadel, you stand a good chance of stopping them inside the walls, but outside—"

He stopped as Adamant nodded. "Very well." The Kirse reached for his controls again, but Torres interrupted.

"Let me—us—go with them. I've been in fighting like this before, many times."

"Very well," Adamant said again. "I will—Silver-Hammer will go with you to work the transporter."

Torres nodded, and turned toward the door, but Tuvok caught her shoulder.

"This is unwise. The chief engineer should not put herself at risk. I will go."

"I'm already at risk—more at risk if we don't help," Torres answered. "And I think we should all come. The more of us, the safer for all of us." *Not to mention,* she added silently, *more people to take over if something should happen to one of us.*

Out of the corner of her eye, she saw Jenar nod, as though he'd read her thought, and Quarante said, "Yes."

Tuvok blinked, the closest thing Torres had seen to an admission of error. "Very well."

Silver-Hammer was waiting outside the door as though she hadn't moved since she'd escorted Torres to the control room. She led them through a shifting maze of corridors, through doors that appeared and disappeared at her command, and finally up a twisting stairway that opened into a long, low-ceilinged gallery. She frowned thoughtfully at the walls, and then adjusted the silver disk in her palm. The transporter sounded, and kept sounding, and then half a dozen doors appeared in the walls. One led outside, clouded sunlight spilling across the stone floor. It opened into one of the enclosed plazas, Torres realized, peering cautiously past the shiny new edge. Then the transporter sounded again, and she turned back to find the room turned into a maze, crossed and recrossed by a dozen half-walls that funneled anyone entering the room toward a central door.

"I've recalled the guardians," Silver-Hammer said. "And there are no other doors into the citadel now."

"Right." Torres stepped away from the door as the first of the dwarf-soldiers filed inside and began taking up positions behind the low walls. She could hear a low humming, growing louder—probably the

Andirrim attack craft, she knew, but put the thought aside.

"Tuvok, if you and Quarante take the last wall, the one to the left of the center door, Jenar and I can take the one on the right."

Tuvok turned to survey the room, and Torres bit down hard on her own impatience. The hum was getting even louder, the Andirrim coming closer, this was no time to delay—

"Yes," Tuvok said. "From that position, we have a clear field of fire, and can use our phasers to advantage."

"They're here!" Silver-Hammer called, from the main entrance, and her words were punctuated by the whine of phaser fire and then the roar of landing jets. The sunlight vanished, and Torres dove for the protection of the wall. Jenar was there ahead of her, his face tense, but his hands were steady as he adjusted his phaser. Silver-Hammer ducked behind another wall, wedging herself in with several of the guardians, and Torres held her breath, waiting.

The Andirrim were expecting trouble, that much was clear. The air suddenly filled with a hail of phaser fire, so bright that Torres and the others could only duck behind their walls, eyes closed, hands to their ears. It stopped as abruptly as it had begun, and Torres forced her head up, blinking hard, to see the first Andirrim forcing their way into the chamber. She fired, and the first row of guardians fired with her, spearing the leading Andirrim with bolts of light. The second Andirrim fell as well, but more came on, and she lost track of how many shots she had fired as the Andirrim bodies began to pile up. She heard Jenar swearing beside her, glanced sideways to see him firing into the oncoming troops, face screwed up with distaste.

"Why the hell don't they run?"

Torres shook her head, fired again, and saw another Andirrim fall while another took shelter behind the row of bodies. And then, as abruptly as the attack had begun, the Andirrim faltered and fell back, ducking back out the door. The first row of guardians started after them, vaulting the bodies, but the hum of engines sounded, and the shadow abruptly vanished from the doorway.

"They're running," Silver-Hammer cried, and rose from her place behind a middle wall. "They've quit the attack."

"Thank God," Jenar said, and holstered his phaser. Torres copied him, shaking her head, and stepped cautiously from behind the protective wall. This hadn't been much of a fight—*a slaughter, really,* she thought, *and I find it hollow to think just that it wasn't mine. The Andirrim commander must be crazy, to have sent them in like this.*

The guardians were busy with the Andirrim bodies, turning them over one by one—all dead, she saw, with some relief, and then one of the Kirse sledges, a dozen paired arms on a low-slung, multiwheeled body, appeared in the nearest doorway. The guardians began to load bodies onto it, stacking them like wood, and she glanced at Silver-Hammer.

"For burial?"

The Kirse nodded. "We can't use them anymore."

Torres blinked, but before she could question Silver-Hammer any further, her communicator beeped.

"Janeway to away team. Report your status."

"Tuvok here," the Vulcan answered, and Torres moved to rejoin him. "We are all safe and accounted for."

"Excellent," Janeway said, and Torres could hear

real relief in her voice. "The ion shield is dropping. The transporter chief says she can beam you up in twelve minutes." There was a pause. "Correction. She can beam you up now, if you can come outside the citadel's walls."

Torres looked at Silver-Hammer, who nodded. "The Andirrim are gone. The courtyard should be safe now."

Tuvok nodded. "Captain, we are going into a courtyard. Tuvok out."

Torres followed him toward the door, averting her eyes from the diminishing pile of bodies. She heard Quarante give a soft hiss of distaste, and Jenar swore again under his breath as he passed the hardworking guardians. Then they were out in the watery sunlight, and Torres heard Silver-Hammer give a soft, mournful cry as she stooped to touch one of the deep gouges in the pavement where the attack craft's landing skids had scored the stone. There were burn marks as well, and Silver-Hammer touched them, too, her beautiful face stricken.

"How," Jenar said, "how can you worry about that when there are all those dead people—?"

Silver-Hammer blinked up at him, her expression genuinely puzzled. "This injury," she began, but her words were cut off by a sudden crack of light that filled the sky.

Torres winced, thinking of radiation, of a dozen other, nasty possibilities, and Tuvok touched his communicator. "Tuvok to *Voyager*—"

"The defense satellites have destroyed the Andirrim shuttle," Janeway answered, flatly. "That's what that was, Mr. Tuvok."

"Understood," Tuvok said. "*Voyager,* four to beam up."

* * *

Janeway stared at the officers gathered once again in the ready room, well aware of the grief imperfectly concealed behind Paris's smile and the concerned look Kim gave him when he thought no one was looking. Tuvok's face was as impassive as ever—no surprise there, she thought—but there was something in Torres's expression that made the captain uneasy. *Something seems to have happened on the surface,* she thought, and deliberately drew herself up to her full height. The murmured conversations stopped as though she had spoken, and all eyes turned to her.

First things first, she thought, and said, "Mr. Chakotay. The ship's status, if you please?"

Chakotay glanced at the datapadd that lay in front of him. "We're in good shape, actually, Captain. We suffered only minor damage, mostly to outboard sensor arrays, all of which has been reported to engineering. The preliminary estimate says it should be repaired in under eight hours."

"I haven't had a chance to give the situation more than a cursory look," Torres said. "We may be able to better that time."

She sounded subdued, Janeway thought, but decided not to pursue the matter just yet. "Injuries?"

"Only minor ones," Chakotay answered, and in the viewscreen the holographic doctor cleared his throat. It was a studied sound, almost theatrical, and Janeway was quite certain that the doctor had carefully studied the physiological mechanisms involved before adding the sound to his repertoire.

"Mostly bruises, and a broken ankle from falling in a Jeffries tube," he said. "However, there is something else that has come to my attention. In examining the body of the Kirse Lieutenant Paris brought aboard—"

"Grayrose," Paris said, softly.

"—I've found a number of anomalies," the doctor finished, and Torres stirred again.

"They use a lot of implanted technology," she began, and the doctor shook his head.

"No—well, of course, yes, they do, I found several such implants, including the primary which certainly contributed to her death."

Paris winced at that, but the doctor went on as though he didn't see the reaction.

"That was a direct link to the shuttle's controls, by the way, which seems to have permitted her to use her natural reflexes as a flyer to control the shuttle. I suspect that a direct hit on the ship created a feedback current that overrode any safeties in the implant and—in essence—electrocuted her. Of course, I can't tell more certainly without performing an autopsy."

"Which we don't want to do without the Kirse's permission," Janeway said. She looked at Chakotay. "I know you informed Adamant that we had the body aboard. Has there been a response?"

The first officer shook his head. "Not yet, Captain."

"I'm well aware that I can't do an autopsy without the captain's authorization," the doctor said. "However, I can and did take tissue samples—purely for therapeutic purposes, of course, hoping that I could do something for her. But when I analyzed them, I got this extremely interesting result."

The viewscreen split, the doctor's face shifting to the side, and a complicated pattern, bright colored symbols against black, filled the rest of the screen. It looked like a DNA sample, Janeway thought, but there were too many red bits, too many similar shapes and colors, for it to be viable.

Across the table, Paris stirred again, brows drawing down into a frown, and Kim tilted his head to one side. "Is that a DNA pattern?" he asked, and only then seemed to realize that he had spoken aloud. "Sorry, Captain."

"It is DNA," the doctor answered. "This Kirse's DNA, in fact. The only thing is, any being with this DNA shouldn't have made it to birth."

"Explain," Janeway said, though she suspected she could guess the answer.

"There are simply too many repeats in this strand," the doctor answered. A light formed on the screen, circled two sections of the display. "You see there? These two segments are almost identical, except half of the second is displaced by one base—and then within those segments there are these repeats—" The light moved again on the screen, marking another three spots. "—that are just the same pair duplicated twenty-seven times. Even allowing for alien genetics, not only was this Kirse unable to reproduce, but her parents probably shouldn't have been able to produce her. This DNA codes for nonsense, not a viable being."

"That's ridiculous," Paris said, sharply, and Kim touched his shoulder.

"Easy, Tom. He's right. That DNA doesn't make sense."

"But Grayrose was fine."

Janeway said, "We've suspected that there was more to the Kirse than meets the eye, Mr. Paris. The question is what."

"There was something," Torres said, slowly, her eyes focused on the middle distance, "something Silver-Hammer said. . . ." She looked up sharply. "She said, about the Andirrim, that they would bury their dead because they couldn't make use of them anymore. Do you suppose they, I don't know, harvest genetic or other material from their dead enemies?" Her expression wavered between queasiness and belligerence.

On the screen, the doctor shook his head. "I doubt it. Certainly this Kirse—"

"Grayrose," Paris said again, and the doctor looked at him.

"Grayrose, then. This Grayrose isn't borrowing any material, genetic or otherwise, from any species other than her own. I'm positive of that." The doctor paused. "The DNA is simply implausibly repetitive, and it can't be anything except replication errors repeated over and over. It's more as though she'd been copied from a copy than anything else."

Janeway frowned, and saw Tuvok shift in his chair. "Yes, Tuvok?"

The Vulcan's brows drew together—not a frown, Janeway knew, but an expression denoting distrust of the accuracy of his information. "When we were in the Kirse's control room, Adamant made a statement that may be relevant. When faced with an Andirrim attack on the citadel, Lieutenant Torres told him he needed to reinforce a section of the wall, and he replied that he was unable to do so, as he was at his limit."

"His limit," Janeway repeated. A number of possibilities were begin to take shape in her mind, everything from the Kirse as some sort of shapeshifting species—*and wasn't the Security Chief of* Deep Space Nine *from the Gamma Quadrant?*—to some kind of linked being, a single mind in many bodies.

"That's right," Torres exclaimed. "Are they some kind of clone? And is that what the machines are for, to make up for the copy errors?"

On the viewscreen, the doctor shrugged. "I've gone

as far as I can, unless you want to authorize an autopsy."

"Not yet," Janeway said, absently, her mind still on the problem.

"Though I doubt they could be literal copies," Torres said, sounding abruptly deflated. "Not given their transporter technology. They haven't been able to get beyond the molecular level on their own."

"Captain," Chakotay said. "We've gotten enough food on board to take us out of this barren patch. And the Kirse have the information we agreed to give them. I think we should take what we have, and get out of here."

Janeway frowned. "On what grounds?"

"First, the Kirse are clearly more than they seem." Chakotay counted the points on his fingers. "Second, they've deliberately concealed that fact for as long as possible. Third, even though we helped drive off the Andirrim, the fact remains that their defense systems are extensive and could be very dangerous to the ship." He paused then, and shook his head with a rueful smile. "Frankly, Captain, I don't fully trust them. They're keeping too many secrets."

"They aren't—haven't been hostile," Paris began, and subsided as Kim touched his shoulder in warning.

Janeway smiled back at Chakotay, acknowledging his concern, but shook her head. "Keeping secrets, yes. But, as Mr. Paris said, they haven't been hostile after we passed their test. And while we can probably make it to the next M-class planet, I for one would feel much better with more food on board." She pushed herself back from the chair. "And I think the best way to resolve these mysteries is to ask them."

"Captain," Tuvok began, and Chakotay spoke over him.

"Captain, I don't think we should antagonize them. Those shuttles could pose a real danger to *Voyager*—"

"We've seen no sign of hostility," Janeway said again. "They may not even realize that we don't have a complete picture of their society—or their biology, whichever it turns out to be. And we still need food badly enough to take one more risk. I'm beaming down. I want to meet them face-to-face."

"Captain." That was Paris, rising to match her. "I—please take me with you."

"You, Mr. Paris?" Janeway paused at the door. She could feel Chakotay's disapproval like heat, could see it matched in Torres's scowl, and bit down on her anger. She was *Voyager's* captain, it was her decision; her responsibility and possibly her death, too, if she was wrong, and she shoved that knowledge aside. "Why?"

"I like—liked Grayrose," the young man said, simply. "I know there's something weird about these people, but I liked her. And I want to be the one who brings her body back."

Janeway looked at him for a moment longer, unexpectedly touched by his words, and nodded. "Very well, Mr. Paris. You can come. Mr. Chakotay, until I return, keep the ship at yellow alert. We'll check in every half hour. If we miss a check, get *Voyager* out of here."

Chakotay looked as though he would protest further, but Janeway lifted an eyebrow, and he sighed. "Aye, Captain."

His tone made it clear that he wasn't happy at all, but Janeway ignored it. "All right, Mr. Paris, come with me."

To her surprise, Adamant himself responded to her hail, and professed himself willing to receive the body and the two humans. He gave a familiar set of coordinates—the garden where they had first beamed into the citadel—and Janeway took her place on the transporter pad, Paris at her side.

"Captain," Chakotay's voice said in her ear. "I ask you once again to reconsider."

"No, Commander. I want answers." Janeway looked at the transporter chief. "Energize."

The Kirse garden was very different by daylight, the enormous flowers furled to tiny white buds, the rich color of the paving stones bleached by the sunlight. The fountain was silent, though it was impossible to tell whether that was normal for daytime or if it had been turned off because of the Andirrim attack. For a moment, she thought the Kirse had chosen to ignore them again, to leave them there with Grayrose's body on its rolling table, but then a door opened in the far wall, and Adamant appeared. Two more Kirse, both winged, followed him, and Revek trailed behind them, hands jammed into his pockets. He straightened, seeing Paris, and Adamant said, "Once again, you're welcome, Captain Janeway. And doubly so for your help against the Andirrim."

"We seem to have a common enemy," Janeway answered. "Adamant, we've brought back the body of one of your people who was killed fighting the Andirrim flagship."

"I did everything I could," Paris blurted.

Janeway gave him a reproving glance, and went on smoothly, "I'm afraid she was dead when we beamed her aboard. We are sorry for her death."

"It was generous of you to bring the body down," Adamant said, and nodded to one of the winged Kirse. He stepped smoothly forward, and tugged the table back toward the open door. Revek moved to help him, but the other winged Kirse waved him away, and moved herself to take the table's end. "Her death will not be wasted."

The transporter sounded again, sealing the wall behind them. Janeway took a deep breath. "There are other things. Things we have to settle before we can finish our transaction."

"Oh?"

It was simulated surprise, she thought, and her attention sharpened. Adamant had been expecting— something. She glanced at Revek, but the human's face was impassive. "Yes," she said, and looked back at Adamant. "When we brought Grayrose on board, our doctor ran tests to see if he could revive her. Although he couldn't, the tests were unexpected in some other ways. Specifically, Adamant, Grayrose's DNA was strange—its segments were incomplete and repetitive, and we can't see any way that Grayrose could have existed. Can you explain this?"

Adamant hesitated, chin lifting like a frightened horse, but Janeway went on without pausing.

"And why were you so reluctant to ask for her body back? For that matter, what are the implants for?"

"Ah." Adamant seized on the last words with some relief. "The implants are made because I am limited—"

" 'I'?" Janeway said. " 'I' am limited?"

Adamant paused again, and Revek laughed softly. "I told you, Adamant, there was no point to it."

"So you did," Adamant said, gently. "So you did." He turned away, and the transporter sounded again, doors opening all along the garden wall. More Kirse appeared, winged and wingless and even a few of the dwarfish soldiers, and in spite of herself Janeway took a step backward, reaching for her phaser. If they attacked, she could take a few of them, buy enough time to transport back to the ship—

The Kirse ignored her, moving to stand beside Adamant, and light flared, growing like the light of a candle flame. She blinked, dazzled, but not before she saw the first winged shape melt—like wax, like snow—and collapse into itself, into Adamant, who glowed brighter as the shape joined his. A second, then a third Kirse were absorbed, and then the light was too bright, and Janeway looked away, shading her eyes. Adamant's voice spoke out of the brilliance.

"I am all of these, if 'I' has true meaning. I am Kirse, all these are Kirse, and are me."

Janeway shook her head, less in disbelief than in denial, and the light faded again. She looked back, and the shape that had called itself Adamant cocked its head at her.

"All this—all these aspects, and this place as well—is Kirse. Does that make it clear?"

"I think so," Janeway began, and wasn't sure if she was lying to herself.

Paris shook his head, hard. "No. I don't believe it. Grayrose—she was different, she was someone real."

"Kirse matches its buds to the people it deals with," Revek said, and his voice was for once without mockery. "It considers it polite to match your interests, your personality." He glanced at the Kirse. "It took me two years to get past that point."

"That's why you said you were limited," Janeway said, to Adamant. "During the attack, I mean." She frowned. "And the citadel, that's also—you?"

"That is so." Adamant—Kirse, now visibly heavy, filled with the potential of a thousand selves—dipped its head in stately acknowledgment.

Janeway glanced around, trying to imagine the situation. The citadel was a kind of shell, like some sea-dwelling creature, but beyond that, the analogy failed her. The Kirse was many in one, like a multiple personality that was fully conscious of all its parts, and that could create bodies to match each of its personas.

"That's how Grayrose always knew what was happening," Paris said, his voice slow and soft, as though he was talking to himself. "She—you—you're all one." He paused. "Does that mean she isn't dead?"

"The part of my flesh that was her is dead," Kirse answered. "But I remember her." For a second, its flesh shimmered and shifted, formed a sketch of a winged female, and Janeway heard Paris's gasp of recognition before the shape disappeared again.

"Grayrose."

"So, Captain Janeway," Kirse continued, Adamant again in outward form. "Are your questions answered?"

"Not quite." Janeway looked from Kirse to Revek and back again. "Why did you conceal what you are?"

Kirse blinked, tipping its head to one side in silent question.

"You knew Revek, so you knew humans didn't understand what you are," Janeway went on. "You could've explained it, explained how you work, but you didn't. Why not?"

"Ah." Kirse looked away, its expression oddly embarrassed, and Janeway saw that Revek was smiling slightly.

"My fault, Captain," he said, and Kirse waved him to silence.

"My assumption, Thilo. You told me how it would be." It looked back at Janeway. "Thilo was distressed by me when he landed, once he knew what I was, and it took time to work out between us how it should be. I—there are few people who come to my world. Most are animals, who come only to steal. When I saw you were of Thilo's species, and therefore all but certainly people, I was eager for company again. I did not wish to jeopardize what might be, and so I held my tongue and told Thilo to do the same." Kirse smiled slightly then. "I was mistaken."

"And the creatures, the ones in the garden?" Janeway asked.

Kirse looked away again, sadness and something like guilt flickering across its face. "A—choice—now regretted, no longer made."

"What do you mean?" Janeway asked, when it became clear that the Kirse would not continue, and Revek cleared his throat.

"They're what's left of the people—sorry, not people, the animals—who have raided the planet. The Kirse used to use them as raw materials, a kind of biological machine. It used less metal than building something whole, and the Kirse is limited to a certain number of aspects."

"You turn prisoners into zombies?" Paris asked, and Revek gave him a look.

"The Kirse doesn't take prisoners. They were dead or dying when it found them."

"Not much of any argument in its favor," Janeway said. The idea was unpleasant—wrong no matter how you looked at it, and all the more upsetting for the fact that she could do nothing about it. The Prime Directive clearly applied, and, as she had said to Chakotay before, she had sworn to uphold that principle.

"That choice is no longer made," Kirse said again. "These that remain—I must use them or kill them, and I would rather have the use."

Paris nodded slowly. "Grayrose said something about that. It makes sense now."

Janeway sighed. She wasn't sure that the remains of the Andirrim—and whoever else had been unfortunate enough to fail the Kirse's test—wouldn't be better off allowed to die and safely buried, but at least the Kirse had ended the practice.

"Are all your questions answered now?" Kirse asked, and Janeway dragged herself back to the present.

"Yes," she said, slowly. It explained everything, all right, all the odd behaviors made clear by an answer she had not begun to suspect, and she nodded again, more briskly. "Yes, Kirse, my questions are answered."

"Then shall we fulfill our bargain?" Kirse asked.

"Yes," Janeway said. "Let's continue the exchange."

Kirse nodded back, the same awkward, learned movement she had seen in Adamant. "I enjoy your company, the company of humans. Perhaps you would care to remain, as Thilo does?"

"Thank you, but no." Janeway took a deep breath. "We—I have an obligation to bring my people home again."

"I understand," Kirse answered.

Janeway looked at Revek. "Mr. Revek. You're welcome to come with us. We have reason to hope we'll make it back."

Revek looked at Kirse, who lifted a long-fingered hand. "It's your choice, Thilo. Your company has been good, but you're a person. The choice must be yours."

Revek smiled then, an open, almost tender smile without irony. "No. Thank you, Captain Janeway, but I think I'll stay."

"Stay?" Paris repeated, and this time Revek's grin held the familiar mischief.

"Yes, stay. I happen to like it here, Tom—think of all the possibilities. Kirse is everyone and anyone I ever wanted." He sobered then, looking at Janeway. "Aside from that, Kirse saved my life several times over when I crashed. I've been rebuilt from the skeleton out—if your doctors were to take a look at me, they'd see more implants than the most mechanized of Kirse's aspects. I'm better off staying here."

For a lot of reasons, Janeway thought, and nodded. "As you wish, Mr. Revek. But if you change your mind, we'll be here for another three or four days while we complete our bargain."

"I won't," Revek answered, "but thanks."

Kirse said, "I will finish your harvest, as we agreed."

"Thank you," Janeway said. "And I'll have my chief engineer beam down to finish the transporter."

"I thank you," Kirse said, inclining his head again, and Janeway found herself bowing back.

"Janeway to *Voyager.* Two to beam up."

The Kirse planet, a blue-green disk streaked with cloud, hung in the viewscreen like a gemstone, vivid against the black of space, its own light drowning the stars. Janeway stared thoughtfully at it, trying once again to see it as it truly was—the home of a single being that could nonetheless become any one of a hundred aspects of itself, one of which was the "citadel" in which it lived—and again failed fully to capture it in her imagination. Each of the Kirse aspects, Adamant and Silver-Hammer and the others, had seemed distinct individuals, and yet she knew the doctor's analysis of the tissue samples taken from Grayrose had confirmed the Kirse's own statement that they were no more individual than images in a mirror. *Well, maybe more individual than that,* she added silently, *but not individuals as we understand them. Not quite.* She shook her head at the gleaming image, glad to be leaving, wondered again if she should make another effort to persuade Revek to leave with them. But he had been certain he preferred to stay, and she pushed the vague sense of guilt away. *Still,* she added, *I'll make sure we're listening for any communications from him for as long as we're in transporter range.* Still, he was an adult, and the choice had to be his own.

She looked back at the screen that was filled with columns listing the supplies already on board, from the various foods to the rootstock for Kes's hydroponic garden. The Kirse had more than kept their part of the bargain, and Neelix was already creating meals from the new stores that were not only nutritious but actively satisfying. A smile spread across her face then, compounded of rueful amusement. More than that, Revek had steered them to a purple-spotted leaf that, mashed and boiled, produced a drink that tasted very close to coffee, and contained enough caffeine to satisfy even the most hardened espresso drinker. She glanced at the mug sitting on her desk. It was almost empty, and she allowed herself the luxury of a second cup, pouring it from the carafe that stood beside her computer console. The supplies wouldn't last forever, of course, and then she'd be back to saving her replicator rations for the real thing, or at least its replicated analogue. *But for now,* she thought, *I'll enjoy what I have.* She took a careful swallow of the bitter liquid, savoring even the heat that stung her lips, and flipped screens to reach a second file.

Voyager's engineers had worked hard to match the Kirse's industry, and Torres's most recent report detailed the last adjustments that needed to be made. They were primarily fine-tuning, fitting the

Federation-styled emitter to the Kirse power source, and Janeway touched her communicator. "Janeway to Torres."

"Torres here." The chief engineer sounded startled, and Janeway frowned.

"How's the final adjustment coming, Mr. Torres?"

"We just ran the first live test," Torres answered. "A success."

This time, it was pride that Janeway heard in the younger woman's voice, and she smiled in answer. "Well done, Lieutenant Torres. When do you estimate finishing?"

"We're done now, Captain," Torres said. "I've turned over the last files to Silver-Hammer."

"Then beam back aboard," Janeway said. "It's time we were out of here."

"Aye, Captain," Torres answered. "Torres out."

Janeway touched the console controls, shutting down the work in progress, and rose to her feet. It was Chakotay's watch; she would let him have the pleasure of taking *Voyager* out of the Kirse system. "Janeway to Chakotay."

"Chakotay here." The smaller viewscreen lit with the words, and Chakotay's face looked out at her. "Any problems, Captain?"

Janeway shook her head. "I've just heard from Torres. Her work is finished, and she's beaming back to the ship. When she and her team are aboard, I want you to set a course out of here."

Chakotay smiled, almost in spite of himself, struggled unsuccessfully to hide his relief. "Aye, Captain. What course?"

Janeway smiled back, knew the expression was wry. They'd survived this crisis, but they were still seventy years from home. *Still,* she thought, *there's nothing we can do except do our best.* She said, "Toward home,

Mr. Chakotay. The nearest point in the Alpha Quadrant."

"Aye, Captain," Chakotay said again, and his image faded from the screen. The Kirse planet reappeared, bright with cloud, and Janeway regarded it thoughtfully. *Someday,* she thought, *we may have to make Revek's choice—but not yet, not for a long time.*

"Take us home," she said aloud, knowing no one heard, and saw the image on the screen shift, the planet sliding aside to be replaced by the familiar stars.

1252.01